"The moment we hit that airfield tomorrow, you'll have been upgraded from bimbo to lover. Lovers are...affectionate. *Openly* affectionate."

"Is this your way of telling me you're going to be touching my ass, Rafael Ortega? If it is, I should warn you that that perk better go both ways." Penny's voice dropped, the low husk making Rafe nearly come in his pants.

Her breasts rose and fell with each heavy breath as he slid one finger into the crease of her robe. "What was the longest you had to go undercover to snare a target, Red? An hour? Two?"

"Three." She failed to contain a gentle shiver as he brushed the top mound of her right breast.

"We don't know how long we're going to be at the compound. We won't be in charge of surveillance. That means we're going to have to be *on* twenty-four hours a day. No second-guessing. No hesitancy." Keeping his heated gaze on her, he lowered his mouth to her skin. "And lovers don't look uncomfortable when the other touches them."

"Is that what you're trying to do right now? Make me uncomfortable?"

"Is it working?"

HEATED
PURSUIT

HEATED
PURSUIT

APRIL HUNT

FOREVER

NEW YORK BOSTON

Copyright © 2016 by April Schwartz
Excerpt from *Holding Fire* © 2016 by April Schwartz
Cover photography by Claudio Marinesco
Cover design by Elizabeth Turner
Cover copyright © 2016 by Hachette Book Group, Inc.

Forever
Hachette Book Group
1290 Avenue of the Americas, New York, NY 10104
forever-romance.com
twitter.com/foreverromance

First Mass Market Edition: October 2016

Forever is an imprint of Grand Central Publishing. The Forever name and logo are trademarks of Hachette Book Group, Inc.

The publisher is not responsible for websites (or their content) that are not owned by the publisher.

The Hachette Speakers Bureau provides a wide range of authors for speaking events. To find out more, go to www.hachettespeakersbureau.com or call (866) 376-6591.

ISBNs: 978-1-4555-3945-1 (mass market), 978-1-4555-3946-8 (ebook), 978-1-4789-1330-6 (audiobook, downloadable)

Printed in the United States of America

OPM

10 9 8 7 6 5 4 3 2 1

*To my children—who've taught me to
smile, laugh, and reach for those dreams
that are high in the sky.*

ACKNOWLEDGMENTS

I wouldn't be seeing my book on the shelf if it weren't for my family and the unending love and support that they've given me each day. Thanks to my husband for understanding when the laundry loads started piling high, and to my children, who were as enthusiastic about having pizza for dinner on day one as they were on days three and four.

My rock star agent, Sarah E. Younger—your encouragement and support have no boundaries. Your guidance, as always, is invaluable and treasured. I couldn't have been blessed with a better soul to guide me through this crazy world of publishing. I'm proud to be a member of #TeamSarah.

Thank you to my editor, Madeleine Colavita, for loving this book and my slightly damaged heroes as much as I do. You've helped me achieve my dream of sharing *Heated Pursuit* with the world, and of making it what it is today. And to everyone at Grand Central / Forever—thank you! You've helped make this experience one I'll treasure forever.

Through the years, I've made so many friends in the writing community—invaluable, amazing, talented friends. As #TeamSarah continues to grow, so does my overwhelming pool of support. And of course, my #GirlsWriteNight crew—Tif Marcelo, Rachel Lacey, Annie Rains, and Sidney Halston. You ladies have been with me through this crazy ride, doling out encouragement when needed, cattle prods when required, and thumbs-up when deserved. To you, I say, #LiftedPensUnite!

My darling best friend and CP, Tif. I never would've thought that in the midst of a busy twelve-hour shift, I would've found my greatest writing champion. If there's one person for which I could say that this book never would've happened without, it's you. You really have been with me from day one: from conception to plotting, to querying, and beyond. Your encouragement and support mean more to me than you'll ever know.

And to my readers—thank you for allowing me the opportunity to share with you my troubled heroes and the women they never knew they needed but now can't live without.

HEATED
PURSUIT

CHAPTER ONE

San Pedro Sula, Honduras

Penny's damp underwear stuck to her skin in an uncomfortable bunch, but it wasn't a man's skillful pair of callus-roughened hands or his dirty, talented mouth that had caused the problem. The blame lay entirely with the god-awful Honduran humidity.

It didn't matter. No degree of sweaty undies or unfortunate chafing would slow her down. *Nothing* could make her turn back, because her family meant the world to her—and Rachel was the only one she had left.

A tingle at the base of her neck made Penny skid to a stop. Her gaze snapped left and right, heart trilling as shadows stretched into human-sized figures and melted away with the twinkle of a far-off light. Nothing looked amiss, but two tortuously slow seconds later, the sound of a boot scraping asphalt had her spinning around with fists raised.

Half-hidden in shadow, the man ducked her sweeping arm and pivoted much too fast for someone his size. In a blink, he reappeared over her shoulder. Months of training and practice brought her heel down onto his large, booted foot and she turned…straight into a hulking black-camo-clad figure.

Holy ever-lovin' god of iron giants.

Behind his ski mask, the man's piercing blue eyes raked down the length of her body. He towered over her by more than a foot, and given the width of his broad shoulders and massive chest, he outweighed her by at least a hundred pounds of solid muscle.

Penny swallowed the fear rising in her throat and did the first thing that popped into her head—she aimed a swift kick between his legs. And then she ran like hell.

Each painful inhale rattled in her lungs as she pumped her legs harder. Her hair whipped across her line of sight, temporarily obstructing her view. Seconds ticked by at an agonizing crawl. Fifty yards. Twenty. The closer her rental Jeep came into view, the louder the echoing pound of foot-steps behind her became.

An inch away from the door, strong hands propelled her face-first into the grimy driver's side window.

"Let go of me." She twisted and squirmed, cursing as he yanked her arms sharply behind her back and pinned them into place with his two hundred–pound frame.

"Ya era tiempo," her captor said, tossing a deep growl of Spanish to their left.

About damn time. Years of studying the language had Penny's heart sinking to her stomach…because she knew he wasn't talking to her.

One dark figure after another emerged from the shadows. Dressed head to toe in matching black fatigues and masks, the metallic glint of weapons flickered off the four bodies like a commando's version of bling. The fact that not a single gun was pointed at her head became a small comfort when a dark van screeched to a halt in front of them.

"Oh hell." She took a deep breath and choked on burnt rubber fumes.

She needed to think, and the hard erection nestled against her ass reminded her there wasn't room for mistakes. If something happened to her, Rachel would be lost forever in the hands of a monster. She couldn't let that happen. She *wouldn't* let that happen.

As if sensing a forming plan, her assailant bent down, his mask brushing against her ear. "*Play nice and you won't get hurt, sweetheart. But if you don't stop struggling, I can't make that same promise.*"

Penny fought against the ice-cold tingle his rough whisper zipped down her spine. Her joints screamed in protest, but she edged closer to the only area susceptible to attack. The second fabric brushed against her palm, she curled her fingers and squeezed with everything she had.

"Fucking hell!" Blue Eyes wrenched her grip free of his balls and tossed her over his shoulder as if she were nothing more than a rag doll.

"Damn it! Let me go!" She elbowed the back of his head, and when that didn't get a reaction, she plowed a fist into his left flank—and the damn man kept walking, not once losing his stride. "Put me down! *Entiendes?*"

Behind her, someone bound her kicking legs while another did the same with her wrists. When a gag came next, she snapped her teeth, nearly catching the hand that tied it into place. A sack over the head later and her world plummeted into darkness before they shuffled her into the waiting van.

Between the musty, stale air and being bracketed between her assailant's rock-hard thighs, it didn't matter that she couldn't see her snug confines. Walls closed in around her, making each breath feel as if it would be the last. She made one last-ditch effort to squirm from her captor's hold.

Blue Eyes' grip locked her into place, her back plastered against his chest.

"*Little viper,*" he murmured—in Spanish—into her ear. "*It's a damn good thing I wasn't thinking about having children anytime soon.*"

"*I'm just glad she didn't grab my balls.*" Another voice chuckled. "*Unlike you assholes, I'd like to expand my gene pool sometime down the line. But I am curious as to why she's down here.*"

"*Me, too. And I'm sure as hell going to find out.*" The familiar voice made Penny's heartbeat stumble.

The tone was the same in Spanish as it was in English—abrupt and menacing even from its distance across the van. But why would Trey be in Honduras? And why the hell had he let his friend turn her into a pancake against the side of a Jeep?

* * *

If someone had told former Delta and current Alpha Security operative Rafael Ortega that he'd have someone tied up in the unit's makeshift interrogation room, he'd have sworn it would've been the drug kingpin, Fuentes, or one of the cartel leader's many henchmen.

Now, three hours after he and his team pulled the hood off the American woman in the privacy of their inner-city headquarters, Rafe still hadn't entirely ruled out the redhead's involvement. Something didn't jibe, and when he couldn't figure things out, it made him goddamned twitchy.

A body search he'd been a lucky enough bastard to perform revealed a single steel blade tucked into her boot and a burner cell phone that hadn't sent or received any calls. No firearms. No identification. That was it, unless you counted breasts that would fit perfectly in the palms of his hands, and an ass that was made to be grabbed—or at the very least, ogled.

For the third time in as many hours, Rafe shifted himself in his pants and walked into the interrogation room. Instantly, he was bombarded with curses that would've had his fourth foster mother running to the nearest church.

"Ah. You missed me," he goaded.

His comment earned him another round of expletives, each one more inventive than the last. He smiled, loving both the challenge and the murderous glint in her blazing green eyes.

Rafe met her glare for glare, not turning when the door opened to emit Trey Hanson, his best friend and former Delta brother. His own black mask still firmly in place, Trey took a position against the far back wall.

"Are you feeling any more talkative?" asked Rafe.

"Go. To. Hell." The redhead tugged on her restraints with each word.

"I've been there. Too dry for my tastes." Rafe let out a mental sigh. This was turning out to be more work than he'd anticipated. "Why are you in Honduras?"

She gave him an eat-shit-and-choke-on-it glare and he covered her hands with his, halting both the damage to her chafing wrists and assessing her sudden surge in heart rate. "I'm losing my patience, sweetheart. Let's try this again. One. More. Time."

Her gaze darted left, to where Trey stood like a six-foot wall ornament, flipping his KA-BAR knife in his hand like Rafe had seen him do countless times when bored.

Something flashed in the redhead's eyes, but when her gaze slid back to him, it hardened to green steel.

The slow, upward curl of her lips alerted him to the smart-mouthed remark about to be unleashed. "Maybe instead of asking me stupid questions you should put some ice on your boo-boo. Untreated swelling could cause permanent damage."

He leaned to within an inch of her face. *Fuck-and-him.* Despite the layers of San Pedro Sula grime caked on her otherwise perfect porcelain skin, a vanilla scent clung to her body. It almost made him forget that her swift kick and good aim were the reason he actually did just get done icing his fucking balls.

"We have ways of making little girls talk," he warned. "And trust me, it's no day at the spa."

Her gaze flickered over his shoulder. "I've never been a spa kind of woman. Ask your mute friend there in the back. After all, we were practically raised as brother and sister."

* * *

Once Penny got over the fact that her surrogate big brother was lounging on the sofa across the room, it was easier to shift her focus—at least temporarily—to Mr. Tall, Dark, and Blue-Eyed.

Rafael Ortega looked like a walking sin stick, not a single ounce of softness anywhere on his body. His broad shoulders could perch a pair of economy-line sedans, and his snug shirt amplified a defined chest and quarter-bouncing set of abs. Everything about the man was rock hard and chiseled, but it was his biceps that had her close to drooling.

Nearly as big as her thighs, they bunched and flexed each time he staunchly folded his arms across his chest, the movement giving her a sneak peek of the tribal tattoo hiding beneath the hem of his sleeve. He was *so* not her type—too large, too intense, and way too brooding. But that didn't stop the butterflies from forming in the pit of her stomach—and a bit lower.

Penny sat on the threadbare couch and forced a smile she hoped looked confident. "Nice place you have. A little compact for men of your size, but nice. Cozy."

"Forget the sarcastic small talk, Penn," Trey growled from across the room. "You owe me a few answers, so let's get to why the hell you're in Honduras."

Fake it till you sell it. The words of her mentor at the bail enforcement agency had her lifting her gaze to Trey's. "I don't owe you a damn thing."

"When you waltz your sweet ass into one of my missions, you most certainly do. You're a goddamned *social* worker. You have no business walking the streets of San Pedro Sula as if you're GI-fucking-Jane."

"I can count the number of e-mails and phone calls I've gotten from you over the last few years on one hand, so don't pretend to know my business. I'm not sixteen anymore. I don't need your lectures, and I sure as hell don't have to explain myself to you. The sooner that sinks into your head, the smoother this conversation will go."

Rafe blocked Trey's path in one step. In a low murmur, the two men exchanged words that pinched Trey's lips into a tightened frown.

A few seconds later, Rafe turned, locking her in his sight. "I think we've gone about this the wrong way, Red."

She matched his disarming half smile with one of her own and watched every line on his already chiseled face go still. "My name's *Penny*. And you didn't seem too concerned about stepping off on the wrong foot when you shoved a gag into my mouth, tossed a sack over my head, and hurled me into the back of a van."

"Had to do something before you ended up injuring yourself."

"Is that why you had me tied to a chair for hours, too? To protect me from bodily injury? You know what would've protected me even more? Not being manhandled at all."

Penny, one point. Blue Eyes, zippo.

His eyes narrowed, taking her bait. "Then the next time you get the urge to take a stroll, do it during the day and not in a seedy part of a foreign city. The only people who trample through the San Pedro Sula warehouse district are either looking for trouble or they *are* the trouble. For all we knew, you could've been a human trafficker looking to make a sale. You were someplace you didn't belong."

"*He* knew who I was." She tossed a blatant glare at Trey and got a stony look in return. "Isn't that right?"

Trey's continued silence turned Penny's insides into a pinball machine. She shifted her eyes to the plans littering the coffee table—schematics, maps, photographs, and itineraries. Considering their dark-wing commando look, none of it was surprising, except for one photo tucked beneath all the others.

Her hand reflexively reached for it, a knot instantly forming in her stomach. Gleaming back at her from the black-and-white picture were a familiar pair of cold, dark eyes.

Someone called her name, but she couldn't answer. Tunnel vision narrowed her focus, darkening the corners of her sight until the harsh stare of the man in the photo morphed into the concerned eyes of Rafael Ortega. Catching her chin between his fingers, Rafe gently forced her gaze upward.

"Talk to me, Red," he demanded gently.

"*He's* the reason I'm here." She met Rafe's gaze, lifting the picture up with a shaking hand. "Diego Fuentes has my niece, *my best friend*. And I'm not leaving Honduras without her."

CHAPTER TWO

News that the same man who brought Alpha Security to Honduras three months ago had also lured a determined Penelope Kline went over like a bomb dropping into the middle of a churchyard. Handling crazy shit was Alpha's specialty. Terrorists. Hostage retrievals. Not bogged down by bureaucratic bullshit, they got stuff done when the government couldn't. Hell, they were currently aiding the Drug Enforcement Administration with an international manhunt for one of the most sought-after drug traffickers this side of the hemisphere—Diego Fuentes.

Penny's grit was admirable, but on the third hour after the dropping of the metaphorical bomb, it was starting to give Rafe a damn headache that an entire bottle of aspirin and the sight of her curvy body couldn't cure.

Three hours of tension. Of glares. Of listening to the faint squeal of the rotating ceiling fan in the background, and they were no closer to talking sense into the redhead than they'd been before. Even Trey, their trained hostage negotiator who could talk himself out of five-point steel restraints, hadn't so much as gained an inch of her cooperation.

Penny Kline had systematically bested each of Rafe's four teammates in the stubbornness department, and for Alpha operatives, it was a hard and bitter pill to swallow.

Sweaty and annoyed, Rafe cracked his neck and prayed for patience as he got *his* turn. "I'm not so sure you're following along, Red. Fuentes isn't a tame little pussycat. He's the goddamned Dr. Frankenstein of the drug world."

Penny leaned against the back of the couch, arms folded across her chest. She cocked up one delicate eyebrow as if something were wrong with him. And hell, maybe there was. He'd always prided himself on being cool and levelheaded. In his line of work, a quick temper got you in tough scrapes. Or dead. But for some reason, this little sprite of a woman put him close to an edge he didn't know he had.

"He also loves dabbling in human trafficking and generalized murder and mayhem. Do you have something to tell me that I *don't* already know?" she asked.

"Do you have any idea what would happen if a man like him got his hands on a sweet little thing like yourself?"

"No, because I'm too busy imagining what a man like him is doing to *Rachel.*"

Her voice caught on her niece's name. Her gaze, previously matching his head-on, lost its ferocity with a few quick blinks. But it was the nibbling of her lower lip that was a red flare shot inches from his face.

Rafe told himself to give her a second to collect herself. But there was too much on the line, and not solely the team's mission to bring down Fuentes before the bastard spread his superdrug, Freedom, to the States. Left to the atrocities of San Pedro Sula, no way could Penny come out whole and intact, and more importantly, she shouldn't have to take that kind of risk. The fact she felt it necessary bothered him a hell of a lot.

Rafe ignored Trey's grumbles from across the room. "If Fuentes has Rachel, *we'll* find her."

A chorus of nods and *hell yeah*s filtered through the group.

"You mean like you've found *him*?" She rolled her eyes with a snort. "I'm sorry. You said you've been down here looking for him for how long? Months? Rachel doesn't have that kind of time. You've said yourself that Fuentes is a monster. If he doesn't kill her or sell her to the highest bidder, then she becomes a walking guinea pig. I'm not going to let that happen."

Trey unfolded his six-foot body from the couch and stood. "And you think you can do any better? Jesus, Penn, we're trained for this kind of shit. You're trained to place children in loving homes and help the elderly work out the kinks in their social security checks. What you're not is a—"

"A social worker."

"That's exactly my point." Trey nodded, looking smug.

"I mean, I'm *not* a social worker." She gestured toward the laptop that sat on the beat-up coffee table. "Look it up. And it'll speed things along if you use the Lebanon County Sheriff's Office database."

Logan, former Marine sniper and resident country boy, was already on it. With his well-worn cowboy boots and chewed-to-hell toothpick sticking out of his mouth, no one but his teammates would've expected it to take him less than a minute before letting out a loud, and obviously impressed, whistle. "*Hot damn.* Looks like our redheaded viper's packing more than a mean kick. She's got a license."

Logan chuckled. Hands propped behind his head, he leaned back so the rest of the team could read the screen.

Trey gawked at the computer, then at Penny. "You're a goddamned *bounty* hunter? What the fuck happened to being a social worker?"

"I got tired of the women in my shelter being afraid because their no-good exes skipped out on parole. And the term I'd prefer you use is bail enforcement agent." An impish grin slipped onto her face as she scanned their surprised expressions. "I may not be a card-carrying member of the Commando Club, but I'm not entirely helpless either. And I'm not flying into this with blinders over my eyes."

Most people chose not to meet Rafe's gaze head-on. When he was young, he chalked it up to the startling contrast of his tanned coloring given to him by his Guatemalan mother and the blue eyes of his Anglo-American father. Then the closer he got to his teenage years, he partnered the oddity up with a fuck-off scowl, and like magic, most people kept their distance.

Obviously, Penny wasn't included in that tally. Not only did she hold his gaze without so much as a blink, but she challenged it with a subtle eyebrow lift. The woman needed to come with a too-intense-for-public-consumption warning label.

"Kidnapping's good business," he pointed out. "This country's filled with all kinds of low-level pond scum looking to make a few bucks. What makes you think it's Fuentes who has Rachel?"

"Because she e-mailed me a picture of him right after he threatened her for sticking her nose in his business."

"What business?"

"The disappearances of young women in the village where she'd been stationed. It didn't take long for her to notice that each one coincided with visits from Fuentes and his men—which was at least once every other week, sometimes more frequent. The bastard had the elders thinking that the wrath of God would strike them down if they so much as muttered a word about it, much less interfered."

Realization started to dawn. "And let me guess...she wasn't so accommodating."

"Rachel loved those people. She loved her job. The NGO she was working for wrote her off as bailing her post, but Rachel wouldn't do that. She wouldn't have gone unless someone *made* her leave."

Hell, it fit. *All* of it. By plucking people in a society where no one would notice, Fuentes solved two of his problems—loose ends and productivity. While remaining stateside, Charlie, Alpha's tech guru, had already gathered intel that led them to believe Fuentes was using the Honduran populace as his own personal test subjects. If Rachel had been about to cause him problems, the bastard wouldn't hesitate in getting rid of her the most efficient way he knew how.

One minute was too long in the presence of a man like Fuentes. Rachel, about to hit a month, was quickly running out of time—if that time hadn't already expired. Penny's stern jaw told Rafe that she knew each and every one of the risks associated with this game of hide-and-seek, and she didn't give a damn—because it was for family.

He didn't have anything in the way of parents or siblings. Hell, he didn't even have a goddamned houseplant. But Rafe understood that fierce loyalty all the same because it's how he felt about each of his teammates.

But that didn't mean she belonged here.

"What are the chances of you staying on a plane if we plop you onto one and fly your ass home?" Rafe asked, though he already guessed the answer.

"I'd be on the first flight back," she said without batting a pretty green eye.

He didn't doubt that for one damn second.

Penny met his gaze. "Look, I know you guys have a job to do here, and putting Fuentes out of commission is an important one. But so is mine. I'll do whatever I have to do to prove I won't be a liability. Put me through the gauntlet. I don't care. But at least give me a chance before you send me on my way. Or *try* to."

Rafe sent a sidelong glance toward his boss. Sean Stone had stayed not-so-miraculously quiet for the last few hours, absorbing everything around him. A man of few words, the former SEAL led Alpha Security with a firm, but fair, fist. No surprise to Rafe, Stone's dark stare hovered over Penny to the point the redhead squirmed—albeit faintly.

"You want a gauntlet, then you got a gauntlet," Stone agreed. His mouth remained in a tight line, nearly obscured by his dark, salt-and-pepper beard. "Whether you stay or go lies entirely in the hands of Alpha's training coordinator. You don't impress him, you go home and leave Fuentes and Rachel to us. We don't have time to babysit and neither does she. Agreed?"

Rafe watched her steadfast gaze bounce from each of his teammates as if trying to figure out in whose hands she'd be placing her fate.

"Agreed." She eventually accepted with a slight nod.

Only then did Rafe let a slow smirk ratchet up the corner of his mouth. Perceptive, Penny caught sight of it. The softly muttered curse that fell off her lips made him grin even wider.

* * *

Penny's heart pounded, the upbeat *thump-thump* making her body vibrate from head to toe. Her arms and legs ached from overuse, and what had been a feminine glow an hour ago was now a profuse fountain of sweat. Not even during her most difficult haul-in did she have to work this hard.

She made a mental vow to punch her bail enforcement mentor the next time she laid eyes on his clean-shaved head. Vince had obviously been training her with kid gloves, and because of it, she was about to have her rear end handed to her on a platter—or more accurately, the floor mats.

In and out. Slow and steady. Hands on knees, she focused on the mechanics behind breathing as she shot a glare at the man standing smugly a short four feet away.

She *had* to go and suggest a damn gauntlet. And then she went even stupider and agreed to put her fate and Rachel's fate in the hands of Alpha's training coordinator. She should've known. She *did* know the second Rafe slowly slid his delectable mouth into a little smirk. Right now the only thing she had going for her was that it wasn't him she'd been pitted against in the hand-to-hand demo. Of course, she wasn't faring all that well against Logan either.

Beneath his sexually themed T-shirt and flirtatious Southern-boy smiles, Logan Callahan was as hard bodied and obnoxious as the rest of his team—something she neglected to see until he flipped her to the floor the first of many times. Now that her eyes were wide open, she was determined to take him down. Just as soon as she could stand upright without fear she'd teeter ass over foot.

"You done already, darlin'?" Head cocked, Logan rocked on the balls of his feet, his blond wavy hair falling in perfect position and not looking at all like they'd been at this for close to forty-five minutes. "Do you want to take a water break? Perch your sweet self in front of the AC? Or how about a nap?"

She drilled the former Marine with a glare that pulled his mouth into a grin.

"*I'll* be taking a nap if someone doesn't do something soon," came a voice from the sideline. "Unless you're trying to knock him over with a bat of your lashes, Red, you may want to actually move."

Penny redirected both her glare and her focus to the man standing to her left. Though the rest of the team held up the wall with their backs and watched as if her match against Logan were better than *Monday Night Football*, it was Rafe of whom she'd been painfully aware.

The man wasn't in-your-face sexy. You wouldn't find him on the cover of *GQ* or walking down a runway wearing a pin-striped suit and expensive cologne. But between his chiseled body and the few days' worth of dark stubble peppering his jaw, he could star as the main attraction in any woman's hottest bad-boy fantasy.

Lord knew he'd fueled her own as she'd lain in bed last night. In fact, the main plot of her personal Rafe-induced flight of imagination involved him getting *really* close. And naked. And a whole lot of sweaty that definitely didn't involve hand-to-hand sparring.

Dream Rafe had nearly sent her body up in flames. His hands. His mouth. Good God, and when he used them together? She was lucky she hadn't set the bed on fire. Never having been the type of woman to be fueled by lust, she found the whole experience a little overwhelming—and a hugely bad idea.

"Have something to say…*Red*?" Rafe's scrutiny pulled her back into the moment. Before she could conjure a snappy retort, he turned to Logan. "Stop giving her time to recuperate. You're not doing her any favors by being too easy on her."

Logan gave him a skeptical snort. "Easy? She looks like she's an axe kick away from passing the hell out."

"Then we'll have proven our point and can send her on her way home." Rafe slid her a condescending smirk. "Which is where she *should* be."

Label it daddy issues or feminist tendencies, but what Penny hated most in the world—besides nylons—was being dismissed. Either Rafe knew that or he didn't care. No matter his reasoning for being a mountain-sized jerk, it sparked an inner fire she hadn't felt for a ridiculously long time.

"Like hell will I be going home." She stepped back onto the center of the mat and crooked her finger at Logan. "Let's go. No napping. No taking it *easy* on me."

Logan looked a bit wary by her sudden rejuvenation. "Okay, but will you go easy on *me*?"

"No." Penny spun. Her fist clipped the blond operative's jaw in a back fist that would've hurt them both if he hadn't ducked when he did.

"Jesus." Logan shot a glance toward Trey. "Why the hell am I the one being offered as the sacrificial fucking lamb? She's *your* not-so-little sister."

"Because you volunteered." Trey smirked. "And I'm not stupid. I saw what she did to Tommy Wilcox when the little shit tried to cop a feel at the homecoming dance. No way in hell was *I* offering."

"You could warn a brother, you know."

Trey shrugged. "Not as fun to watch."

"Are we going to do this or what?" Penny asked, drawing their attention back to the task.

Logan, looking less eager than before, stepped back onto the mat. Penny mirrored his movements when he made his approach. No way in hell was she backing down. Her renewed fervor had less to do with tossing the cowboy operative to the floor than it did wiping the bemused grin off Rafe's face.

And she'd be lying to herself if she didn't admit that a small part of her wanted to impress the hell out of him, too.

Crazy. Pure insanity considering she told herself years ago that men with the GI Joe Complex were strictly off-limits. She abso-freaking-lutely appreciated everything soldiers did for their country. The duty and loyalty that ran through their veins produced true heroes. But she knew from experience that that kind of allegiance often put people who weren't dressed in Army green—or Navy blue—into a second-tier spot of importance.

Been there. Done that. Had the daddy issues to prove it. And most importantly, not doing it again.

Keeping a safe distance from anything or anyone who couldn't offer her a first-place ranking was paramount. And she'd get back to it—*after* she demonstrated to Rafe and the others that she wasn't a liability.

The glint of the mock knife in Logan's hand snapped Penny back to reality. He deftly tossed it from palm to palm. Her eyes tracked it like the pendulum of a clock. The second he lunged, she dodged left. The quick-ducking side step made him miss by inches. It was poetry in motion as she found her groove.

Lunge and evade. They moved in an unchoreographed dance that paraded them around the mat. On their third pass, her sneaker snapped against his wrist, sending the knife flying.

"Save the acrobatics for the circus," Rafe growled from the sideline.

Logan's gait glided over the floor as he and Penny circled.

He flashed her a quick wink. "I don't know, Ortega. Some of those gymnastic moves could be pretty damn inspiring in the bedroom."

"Aw, have things become so deficient you'd resort to getting your butt kicked to spice it up again?" Penny ignored the fact her words came out sounding like an asthmatic phone-sex operator and continued to tease. "Maybe you should be the one taking that nap. You're slowing down."

"No way in hell, darlin'. You caught me once. Not gonna happen again."

Male laughter erupted from everyone except Rafe. A split second later, Logan charged in a frontal assault. Grabbing onto his forearms, she used his forward momentum and propelled him across the floor like a two-hundred-pound paper airplane.

A second from his face hitting the mat, he ducked into a roll and came back to his feet. When he turned, she was there with a sharp elbow jab to the gut. Logan doubled over with a grunt, giving her the opening she needed. Lowering her center of gravity, Penny gripped the back of his shirt and with a throaty growl, tossed him over her shoulder and onto the mat.

Again.

Logan looked momentarily stunned. "Well, hell, darlin'. You may be small, but you've got some skills."

Penny chuckled as she wiped the stream of sweat off her forehead. "I think there was a compliment in there somewhere, so thank you."

"You're welcome. And I'll give you another one by asking you to have my children. I mean, just imagine them… beautiful, sassy, redheaded ones with fast reflexes." He got back to his feet with a groan. "That's if I can have children after that elbow drill. Shit. I think I need a medic, Kincaid."

"If it were an arm, leg, or even your head, I could be convinced to give you a hand, but I'll be damned if I'm going anywhere near your junk... or your ass. You're on your own, man," said Chase Kincaid, the blond Viking standing next to Trey.

Penny snorted on a laugh. As far as ending notes, this felt like a pretty damn good way to finish the day. Preoccupied with her mental pat on the back for not looking like a complete damsel, she didn't register the looming figure at her back until twin logs wrapped around her middle.

It was freaking déjà vu.

CHAPTER THREE

Rafe could deal with a lot of shit, but watching Penny spar with Logan wasn't one of them. As a matter of fact, it felt like having a hot poker repeatedly shoved through his eye socket. He lost count of the number of times he'd nearly made an ass of himself and stopped the whole damn thing. But the real challenge came in the form of the hard-on that sprang to attention the second it was *his* hands on her lithe body.

Nothing like a raging erection to become the physical symbol for pissing on the Man-Code Book of Ethics. Now that his body pressed flush against hers, he may as well have set it ablaze and buried it under six feet of cow shit. Because the code didn't give a rat's furry ass if Trey and Red shared the same blood or not, or if they'd basically been estranged the last few years. They were related all the same. Pseudo-siblings. Hands off was hands-fucking-off.

Rafe could attempt to pass off his draw to the redhead as concern for her well-being, but she'd held her own against Logan, using speed, agility, and creativeness not only to keep the playing field even, but to occasionally take the lead. Even bullying her into quitting hadn't worked.

A confident woman with the ability to make a grown man literally fall to his knees was fucking sexy as hell. Her fortitude. His erection. Their mission. All wrapped up in one special package, it meant he was triple-fucked. In his pants, his cock twitched its agreement.

Distracted by the inopportune hard-on, he hadn't realized Penny had gone still in his arms until she drilled her foot into his instep and slipped from his hold. Rafe sucked in a curse, blocking a back fist to his nuts with only centimeters to spare.

"Nice try, Red." He twisted her around until her back met his front again, and coasted his mouth over the shell of her ear. "You're fast, I'll give you that, but you can't rely solely on speed. You need to always pay attention, be aware of your surroundings every damn second. And for fuck's sake, never underestimate how much your opponent wants to kick your ass—or worse."

At Penny's feminine growl, Rafe realized he'd just broken every single one of his fucking words of wisdom. She clapped her palms over his ears, making them ring like a church bell. And then his feet went airborne.

Five feet two inches of compact curves swept his legs out from beneath him and dropped him flat on his fucking ass.

"Well, now I don't feel too bad." Logan laughed gleefully, followed by the snickers of the rest of the team.

"I'm not fixing your ass either, Ortega." Chase snorted on a chuckle.

"What were you saying about always staying alert?" Hands braced on her hips, Penny hovered over him. Her brilliant smile sucker punched him a second time.

Before he could think through the repercussions of his actions, Rafe wrapped his hand around her wrist and tugged her off balance. Her body landed on his with a loud grunt. And then with one arm banded around her waist and one hand pinning her arms above her head, he rolled until he came out on top. Literally.

From an inch away, her lush lips pressed into a firm line that reminded him of a royally pissed—and helpless—pixie.

"What was your question again, Red?" He struggled not to smile when her eyes narrowed into catlike slits.

It took every ounce of his willpower not to ogle the impressive cleavage left exposed by her fitted tank top. But he didn't need to look down to feel the slight poke of her nipples against his chest.

"My. Name. Is. *Penny*." Her terse reply pulled him away from the mental image of him laving her perky tips with his tongue. "And you tricked me."

"Do you think Diego and his men are going to use the rules of engagement?" He lifted one dark eyebrow. "He'll use every dirty, underhanded trick in his arsenal to get what he wants, and if you think otherwise, we're putting your sweet little ass on the plane right the hell now. Pouting and stomping your foot isn't going to do shit."

"Right now you're lucky my foot is otherwise incapacitated."

The woman threw him too far off his game to worry about pissing her off. Her being angry at him meant he'd be less likely to imagine fucking the attitude out of her. As pleasurable as that would be, he couldn't let it happen...which meant he needed distance.

He released his hold and backed onto his haunches. Before he could stand, Penny braced the soles of her sneakers solidly on his chest and shoved. When his back hit the mat, she followed, her legs straddling his waist. He gave her a moment to realize her mistake before clamping his hands on the swell of her hips and rolling them until their positions reversed. Again.

The layers of clothes between them may as well have disintegrated, and probably would if they stayed in this position much longer. Rafe groaned, the blood flow to his brain instantly diverted southbound. The more she squirmed, the harder his growing cock pushed against her mound. He knew the exact moment she registered his erection for the monster it was, because her eyes widened and her mouth slackened a fraction of an inch.

Taking her in a kiss would've been all too easy. One taste. One taste was all he needed to get her out of his head.

"Christ, I think I need a smoke." Logan's mutter reminded him they were far from alone.

Rafe pushed to his feet with a mumbled curse. He needed to bury this attraction in the fucking sand because despite her sly smirks and truckload of stubbornness, he'd bet his Civil War Smith & Wesson that Penny Kline wasn't the type of woman for a no-strings romp—and that was all he was good for.

He didn't *do* relationships. Weekends of sexy fun—sure. One-night stands—hell yeah. Marriage and picket fences and two-point-five children—no fucking way. A second reason why maintaining distance was best was boring a hole into the back of his head with the tenacity of a heat-seeking missile.

Trey. Best friend. Delta brother. There was an unwritten rule about fucking your best friend's almost little sister.

Rafe ignored Trey's displeased glower and paused at the training gym door.

Stone's gaze caught his and his boss asked simply, "Verdict?"

"I'm not signing off on her until I know without a doubt that she can keep her shit together out in the field. It's one thing to defend yourself with comfy mats cushioning your fall. It's an entirely different scenario out there in the real world."

"What are you suggesting?"

"A field demo where anything and everything can happen. We toss shit at her and see how she reacts. Dropping two of us to the floor in a gym doesn't prove she's going to be able to do it when Fuentes or one of his goons comes at her with a knife—or worse." He threw an unapologetic glance over his shoulder. "Wish I could say that I was sorry for being so blunt, sweetheart, but I'm not."

Penny glared at him from the middle of the room. "No need to apologize to me, *sweetheart*. Let me know when and where and I'll somehow manage not to crawl into a corner and hide."

* * *

With Rafe and Sean making their cover appearances at the local bar and the others scouring the city looking for leads, Penny sat alone on the enclosed back porch of Alpha's safe house. Sirens whirred far off in the distance and from a few blocks over, someone triggered a car alarm. She ignored it all, trying to make sense of the last few months.

When Rachel had come to her with the idea of the two of them volunteering with Youth Worldwide, Penny had thought it was a good idea with the promise of once-in-a-lifetime excitement. They'd made plans, shopped until they were nearly dead on their feet, and then because of her big job switcheroo, Penny hadn't been able to get the time off for a trip of that magnitude. Still, she'd encouraged Rachel to go, never for once thinking that she was sending her straight into danger.

Guilt and fear crushed Penny's chest like an anvil, and the more she willed the forming ache away, the heavier it became. Rachel's abduction was *her* fault, and if anything happened to Rachel while in the hands of Fuentes, Penny had no one to blame but herself.

She definitely couldn't blame Rafe and the others, and she couldn't condemn them for being wary of her abilities. Heck, *she* was wary of them.

Even though she'd turned in her social worker's briefcase for a pair of handcuffs and she had a bail enforcement license in her wallet, it hadn't been without a whole lot of *I-must-be-losing-my-mind* freak-outs. And technically, she hadn't finished her mentorship requirements with Vince. But wrapping things up had been the last thing on her mind when Rachel hinted that she thought she was in trouble.

Penny hadn't hesitated to drop everything. Yeah, Rachel was her niece despite their three-year age difference, but she was also her best friend—her sister. There was absolutely nothing she wouldn't do for her, but she couldn't do any of it if Rafe and the guys sent her home.

Reservations over Rafe's real-world demonstration weighed heavily on her mind. No doubt it would be brutal. The look he'd sent her way before leaving the training room that morning sure hadn't given her the warm fuzzies...or the impression that it would be a cakewalk. Her imagination had run the gamut from chin-ups off the side of a building to stopping a bullet with her teeth. Part of her hoped to have another chance to flip him to the ground—*without* the mat—but she didn't think she'd be that lucky a second time.

As the bug zapper on her left went crazy, twin male voices drifted over the backyard's ten-foot security wall. In a city where buildings were practically built on top of each other, overheard conversations weren't abnormal. But at the mention of Freedom, Penny found herself tiptoeing toward the cement barrier that separated the yard from the alley.

"*What's that stuff called again?*" a man asked another in Spanish.

"*Freedom,*" answered the second. "*I'm telling you, Fuentes scored the big one with this shit. A few tastes and you have an instant following. They'll come back for more and will do anything to get it.*"

"*Sounds too good to be true.*"

"*Head down to El Sótano. It's a fucking playground down there, especially with the old man himself doling out a few early advances. But the real fun will be when it hits those American bastards. Freedom is really going to ring then.*" The man howled in laughter at his own twisted joke. "*And soon. Really soon.*"

Fuentes being confident enough in his product to already leak it to the general population twisted Penny's stomach into a cold, hard knot. The men continued their conversation as they walked away.

Penny ran into the house, skidding on her heels at each turn. By the time she peeked out the blackened front window, the men were nothing more than black blobs down the street. Frustration pulled a growl from her throat and her disposable cell from her pocket.

She started hitting button after button, ticking through the list of phone numbers Logan had preprogrammed earlier.

Each call ended with a no-service message or no answer, even the one to the bar. When a second round of calls yielded the same result, she barely resisted the urge to punt the piece-of-crap phone into the wall.

Five excruciating seconds ticked by before she admitted what she had to do, regardless of the animallike snarls it would incite, most of them probably from the Master Growler himself. Rafe could deal with it because she didn't have a choice. With Rachel, each second counted.

* * *

Finding an adult version of a dress-up box stuffed in the safe house's far back closet had been both a blessing and a curse. With a dark-haired wig and barely ass-covering leather skirt, Penny blended in with the local girls who were perusing the four dilapidated city blocks toward *Tres Brujas*. But with the fishnet stockings and thigh-high leather boots came a whole lot of stomach-souring leers and unwanted gazes.

She ignored the catcalls and whistles, breathing a little sigh of relief when the door to the bar came into view. *Tres Brujas* looked like the quintessential seedy neighborhood bar, the former redbrick building aged brown over time. Metal bars adorned four of the broken front windows, letting the loud thump of music spill onto the street without interference.

Penny pulled open the door. At least a half-dozen stares immediately slid in her direction. "No going back now, Kline," she murmured to herself, stepping inside.

She took a moment to scan the room, finding Sean in the far back corner. The Alpha leader looked larger than life and lethal as he filled the line of shot glasses in front of him. As far as keeping covers during their prolonged stay, this one seemed to fit him well. He appeared to keep the chat down to a minimum, moving briskly up and down the length of the bar, serving one customer after another.

Penny battled her way through a sea of wandering hands and slinked to the room's periphery. When she finally reached the counter, Sean was gone and she needed a bottle of disinfectant.

"*Are you looking for some fun tonight? How much?*" the man on her left propositioned her before she planted her bottom on the only empty stool.

"*Sorry. I'm waiting for someone,*" she replied coolly. There'd be no way in hell she'd give him the time of day even if he hadn't mistaken her for a hooker. With long, unkempt, stringy hair, it looked as though he hadn't seen the damp side of a shower in weeks.

An older woman stepped through a swinging door and stood where Sean had been only minutes before. Her gray eyes zeroed in on Penny almost immediately. After scanning her from the tip of her fake hair to her on-display cleavage, she broke into a sly smirk.

Beside her, Penny's admirer clamped his mouth shut.

"*Stop bothering my pretty customers, Roberto. Or I'm going to cut you off for the night, and this time, I mean it,*" the sixty-some-year-old warned with a husky voice.

"*It's too early for that, Maria. You can't do that to me.*"

"*This is my bar and I'll do what I want and when I want it. Now, if you know what's good for you, you'll keep your mouth closed and keep your eyes and your comments to yourself. Understood?*"

"*Yes, Maria.*" Next to her, Roberto went dutifully quiet. Man, Penny needed to learn how to wield that kind of power.

Maria turned her attention to her. "*Very pretty. And very brave, sweetheart. You're looking for one of the boys?*"

She wouldn't call Rafe or Sean boys—not by a dozen years and a hundred pounds. But this woman had obviously linked her to the guys. "*I...yes. No one answered their phones. Are they around?*"

"*Stay put and I'll find someone.*"

The second Maria slipped into the back, Penny's unwanted admirer shifted closer. His meaty hand landed on her thigh and shifted higher each second. "*A woman doesn't wear that kind of outfit unless she's looking for a good time. And I'll give it to you, baby. I can fuck with the best of them.*"

Penny averted her gaze. "*Somehow, I highly doubt that.*"

"*Let's get out of here before the old lady shows up again and I'll prove it to you.*" Flashing a yellow smile, the brute gave her leg a painful squeeze. She bit her tongue to withhold even an ounce of emotion and casually palmed his jean-covered erection. One second. Two. She counted to three before applying pressure, and watched his complexion pale.

He shifted uncomfortably in his seat. "*Get your hand off me, you little bitch.*"

Eyes wide in mocking innocence, she replied, "*Then I suggest you do the same.*"

"*And now, before you lose it,*" came Rafe's low, menacing growl.

Her admirer turned toward a steel-faced Rafe and went from pale to ashen in a split second. The man's eyes darted left and right, looking for a route of escape around Rafe's hulking frame. A dark shadow slipped over Rafe's face as he leaned into Roberto's personal space. "*Do you know what I do to men who touch what's mine?*"

The man quickly lifted his hands. "*I-I didn't know.*"

"*Which is the only reason why you still have fucking*

hands." Rafe barely spared the man a second glance as he effortlessly plucked Penny off the stool. "With me. *Now.*"

"Rafe, I—"

"Later."

He took her hand and linked their fingers, guiding her to the back of the bar. His pace was brisk, only slowing to return the occasional nod or knowing smile to a passing customer. No doubt they thought he was taking her somewhere to screw her senseless, and he did nothing to deter the beliefs as he palmed her backside and urged her into what was easily the most disgusting men's bathroom she'd ever seen.

He checked each stall before turning toward her with a lowly snarled, "Red."

"Before you get all growly," she interjected before the lecture began, "I tried calling—*all* of you. Even here. *All* multiple times before I finally gave up. And yes, I know it's dangerous, but I really had little choice, and it's not like I walked here with an American passport stamped to my forehead."

Awareness flashed through her body as his gaze dropped to the leather bustier fluffing up her C cups. No longer the vivid blue, his eyes darkened with an intensity that made her heart skip a beat. And she couldn't really fault him for it, because her own gaze admiringly tracked the way his T-shirt stretched across his chest.

"You dirty up pretty good, Red." Rafe broke the sudden tension first. Only when she crossed her arms over her chest did his gaze drift north of her boobs.

She cleared her throat and winced at the sudden dryness. "It was surprisingly easy, and that's something I'll have to eventually think about, right along with why five men had a chest full of women's clothing."

Rafe's lips twitched. "Both the house and the clothes are

Maria's. She's the team's unofficial den mother and starting point of the Yellow Brick Road to Lowlifes. No one wants to see Fuentes put away more than her. But enough about Maria. Why the hell did you leave the house?"

"The drug dealers who decided to talk shop over the fence."

He casually leaned back against the sink. "What dealers?"

"Two men—I couldn't see their faces. But they talked as though Freedom had already hit the streets and referred to some place called *El Sótano* as being Fuentes's ultimate druggie playground."

If she hadn't been watching Rafe closely, she would've missed the slight twitch in his jaw. "You sure he said *Sótano*?"

"As certain as I am that he also identified Americans as being next on the hit list."

"Did they say when?"

Penny shook her head. "They just said *soon*. If Fuentes is already slipping this superdrug to the general public, that means we've already run out of time."

The bathroom door opened. Rafe tugged her forward, pinning her between his rock-hard body and the wall. All of her pleasure senses rose instantly. Eyes closed, she counted to five in hopes of dampening the physical response to his closeness. She failed. Miserably. Counting to a hundred wouldn't have done a damn thing, especially when his mouth brushed over the curve of her neck.

Her breath quickened to the point that her fingers tingled where they fisted in his shirt. He trailed his large hand over her hip and down the length of her bare thigh. Stopping at her knee, he pulled her leg around his waist and inserted himself between her spread thighs.

Her body needed no further coaxing to come alive, ultra-aware of every ridge and valley and the closeness of their bodies. And damn the man for smelling so good while standing in the middle of a smoke-hazed sweatbox. She fought the urge to rub herself against all that hard muscle, but then he took the decision out of her hands when his hips lightly brushed against her stomach.

A whimper slipped from her lips as he took a gentle nip of her neck. Her neck was her hot spot, something her pathetically few lovers had never taken the time to realize. But Rafe may as well have brought a lunch and stayed for the day.

His lips nibbled on her from shoulder to ear while his free hand gave her ass a firm squeeze. A girl could only take so much temptation. Penny gave into the urge to roll her pelvis into his, satisfied when the move coaxed a soft groan from *his* throat.

With each brush of Rafe's rock-solid, jean-covered erection, Penny's thong dampened even more. If the firmness rubbing against her mound was any indication, Rafe Ortega was huge and hard. *Everywhere*. Another few seconds and she officially wouldn't care that their visitor was on the other side of the room, emptying his bladder.

The stranger did his business and walked out without giving them so much as a cursory glance. Once again alone in the small bathroom, the temperature escalated a good thirty degrees.

"Rafe," she huffed out breathlessly. "Please."

Too bad she didn't know what she was asking for. To stop? To rip off her clothes right there, hygienics be damned, or the reason she came out to *Tres Brujas*?

Rafe must have interpreted it as a hard stop because, dragging his hands over her thighs, he returned her to her feet and stepped back. Slightly. Every inch of her hummed, and the rapid rise and fall of his chest told her that he wasn't as unaffected as his expressionless face would have her believe.

Clearing her throat, she smoothed his rumpled shirt and prayed he didn't catch the slight tremble to her hands. "So... Freedom. Fuentes. Where do we go from here?"

"Nothing we can do here. I don't know why you couldn't get through to the guys, but I'll check it out, make sure they haven't stumbled into any problems. Give me a few minutes and we'll head back to the house. In the meantime, do you think you could keep your nose out of trouble?"

She braced a hand on her hip. "I had nothing to do with that guy not being able to take a hint. I didn't *invite* him over."

His eyes twinkled with a wicked gleam. "Sweetheart, the second you shimmied your sweet self into that getup, you invited any man with a pair of eyeballs to attempt to enjoy the wonderland that's your body. If I hadn't come along when I did, you'd have been up to your pretty little chin in some serious shit."

"I think I held my own pretty well."

"No doubt, but what would you have done when half a dozen admirers surrounded you? You only have two hands, Red. You can't grab them all by the balls."

Penny opened her mouth, ready to fire off a flaming retort despite the fact he had a point. But before she could retaliate, he turned her around and ushered her to the front of the bar with little more than a palm against the small of her back. He tucked her on a stool directly in front of Maria's knowing grin and disappeared from view.

"*Very, very brave, sweetheart,*" Maria repeated her earlier sentiments, chuckling.

"*Is he always so... growly?*" Penny asked.

"*Rafael?*" Maria tapped her chin in thought, then smirked

wider. *"No. Perhaps it is you that brings out the animal in him, yes?"*

Penny would've fallen off her stool in laughter if she hadn't been leaning against the bar. She couldn't imagine being responsible for bringing out the animal in anyone much less a man like Rafe. She dated, sure. Maybe not very much in recent months. And most definitely not men who growled and palmed her ass and called her sweetheart.

Still, she hadn't imagined the lustful look in Rafe's eyes. She let herself bask in the fact she'd been the one to put it there until he reappeared on the edge of the dance floor with an attractive brunette butted up against his groin.

Evidently he hadn't felt her news or their bathroom make-out session dire enough to skip a dance—if what he and the brunette were doing could be considered dancing. It was skewed heavily in the direction of foreplay with clothes on, and the woman attached to the front of his jeans looked more than willing to remedy the clothes situation.

Jaw clenched until it ached, Penny breathed through the sudden rush of unexpected anger and turned to Maria. *"When the Walking Pheromone's done, tell him I headed back."*

Maria snuck a glance toward Rafe, her frown lining her forehead. *"I don't think it's a good idea you leave, sweetheart. You should wait."*

Yeah, she should. And as much as she didn't relish the idea of heading back onto the streets herself in this part of the neighborhood, there was no way in hell she was going to watch Rafe get a vertical lap dance either. She waved off the older woman's concern. "I'm good. It was nice meeting you, Maria."

At the exit, she tossed a second glance over her shoulder. All she could see was Rafe's wide hands bracketing the attractive woman's hips, his head tucked into the curve of her neck.

Nope. Not staying another second.

CHAPTER FOUR

Extracting himself from Rosa's talons hadn't been easy. The woman was all hands and no ears. By the time Rafe had finally managed to extricate himself from her grasp, Maria had clapped him upside the head so hard he saw fucking rainbows. Knowing Penny witnessed the exchange and got the wrong idea bothered him. And the fact that it *bothered* him, bothered him.

"I can't believe you lost her," Trey grumbled from the surveillance van down the street.

Despite the fact their positions spanned the four-block length between *Tres Brujas* and the safe house, communication earwigs linked Rafe with each of the team. He didn't need to see his friend's face to know that a scowl was probably firmly etched in place.

"It isn't my fault she's allergic to listening. I planted her ass on the stool and told her to stay the hell put," Rafe said, halfheartedly defending himself.

"Allergic is one way to describe it. In case you don't already know, telling Penn to do something only guarantees she's going to do the exact opposite. Basic Penny 101, brother. If we're going to be letting her stick around, you best learn that pretty fucking quick."

"Quick. You hear that, Callahan?" Rafe goaded Logan. "That would be the exact opposite length of time it's taking you to get a bead on Red. Pick up the pace or I'm making a motion to replace you with another loud-mouthed Marine with bad fashion sense."

"Hey now." Logan's keyboard clacked in the background. "Don't be hating on my T-shirts, man. And as for finding our little lady...pinpointing her in a sea of white fuzz isn't exactly child's play. San Pedro Sula is in serious fucking need of upgrades. You all are sure you don't see a thing? Maybe the surveillance equipment at HQ is on the fritz and she's already lounging back with a sangria."

"Or maybe she's fucking with us because Ortega was getting too friendly with the locals," Trey jived.

How the hell could this woman disappear? On *his* watch? Rafe's bird's-eye view from a rickety fire escape let him overlook the alley across the street. To his left, a stray dog barreled after paper garbage that skidded across the wet ground, and just inside the mouth of the alley, a young couple battled it out with a lot of pissed-off body language.

Rafe half wished the dipshit boyfriend would do something stupid so he could pound out a few aggravations, because while on an op, there was no other pleasurable way to relieve stress. It's not like they could run down the street and hit the weight machine at the local gym, and sex was fucking out of the running. Mixing business with pleasure ensured a mission went straight to hell. *Fast*.

A three-month station. Five men. And a shit ton of testosterone. Rafe and the team probably had enough morning driftwood on any given morning to build themselves a fucking yacht.

About to suggest resetting shop closer to the safe house, Rafe saw the lowlife across the street give his girlfriend a hard shove. The echoing crack of her head hitting brick made him wince. Getting involved in San Pedro Sula's daily grind wasn't the reason Alpha Security was there, but sometimes interventions couldn't be helped—like dealing with run-of-the-mill assholes.

Rafe shifted to make his move when the familiar clickclack of heels echoed on the deserted street. His body stiffened as Penny, still dressed head to toe in the painted-on leather number, rounded the corner. Her gait slowed as she observed the quarreling couple.

"Keep it moving, sweetheart," Rafe murmured under his breath, wishing he could keep her walking by will alone. Prepped to move in case his will wasn't enough, he announced into the mic, "I got her, but she's about to poke her nose where it doesn't belong. Corner of Del Sol and Ramones."

Penny changed directions, headed straight toward the abusive bastard.

"*Fuck!* She's on the move. We gotta get down there. *Now.*"

Rafe half skidded, half flew down the fire escape. "I'm going to have to go in hot. ETAs?"

"Logan and I are nowhere close." A slam of a car door announced Trey had left the surveillance van. "Stone? Chase?"

"I'm on the move, but there's no way I'm making it first," Stone announced.

"Me neither." Chase could be heard cursing out a taxi that

decided to play chicken with him as he crossed the street. "Rafe?"

"Almost there." Rafe's feet barely touched the ground with his mad dash. His eyes locked on the petite form more than twenty-five yards away, and he narrowed both his vision and his thoughts to one thing.

Getting to Penny.

* * *

The second Penny turned the corner, the hair on her arms stood on end. She saw the man first. He was pressed and primped, an aura of self-importance radiating off his immaculately trimmed hair and high-end shoes. His clothes hugged a tall, rangy build too perfectly for them to be anything but tailor-made, and on his wrist, a gold watch glittered beneath the barely working lamppost.

For this side of the city, his dress alone rose her internal alert system...and then his body shifted and she caught a glimpse of the young woman.

One eye nearly swollen shut, the brunette gasped, eyes frantically searching for a means of escape despite the fact the man had one hand curled around her throat.

To the bar and back—Penny's plan to return to the safe house was first dodged when she'd had to bypass some kind of drug bust, and then again by a growing group of questionable loiters. Somehow she'd miraculously found herself back on the main road...and now this.

Penny mentally cursed the fact that there hadn't been anywhere to stash a weapon in Maria's outfit.

"*Did you hear what I fucking said?*" The tall man backhanded the brunette so hard Penny's teeth ached in sympathy.

She couldn't walk by and do nothing, and there wasn't time to trace her steps back to the bar. If anything, she could distract the jerk from doing further damage until either one of the guys happened to swagger by or someone with a phone and a direct line to the police crossed her path.

"*Do you know where I can find a taxi?*" The Spanish rolled off Penny's lips effortlessly.

"*Back off, bitch,*" the man snarled without looking in her direction.

She cocked her hip, slightly insulted he'd dismissed her as a nonthreat without a single glance. Still determined, she pulled her bail enforcement skills to the surface and forced a smile into place, becoming the bar-hopping annoyance this man expected.

She stepped forward as he raised his hand to gift the young woman another punch. "*I think I'm lost. Maybe you can help me find my way home.*"

"*Leave before I realize two of you means double the fun.*"

The man's head whipped in her direction. His dark, impenetrable stare drilled through her armor and snaked a sliver of fear up her spine. There was no emotion on his face except wild, raw, and nearly unrestrained *rage*—and now she had both his attention and the attention of the cowering woman against the wall.

"*Please,*" the young woman rasped, begging for Penny's help. "*Help me.*"

With a growl, the man released his hold on the woman and swung in Penny's direction. She ducked, the momentum of his botched punch sending him into a sideways swagger. It didn't take long for him to regain his balance and come at her again, this time with a small glint of metal in his right hand.

"*Not so talkative now, are you, bitch?*" he jeered, sidestepping toward the left.

Penny's heart instinctively shot to her throat, but she pushed it down and focused, never letting his hand leave her line of sight. She hiked up her minuscule skirt, centered her balance on the damn high-rise boots, and waited for him to make the next move.

He didn't keep her waiting long. He lunged. A quick spin to the right and he stumbled past. Like the training exercise with Logan, she snapped a roundhouse kick against his wrist. There was a loud crack on impact, and then they both watched as the serious-looking blade skidded beneath the nearby Dumpster.

Her attacker leapt to attention first. Penny didn't see his fist until it caught her jaw. Colorful starbursts exploded across her dimming vision.

One, two, three. He slammed her into the nearby wall, giving her no time to recuperate before driving a fist into her left flank. Her head spun. Her torso ached. But the sound of his victorious laugh cut through her pain like heated steel through butter.

With a warrior's yell falling from her lips, she whipped a clenched fist into his face, making impact hard enough to stun him for the knee she drilled into his midsection. The second he doubled over, she followed it up with a second—and final—ram into his face. Bones crunched and the asshole dropped. Hard. And most importantly, unconscious.

Fits of nausea forced Penny to lean heavily against the wall. She didn't even attempt turning around when another dark shadow entered the alley. Somehow she knew it was Rafe. He stepped into a beam of light, and the look on his face nearly took her breath away all over again. Muscles tensed, he glanced from the scumbag on the ground to the woman cowering by the Dumpster. When they returned to Penny in a visual scan, his eyes softened.

"Are you okay?" No yelling, no cursing, no getting in her face and calling her ten shades of stupid. His gaze darted over her face as he took a hesitant step closer.

"I'm good. No worries." She waved him off with a forced smile, afraid she'd burst into a puddle of tears if he touched her for even one second.

Her humorless laugh was the wrong move. Pain rippled around her side, each wave stronger than the previous until her knees buckled with the effort to remain standing. A tight-lipped hiss was all it took to find herself in Rafe's arms.

He became her support. Firm yet gentle, he tucked her against him and didn't flinch when she gripped the back of his shirt, probably taking off the first layer of skin.

"Slow and steady," he ordered gently. He caressed his palm over her battered torso. "No sudden movements, okay? And it's probably best to save the yoga breathing for when you don't have a few broken ribs."

"I don't think anything's broken." Her voice went tight, and she was afraid to breathe too deeply.

She sent him a weak smile and got an unidentifiable look in return. It froze on his face, his vivid blue eyes homing in on hers. The power of that one single look made her throat convulse. Years of growing up amidst tough, seasoned military men, and not once had one made her the least bit nervous. Until now. There was something about Rafe that made her unsteady and a little bit unsure of herself. And she wasn't sure she liked it.

Behind Rafe, the remaining team staggered into the alley. Their expressions ran the gamut from amusement to concern, maybe a bit of appreciation. Trey's, however, was all anger.

Red faced, he stopped no less than two feet away.

"What the hell were you thinking?" Trey's voice boomed, breaking the tender silence. "Were you trying to get yourself killed?"

"No. I was trying to get between a pair of decent-sized fists and her." Penny tipped her head to where Chase stepped over the man on the ground to get to the young woman. The brunette cringed away from him at first, but he got down to his haunches, speaking to her in a low murmur. "Five more minutes in that jerk's company and she wouldn't be able to tell you a thing."

"One wrong fucking move and you wouldn't be able to either."

Logan interceded, blocking Penny's view of Trey's scowl. "Take a breather, man. Our little lady did fucking incredible. The ass-hat never saw it coming." He flashed her a wink and earned himself a glare from Rafe when his congratulatory pat on the back made her wince.

"Shit." Logan cringed. "Sorry, darlin'. You're going to be one big-ass bruise in twenty-four hours. You know that, right?"

Penny groaned, half chuckling. "Aren't you supposed to be the Southern gentleman of the group? You're not supposed to remind me that I'm going to look and feel like death warmed over piping-hot coals."

"Hell, honey, you'd look rock-star gorgeous even on your worst day."

"Thank you for being such a good liar," Penny teased.

Sean stepped forward, eyeing the scene around them. "Our contact in the *policía* is on his way, which means the rest of you better make skid marks." With a semi-amused shake of his head, the Alpha team leader asked her, "How you holding up? Does Chase have to patch you together with glue and tape?"

"I think everything's in its proper place." Though she couldn't imagine feeling any more sore if she'd wrestled with a professional linebacker. Purposefully ignoring the gazes of both Trey and Rafe, she asked, "So, did I pass? There can't be anything more real world than what just happened, right?"

With a laugh, Sean gave her arm an affectionate squeeze. "I think we'll keep you around for a bit, but I don't think we should unleash you on the rest of the world just yet. Go back to the house with the guys; put yourself back together."

Her gaze slid to the young woman now sobbing into Chase's shirt and her heart ached. "What's going to happen to her?"

"My contact will get her to where she needs to be." Sean glanced down to the man on the ground who stirred faintly with a groan. "We'll get him where he needs to be, too. It'll be a long time before he thinks about hurting someone like that again."

Penny said a prayer of thanks that she was where she needed to be, too. Only a fool wouldn't admit that she was way out of her element. She needed Alpha Security, their contacts, their brawn, their help. And at that very second, she would admit, she also kind of needed Rafe's arms.

Logan shifted into her line of sight, mouth curled down into a frown as he peered into her face. "Hey, are ya feeling okay, Penn? Shit. She doesn't look so good, Ortega. I think she's going to pass out on us."

The scents of the alley dulled. Lights dimmed. With every passing second, Penny's head swirled more. Rafe's warm hands gently pushed her hair from her face. There was a soft curse and a muffled string of expletives. By then, his voice barely cut through the thickening fog. It was the last thing she heard before darkness rippled over her head and her legs folded in on her.

"We got to get her out of here."

CHAPTER FIVE

Each hour since returning to the safe house, Penny down-graded her status a bit more. First, she felt like she'd been tackled by a linebacker. Then, a linebacker and maybe one of his defensive-end friends. By the time morning came around, wrestling with the professional football league's entire roster would've been considered a step up.

Thankfully alone for the time being, Penny eyed the couch like it was an obstacle in one of those reality ninja shows, and it may as well have been. She bit her lip and gingerly lowered herself to the edge of the cushion. It was nowhere near comfy, but it would have to do because another inch back meant rolling to the floor to get back up, and there was no returning from that regardless of time constraints and probably a forklift.

She'd barely tucked her ice pack against her ribs when a second bag of frozen peas dropped onto the cushion. Rafe leaned against the doorjamb to the kitchen entryway, no doubt having seen the spectacle of trying to get comfortable. Too sore and too spent, she didn't care. She'd already hit her embarrassment quota earlier when Logan recited in explicit detail how Rafe carried her to the van and then into the house. Unconscious.

"For your ribs," Rafe clarified, when she didn't say anything. "You must be hurting."

"Thanks." As she attempted to stabilize the second bag over her right kidney, she realized that there actually was an inch of room left for embarrassment. The stupid thing dropped out of her numb fingers twice before Rafe stepped away from the door, hand outstretched.

"It isn't going to do you a damn bit of good like that."

"I'm good." She shook her head.

He pointedly glanced at his hand. And waited. "*Red*."

She was in too much pain to protest. "Fine. I'm not good, but I honest-to-God don't think I can move right now. Maybe in a minute. Or sixty."

"You need ice now, not in an hour."

"I'm sure you saw how long it took me to actually sit down. It'll take me at least double that to get up again. An hour's the best I can do."

The lines around Rafe's mouth smoothed as he scanned her face. He surprised her by draping her arm over his shoulder and gently easing her up into a standing position. "Lean on me. Easy does it."

"And here I was about to do a handstand." Her gaze dropped to the sight of his threatening smirk. "Sorry. I tend to get a little bitchy when I feel like I've been hit by a Mack truck."

"It's good to know you have the ability to turn into even more of a smartass. But just so you know, you look like you've been leveled by a *fleet* of Macks. Lift your shirt. Or better yet, take it off."

He didn't so much as bat an eye at her skeptical glare. This time, he smiled—an honest-to-God, dimple-inducing smile. The rare action brought a tuft of lines to the corners of his eyes.

The man was a walking personification of intimidation, but this version, with his gentle touch and laugh lines, didn't just take her breath away. It sucked the oxygen straight from her lungs and melted every still-functioning brain cell. Even in thought, she was only able to form one- or two-syllable words.

Hot. Body. Everywhere. Okay, so the last word had a third syllable, but it took a lot of effort. At least the sudden burst of arousal meant her organs weren't poised on the brink of shutdown.

"Sweetheart," Rafe said, grinning wickedly, "it's really unfair to look at me like that when you're not capable of acting on it. We got to get that ice where it's going to do some good, and to do that, I need skin. A lot of it. No need to be modest. It's only the two of us."

Penny didn't know if it was worse knowing they were alone or trying to figure out what he meant by that statement. Did he *want* her to act on it? Or more importantly, did she want him to do the acting? Her head told her no, but the little flutter in her stomach called her a big, bruised-up liar.

"Where did they all go?" she asked, hoping to steer her thoughts away from where they were currently directed.

"To look into a lead across town, and Maria said she was going to make a stop at the market and pop in later. She said something about fixing you from the inside out. Warning, though—that usually means tequila. Sip lightly."

"Good to know." Her lips slid into a small smile.

"Are you done procrastinating?" With a lift of his chin, he gestured toward the shirt. "My clothes aren't going to come off on their own."

Penny looked down at the T and sweats she'd slipped into after her shower. *His clothes*. She'd known they weren't her belongings, which Logan and Trey had commandeered from a reluctant motel manager that morning. But she'd been so thankful not to have to shimmy into snug yoga pants that she hadn't considered how the extra-large shirt and sweats had ended up on the bed. Now it made sense, and so did the scent of clean soap, musky man, and gun oil.

Rolled into one, it was Rafe.

"I could've given you one of Logan's shirts," Rafe said, interrupting her thoughts, "but the only thing he had clean had a cartoon picture of a nurse with supersized breasts."

"In that case, thanks for the clothes." *And thank God she'd struggled into a bra.* She lifted the hem of the shirt halfway before sucking in a sharp breath.

"What's wrong?" Rafe asked immediately, sounding concerned.

"It appears my ribs aren't liking the whole yoga stretch thing." She mentally cringed at what she was about to ask. "I'm assuming you have practice with taking off a woman's clothes?"

"It's practically my favorite pastime."

"I don't doubt that in the least." She matched his smirk. "Do you think you can help a girl out?"

Rafe's blue eyes glittered in mischief. "It would be my absolute pleasure."

They worked together to slowly lift the shirt over her head. Each brush of his fingers sent a small zap to her nerves, nerves that traveled down her limbs and coiled low in her abdomen. Although his gaze never strayed from her face, it felt as if he'd scoured her from head to toe.

"My clothes look better on you than they do on me." The low timbre of his voice caressed her like slightly roughened silk.

She choked back a laugh. "I look like I'm playing dress-up."

"This is the kind of dress-up I can fully get behind. As far as hobbies go, it may be a close second to the removal of clothing." His gaze briefly dropped to where her nipples practically pushed their way through her lace-covered bra. "Or maybe not such a close second."

Penny's face heated at the unspoken innuendo. But it was the softening of his eyes as they landed on her bruised torso that made her heart do a funny flip. At two hundred pounds of solid, lethal muscle, the man was a walking weapon, yet he traced around the edge of her black and blue as if cotton balls tipped his fingers.

"I think it looks worse than it feels," she murmured, uncomfortable by the sudden shift from teasing to serious. Goose bumps followed the path of his touch.

"Why didn't you tell someone it was this bad? This has got to hurt like hell." His voice deepened the longer he examined her ribs.

"It doesn't tickle."

"I'm not kidding, Red. If that punk had had a gun on him, you could've had a few holes to go along with the bumps and bruises. And then it would've taken a hell of a lot more than a bag of frozen peas to fix you. You were lucky."

"Well, Lucky is my middle name," she joked.

He didn't look humored. Mouth tight, he grabbed an ACE bandage from the table and stepped close enough for her to see the small flecks of silver in his eyes. The warmth of his body suffused hers as his arms spanned entirely around her waist. Gentle and sure, he secured both ice packs into place.

A fresh, soapy scent clung to his body. His shirt, slightly dampened, molded itself to the hard planes of his chest. She closed her eyes to combat the need to use his body as a pillow.

"Lucky really is my middle name." She babbled the first thing that came to mind so she didn't envision his hands running over every square inch of her skin. "It was my father's handle when he was in the Navy. He never got the son he wanted, so I guess he figured that it was the only way for him to relive the glory days."

"Where's your dad now?" Rafe's gaze flickered up to her face and back down to his task.

"His doctors had been telling him to take it easy for a long time, but easy wasn't in Admiral Michael Kline's vocabulary. He had a heart attack a year ago while doing a carrier-to-carrier helo hop."

"And how does the rest of your family feel about you traipsing all over Honduras looking for a madman?"

"There's only been Rachel and me for a long time—and Trey's mom." Thinking briefly of the woman who raised her, a wave of guilt slammed into her. "I may not have been totally candid with Sophie about everything that's happened down here. She's had enough to worry about with Trey going MIA as frequently as he does. I didn't want to add to it."

Ever since she'd seen the camaraderie Rafe and Trey seemed to have, a nagging question kept popping into her head. "Can I ask you something?"

"You can ask. I don't lie, so if it's something I don't want to answer, I won't."

"Fair enough." She nodded. "You've known Trey for a while, right? Before the two of you joined Alpha?"

He picked up the tape and began securing the bandage. "We've known each other since our Ranger days. And then we were placed on the same Delta team. We've saved each other's asses more times than I count."

"So you're close?"

Rafe's gaze flickered up to hers. "We're brothers."

"Did he ever once—in all the time you've known him—mention his family? His mom...Rachel?" *Me*, Penny thought.

Rafe's silence told her what she already guessed, but that didn't stop the dagger-to-heart sting in her chest. Years of practice was the only thing keeping tears from welling.

"You said that it had been just you and Rachel for a long time, but your father died last year," Rafe finally spoke.

"He did. And I meant what I said," Penny mumbled.

The sudden charged silence opened her eyes. Rafe stared so intently she averted her gaze. Even with the ice packs firmly in place, he'd only moved to give her chin a gentle tug up. The intensity on his face made her squirm. On the outside, he fit in with the dangerous clientele at Maria's bar. Lethal. Dark. Dangerous. But the hard outer package wasn't what unnerved her.

Bright blue and a hint to his mixed heritage, his eyes darkened and dropped to her mouth. Something told her a kiss from Rafe would be as dangerous and uncontrollable as the comfort gained from being in his arms. To give in to either urge would pop apart her safely bubble-wrapped life. But damn, she wanted a taste of both.

"We'll find a way to get Rachel back, Red." Rafe's voice lowered, his thumb caressing the corner of her mouth. "You don't need to subject yourself to...*this*."

"*This* is nothing compared to what Rachel's probably going through. If it brings her home, I'll go through *this* and a hell of a lot more." Her voice caught in her throat.

Years of keeping tears at bay ended when moisture brimmed her eyes. Man, she was a raging mess, so near the edge that a few nice words and a simple touch could push her right over the cliff.

She *hated* crying, loathed the exposed feeling it always left behind. And that's how she'd felt since that last frantic e-mail from Rachel. Exposed and open. Standing this close to Rafe, feeling the scorch of heat building with their prolonged silence, only made that sensation worse. The man was a walking, breathing supernova. There was no way she wasn't going to get burned.

"I really appreciate the fact that you and Alpha are willing to help me find her," Penny said truthfully. "It's not like I don't trust you all, but—"

"But she's your family," he finished.

She swallowed the forming lump starting to clog her throat. "My *only* family. I can't with good conscience step aside and watch others do for her what I should be doing myself."

Rachel always came first, and Penny knew the feelings were returned. It was the way it had been even when her father was alive. Because even as a young girl, she'd quickly come to the realization that unless she slipped into Navy dress whites and memorized every tactical maneuver from *A History of War and Conflict*, she wasn't enough to keep a man like her father content and happy.

The look on Rafe's face was unidentifiable—lips tightened, eyes narrowed. His gaze roamed her face as if trying to memorize every slight dip and freckle.

"This isn't going to be a walk in the park." His voice drew Penny from her daze. "We *don't* know more than we *do*, and Fuentes always seems to keep one step ahead."

"And here I thought he'd erect flashing neon lights that would point us in the right direction."

Rafe's large form, still less than an inch away, chased the chill from her body. The seriousness of the moment was slow to drain away, but it did, replaced by something infinitely more dangerous. A sense of security. Protection. Penny couldn't remember the last time she'd let someone hold her.

Rafe's hands steadied her as she lifted onto her toes and touched her mouth over his. It started off as a faint brushing of lips, but then Rafe's fingers slipped into her hair and his mouth moved with hers. His near-instant reaction threw her so off-balance, she clutched his shirt and leaned closer, gently taking his bottom lip between her teeth.

Her chest flush against his, Penny appreciated the stark contrast of his hard body and soft touch. His large palm skated up her back, catching beneath the hook of her bra while his other gently held her in place for the slow tangle of lips and tongue.

As far as first kisses went, this was high up on her list of best kisses ever. Like, the very top. She savored every glide of his hands and shift of his hips. Her hardened nipples brushed against his shirt while his thick erection pushed against her stomach.

Rafe's touch was better than any ice pack or drug—right until her body protested her desperate need to get closer by blasting a shot of pain between her ribs. She sucked down a hiss.

Rafe ignored her disapproving whimper and pulled away. Their heavy breaths mingled as their chests rose and fell. She couldn't even remember her own name as his gaze scoured every inch of her face. "We better stop right here, Red. I don't want to hurt you."

She almost asked if he meant emotionally or physically, because she could take physical pain as long as he kept touching her. Before she had the chance to make a fool of herself, booted steps thudded up the back porch.

Rafe reacted in an instant, pulling a gun from the back of his pants before turning toward the open doorway leading into the kitchen.

Chase barreled into the house first. "We've got a fucking problem on our hands."

Rafe tucked both his Glock and Penny's half-naked body at his back. "Plan B?"

Sean's face looked even grimmer than normal as he stepped into the kitchen. "We're moving straight to D. As we speak, Charlie's polishing up everything we have for the grand appearance of shipping magnate Rafael Manuel. It's all or bust."

Penny peeked from around Rafe's large body. "Who's Rafael Manuel?"

"Our Hail Mary," Rafe answered, face grim. "And you're looking at him."

CHAPTER SIX

Eerie red and blue lights pierced through the darkness, pulsing to the beat of the music as they flickered over the sea of scantily dressed bodies. Smoke, sex, and wealth. The basement club of *El Sótano* reeked of all three.

Penny's eyes slowly adjusted to the dim lighting, and when they did, she did a double take. Groups of twos and threes swayed and moved. Hands touched and probed, some not bothering to hide the fact that they were having sex on a very public dance floor.

Plan D, which involved Rafe posing as a self-made millionaire and her as his American arm candy, was about to take a very interesting twist.

Stepping onto the main floor of the basement club, Penny skirted around a wandering hand and huddled closer to Rafe's side. "Until a minute ago, I didn't think it was possible for me to feel overdressed."

He settled a hand low on her hip. A tingling heat brushed

over her everywhere his head-to-toe scan traveled, confirming that after two days of rest and ibuprofen, she was most definitely on the mend.

Rafe's wicked grin widened. "Trust me—you look perfect."

That comment from any other guy would've sent her eyes into a massive roll. But when Rafe said it, she believed him. And she was also back to feeling naked. Calling her outfit a *dress* was probably overstating it by a few square yards of fabric—a silky green scrap of cloth, maybe. And again, her ensemble was compliments of Maria's dress-up chest.

Rafe's blatant approval made her equal parts nervous and confident. On the tail end of that realization came the knowledge that before him, she'd never met a man who made her feel either, much less both.

A dangerous excitement made her forget they basically stood in the middle of a vertical orgy.

Thank God he couldn't see her blush. "How are we going to find Fuentes in this madhouse?"

"We're not going to have to. His men told him we were here the moment we gave my name at the door. Now we relax and wait for him to come to us."

Rafe nestled a series of erotically light kisses from her bare shoulder to the sensitive spot just under her ear. Penny trembled on contact.

"Relax," he murmured against her skin, "or I'll have Chase pull you out quicker than you can lift that lethal knee of yours."

When his tongue flicked the lobe of her ear, Penny's eyes closed on a sigh. "If you want me to relax, stop making out with my neck."

Rafe let out a soft chuckle. "Distracting you, am I?"

"Not in the least. I'm fine," she lied.

"So you say, and yet your fingers are practically ripping a hole through my shirt and your heart is beating a mile a minute."

Damn the man for being so perceptive.

As if making his point, Rafe's mouth traced the hollow of her throat where he could no doubt see her heart's frantic pace. "Fuentes is a greedy enough bastard that he should take the bait regardless if you're here or not. No one would think any less of you if you chose to sit this one out."

"Maybe not, but I would. Everyone agreed that having a sidepiece on your arm would help with getting—and keeping—his attention."

"And it will. Beautiful women have always been his weakness. I'm just saying that your presence isn't *required* for this plan to go the way we want. Think of yourself as an additional insurance policy. An extra something-something. A way to improve our odds."

"It's bad enough that we've had to wait two days to make sure everything was in place. I'm not taking any additional chances with Rachel's life. If my being here increases our odds of getting him off the streets and bringing Rach home, then I'm happy to play bait. It's not like I haven't done it before."

Albeit reluctantly, Penny admitted to herself. And not without Vince as her backup, but no one really needed to know that part.

"Playing bait to parole jumpers and tax evaders is a hell of a lot different than flaunting your wares in front of a man like Fuentes," Rafe warned.

"If you think you or any of the guys can fit into this dress, I'll gladly stay behind, but I should probably warn you that panties are a no-go."

This time, Rafe was the one who stiffened. He pulled

his head back far enough for her to see that his eyes had turned stormy blue, and she grinned internally, somewhat giddy that she'd been able to get a reaction out of the usual man of steel.

She added, "I also suggest that when you compare a woman to something, you use a beautiful sunrise or the breathtaking glow of the moon. You do *not* compare her to your collision insurance or make her sound as if she's part of a blackjack deal. If I say I'm fine, I'm *fine*."

He flashed her a wicked grin. "So you're telling me that unlike most women, you actually say what you mean? I knew there was something special about you."

The approach of a well-dressed, paunchy older man cut off her retaliating comeback. His overly wide smile refracted the colored strobe lights, making him look like a rotund, moldy-toothed troll as he introduced himself as the club's manager. Two seconds later, he led them toward the VIP section of *El Sótano*.

Rafe's hand caressed the bare patch of skin just above the curve of her behind. A few appreciative leers slid her way, but most of the male patrons were focused on their escorts— most women, but there were a few men intermixed into the group. Sharply angled collarbones and sunken cheeks seemed to describe the majority of them. Their emaciated bodies danced robotically to the music, but it was their eyes—empty and blank—that twisted Penny's insides in a slow roll of revulsion.

What if Rachel was just like them? Just as hollow. Just as sickeningly obedient. On Penny's left, a brunette knelt on hands and knees and pleaded with the man in front of her, no doubt for whatever drug was running low in her system.

A mental image of Rachel being subjected to the same treatment made Penny stumble.

"Easy, Red." Rafe caught her and kept their feet moving.

"*Rafe*. We've got to do something."

"We're doing this for them, too, sweetheart. Just keep moving."

Two armed guards stood vigilant outside the cordoned-off section of the club. Neither spared them a second glance as the manager ushered Rafe and Penny into the VIP room. By the time the heavy, velvet curtains fell back into place behind them, Penny fought to control the drop of her jaw. The sexual proclivities of the partygoers out front had nothing on the men and women in here.

Tucked in the far-back corner of the room, a large, opulent bed was shielded—only partially—by sheer harem-like curtains. It did nothing to hide the fact that the bed was occupied by more than one couple. And on a plush couch a bit closer to where she and Rafe stood, two women were face-down in one male patron's lap, taking turns in a sexual act she was glad she couldn't actually see.

This time, Penny didn't flinch—or gawk. She lifted her chin and reminded herself, *This is for them all.*

* * *

Rafe clocked five seconds in the private room until they snagged the attention of the first curious set of eyes. He trailed his hand up Penny's back and savored the coinciding quiver of her body as she turned toward him.

She wasn't the strongest, or the most qualified, but she wanted this impromptu mission to succeed the most. Watching her go head-to-chin with Trey when he'd dared to attempt to put a stop to it had been a beautiful thing. Entertaining as well as enlightening.

The woman didn't intimidate easily.

With a forced smile in place, she slid a hand up his chest and around his neck. Her lips brushed against his ear, making his heart somersault. "We should probably get ourselves into a better position, someplace that will give us a three-sixty view without it being obvious."

He inwardly groaned when her gaze slid toward the dance floor. Talk about throwing a starving man into the short line of a buffet. But he let her take the lead, their fingers threaded together as she dragged him to the middle of the dance room.

He couldn't help but enjoy the exquisite view. A couple days' rest and ibuprofen sure did her body good. Her firm ass swayed gracefully in front of him, a sweet though painful reminder of what she admitted earlier *wasn't* beneath the killer dress. He mentally chanted *Do not touch*, but when it came to Penny and all the things he should and shouldn't do, he was deaf.

And technically, it was his job to touch, something of which she reminded him the instant she stepped flush against his body. This time when he brought his hand over the flare of her hip, she wasn't the only one who shivered.

Rafe had been with his fair share of women through the years. He wasn't a monk and they smelled too damn good to avoid forever. But any involvement remained casual and easy, and he made sure that fact was known right from the beginning.

Sometimes, the woman got it. Other times, she didn't. Always, he broke things off before emotions complicated things—and he'd never once been tempted to *see* how things went, because in his experience being shipped from foster home to foster home, the more you hoped things worked out, the increased chance there was for disappointment.

What Penny conjured in him with a faint touch was new. It was distracting and dangerous. A lot banked on him keeping his head on straight, something that had no chance in hell of happening when he slid his hand over her hips and pulled her close.

"What's wrong?" Penny's soft question kicked him out of his erection-induced stupor.

"Nothing." *Except he was losing his damn mind.*

She glanced up from where her hand absently stroked his chest. He couldn't blame her for not believing him, because he didn't believe himself. Especially not after she laid that kiss on him back at the safe house. It was days later and he was still reeling from the way she'd nearly melted in his arms.

This was unlike any lust he'd ever felt. His body ached when she wasn't close enough. Her scent invaded not just his nostrils, but his entire damn thoughts. He needed her. To be *in* her. Around her. The only emotion stronger was the need to keep her safe and unharmed—laughable since she'd proven multiple times already that she could take care of herself.

Worn down from the effort to maintain both a physical and emotional distance, Rafe tossed his reservations on their ass and inserted a leg between her warm thighs. As far as maneuvers went, it was the tamest of what was happening around them. Couples danced, hands roaming and pillaging beneath undergarments. One partner. Two partners. A few couples down, one man had four overzealous women attending to his every need.

If anything, he and Penny stood out like saintly sore thumbs. Arousal smoldered in her eyes as she fixed her gaze on his mouth and enflamed his own. He gently shifted his leg and her stance widened, the distractingly high slit in her dress making it easy for her to straddle his thigh.

"Tell me when to stop, Red." Head bent, he trailed his lips along the curve of her bare neck. He fucking loved the way she always smelled of lilac and vanilla. He drew his tongue out for a quick taste only to find her pulse beat nearly as fast as his.

Each provocative sway of their bodies brushed his cock against her stomach, a steady and persistent pressure that had him fighting the urge to thrust into her softness.

Her fingers massaged the nape of his neck. "Would a lover really tell you to stop...*Rafael*?"

"If she ever felt uncomfortable with the progression of things, she'd damn well better. I'm following your lead on this one, sweetheart. If it were up to me, we'd be going somewhere with a lot fewer eyes."

And that was the damn truth. Cover or not, he wanted her. He also didn't want to scare the hell out of her or push her even an inch past her boundaries. When a shadow of uncertainty shimmered in her eyes, Rafe worried it was too late.

He nudged her gaze back to his with the crook of a finger. "Those were some heavy thoughts rolling around in there just now. Care to share them?"

"Not particularly."

"Red, if you're having second thoughts about this, you need to tell me. And it's more than the danger it could bring. I don't want you to feel you have to drop to your knees and su—"

She silenced him with a finger to his lips. "Stop. Trust me—you're not the only one eyeing that relatively dark corner of the room."

"Then what is it?"

"You constantly checking to make sure I'm all right makes me feel as though you don't trust me."

"It has nothing to do with trust—in you or your abilities. I've seen you in action, remember? I witnessed firsthand what kind of damage you can do. Call me a caveman, but

I'd be concerned even if you were one of our female operatives."

"Do you even have any female operatives?"

"Not yet," he admitted hesitantly, "but I'm sure it's just a matter of time."

She nailed him with a look that could've easily surpassed Maria's best hairy eyeball. "So you're saying that you'd give a female operative on your team a chance to back out of a mission?"

Rafe recognized the land mine he was about to step into, but it didn't make him back away from the truth. "Truthfully, I don't know. But this assignment isn't our regular grab-and-go. Besides polishing up our backgrounds, there wasn't much time for all the other shit that goes along with an operation like this. Like setting limitations. Expectations. I want to make damn fucking sure I'm not making you cross any lines you're not willing to cross."

Penny studied him a moment before gifting him the slow curl of her mouth. "You'll know I've reached my limit when I knee you in the junk. Okay?"

"Do you think you can tell me *before* that happens?" Rafe requested with a faint grin. "My junk's never going to be the same as it is."

Penny didn't have time to reply when they were approached by a server with an offer to join none other than their target himself—Diego Fuentes.

* * *

Impeccably dressed in a suit that easily cost more than two of Penny's paychecks, Diego Fuentes looked the part of the polished businessman. His more salt-than-pepper hair pegged him to be somewhere in his midsixties, and though he smiled as she and Rafe approached, there was no hiding the emptiness lurking in his eyes. Cold and hollow, they conjured a combo surge of anger and nausea that pitched her stomach to the side as Rafe accepted the man's hand.

"Señor Manuel, it is an honor to finally meet you." Diego's too-white smile flashed. "I have heard a great many things about you and your company."

"And I've heard many varied things about you as well, Señor Fuentes." Rafe's arm, linked solidly around her waist, tightened as she stiffened in response to his remark.

Fuentes paused a moment as if shocked that someone would speak to him so candidly, but when he let loose a low laugh, Penny slowly let her muscles relax.

"I have heard you are a straightforward man, Rafael, and this I like. And who may I ask is this exquisite creature draped on your arm?" Diego brought her hand to his lips as his eyes dropped in a breast-to-ankle assessment.

Rafe introduced, "This is Nell Hanlan."

At the brush of Diego's lips, Penny nearly vomited her internal organs on the man's thousand-dollar shoes. Screw boiling water and gallons of disinfectant. To feel clean again, she'd have to skinny-dip in a vat of flesh-eating acid and then rinse off in a pool of bleach. It took the man forever to release her hand, and when he did, she barely refrained from wiping it on her barely there dress.

"*Americana?*" Diego's wandering eyes made her skin crawl. "With hair as brilliant as a ruby and skin as flawless as I have ever seen, you are no doubt a model? An actress?"

She forced out a small string of giggles. "Actually, I *am* an actress, but I've been waiting tables until something that suits me comes along. Rafael's helping me."

"No doubt he is a good ally to have, *sí*? Please, join me."

Diego swept his hand toward his table, whose only occupant was a dark-haired young woman.

Penny smiled at the brunette but got nothing in return as Rafe ignored the extra chairs and pulled her onto his lap. The woman was an empty void—not a twitch of lips or a jealous sneer, and only after a full minute did the woman finally blink. Once.

"Tell me, Rafael," Diego said as he dismissed a nervous waitress after she appeared with two more glasses of whatever brown liquid was in his tumbler. "Your business seems to have come quite a long way in such a short period of time. One who has his hand into exports cannot seem to have a business conversation without Manuel Shipping mentioned. Have you ever thought about expanding?"

Casually resting one hand on the inside of Penny's thigh, Rafe stroked his fingertips over the sensitive back of her knee. An arousing combination of innocent touch and gentle caress, the contact would've awoken every flammable cell in her body if it weren't for the fact that they sat with the monster who had Rachel and God only knew how many others.

This was the exact direction they'd hoped to go in, yet Rafe looked as if he hadn't a care in the world. He lifted a shoulder in a barely noticeable shrug. "I already own one of the largest shipping companies this side of the hemisphere. Why would I need to expand?"

"A shrewd businessman is always looking for new ventures. What would you say if I informed you that I have the perfect arrangement already planned for the two of us?"

The corner of Rafe's mouth lifted. "I'd think it would be a little presumptuous, but I'd hear you out. I should warn you, Señor Fuentes. I maintain high expectations in my business relationships. Both my name and my company's hold quite a bit of weight in the import and export business. When involving both in *arrangements*, I make absolutely certain the payoff is worth the risk of ruining my reputation."

"That is understandable. And smart." Diego nodded.

"So you understand why I'm going to have to demand a show-and-tell—everything from the manufacturing process to your testing facilities. And it goes without saying that I'll be critiquing the distribution means you already have in place. In order to make this worth the risk, I need to know for certain you possess a top-of-the-line product from start to finish."

"I assure you my product is pure—and unlike so many out on the market." Though he was smiling, an underlying edge crept into Diego's voice.

"I didn't get to where I am today by relying on unproven assurances."

"I'm afraid I cannot do as you ask, my friend." Diego kept his posture relaxed as he sipped his drink. "If it is a sampling of the product you request, of course. I will have some to you within the day. But your other wishes I am afraid I cannot grant."

This was it.

Penny feigned preoccupation with the softness of Rafe's hair while silently screaming at him for playing too damn hard to get. This was their opening, their chance to get on the inside. But his face was a blank slate as he slid his hands to her hips and gently guided her off his lap.

Rafe gave his head a faint, disappointed shake. "I'm truly sorry to hear that, Señor Fuentes. I really am. But I can't go into business with a man who can't see beyond his own challenges—and for you that would be the Honduran government and the American Drug Enforcement Administration."

Their imminent departure startled the older man to his feet. Lips curled into a snarl, he looked five seconds away from bursting the bulging blood vessel at his temple. "To whom do you think you are talking? Some inconsequential street urchin?"

Rafe tucked an arm around her waist and stated blandly, "I thought I was speaking to a savvy businessman, one who understood that you're the one in need of a new avenue to export your product. I may be fairly new to this game, Señor Fuentes, but I assure you that I didn't start yesterday. Money is negotiable. My reputation is not. Before putting it on the line, I need to make sure the benefits far outweigh the risks. If you can't agree to those terms, then we're done here."

Penny hissed under her breath as he led them away from the table, "What the hell do you think you're doing?"

Rafe mumbled back, "Wait for it. Three, two..."

Six steps from the table, one of Diego's seven-foot watchdogs blocked their exit.

Fuentes slowly approached. Penny didn't know what was worse, the man's sickening smile or his blank, cool stare.

"While I do not agree initially to those measures," Fuentes said, addressing Rafe, "I would like to extend to you an invitation to my home. Maybe we can search for a viable solution and build a partnership that would appease us both. A few days, so that we can reach an agreement."

Diego's dark, soulless eyes settled on Penny. "And I insist that you bring your beautiful señorita. It has been far too long since a striking, vivacious woman has graced the grounds. My only stipulation is that your security stays behind. As you pointed out, I am a man in need of keeping many secrets and the location of my home is one of them.

I'll have one of my men meet you at my private airstrip and they'll escort you the rest of the way."

Rafe stayed silent for so long Penny nearly pinched him. Finally, he accepted Diego's hand. "Name the meeting time and we'd be pleased to join you."

CHAPTER SEVEN

Rafe enjoyed a good silent moment. He far preferred it to incessant ramblings and incoherent speeches, which is why it took him off guard when ten minutes into his and Penny's drive toward the city's posh tourist district, he felt ready to burst from his skin.

Curses. Mutters. Mumbles. Even the mother of all rants. He didn't care which avenue Penny chose to take, he just needed to have some kind of clue as to what was going through her mind. But it didn't look like that was about to happen. From the driver's seat of their rented luxury car, Chase glanced back, no doubt coming to the same damn conclusion.

Thirty minutes later, they pulled up to the hotel where Rafael Manuel and the lovely Nell Hanlan spent their nights while on vacation. Through the lobby and the elevator ride up to the penthouse suite, Rafe kept an eye on the stiff set of Penny's shoulders while ignoring the growing tension in his own.

They were supposed to set up a meet, get the intel they needed, and then coordinate the takedown of the entire Fuentes organization with every available government agency. End of operation. Game over. Bad guy in fucking jail. None of them had seen this shift in the plan.

When they finally entered the suite, the looming silence shattered with Trey charging across the room like a bulldozer.

"What the hell were you thinking, Ortega?" Trey demanded. By the look on his face, he'd been brewing a foul mood probably since Rafe and Penny had left the club. "Do you seriously think I'm going to allow you to sweep Penn into that psycho's lair with a fucking army much less with no one as backup? What shit have you been smoking?"

Rafe kept his head cool. "In case you misheard, it wasn't exactly my idea."

"But you fucking agreed!"

"*Allow* him?" Penny's gentle tone froze all five men to their spots. Instead of shrinking as she kicked off her heels, her stature grew. She glanced pointedly at each of them before landing on Trey, and never once raised her voice. "If Rafe had insisted on bringing any kind of security, it would've made it look like he had something to hide."

"Yeah, but he didn't need to agree to letting you tag along," Trey argued.

She shrugged. "Fuentes likes women. Isn't that why we thought sending me into the club with Rafe was a good idea to begin with? We got his attention. We got in. I'm not going to question why, and having been after this guy for months, neither should you."

"We shouldn't, but we are," Stone interjected. "Too many innocents have been affected by Fuentes. We're not eager to add to the tally."

"My name was added to that list the moment the bastard took the only family I have left!"

As the rest of the team focused on Penny, Rafe's gaze cut to his best friend. If he didn't know Trey so well, he would've missed the minute twitch of his left eye. Faint, quick, and only happening once before Trey pulled himself back together, the brief flicker was his friend's only physical show of weakness.

Rafe treaded carefully, clearing his throat. "I think what Stone means, Red, is that playing arm candy for a few hours is a hell of a lot different than having you under Fuentes's roof—literally."

"Then I won't do it."

"Thank fucking God," Trey mumbled.

When Penny folded her arms across her chest, fluffing up the already impressive view, Rafe knew there was more. "If you can tell me right now there isn't the slightest chance Diego will rescind his invite if I back out, then I'll stay behind." No one could make that claim, and the grim smile on her face indicated she knew it. "No? Then I'm going."

Stone perched on the edge of the couch. His gaze was stern, but his voice surprisingly gentle. "You have to understand something, sweetheart. We have no idea where the Fuentes compound *is*. The entire international alphabet-fucking-soup has been trying to track the bastard down for years. We're their last line of defense before they have to tuck tails and admit they've fucked up."

She tossed her hands up in the air with a growl. "Which is why it doesn't make sense that you'd be willing to risk the chance of Fuentes telling us to bug off! You've never gotten this close before."

Trey intervened. "You'd be going into this op dark, Penn—no backup if things go to shit. No support. We can't send you in with wires or run-of-the-mill tracking chips, because the paranoid bastard has the capability of finding them. It'll just be you and Rafe. And if things go to hell, it'll be the two of you and the Honduran rain forest."

"Good thing I was a Girl Scout, then, huh? I wasn't blowing smoke up your skirts when I said I'd do anything to get Rachel back. The question is are you going to *let* me?"

Fuck no. The red-blooded man in Rafe wanted her sweet ass on a plane. Out of sight. Out of mind. And out of danger. But the trained operative grudgingly admitted that she had a point. Her leaving at this juncture in the game would make their job more difficult than if she stayed.

Still, it wasn't Rafe's call to make—thank fucking God.

Stone, looking a hell of a lot like a gargoyle, went quiet. That alone wasn't what alarmed Rafe, because the Alpha head often kept his thoughts under a tightly sealed wrap. What had Rafe holding his breath was the way Stone tapped his fingers against his thigh...as if he was in deep thought.

And then his boss's gaze shifted to him. *Fuckin' A.*

"The decision's yours, Ortega." Lips pressed into a thin line, Stone's expression looked anything but thrilled. "You're the one going on the inside with her. I know I don't have to remind you that you're going into this deaf and blind. Bail enforcement or not, Penny's not Alpha trained. That means on top of everything else you're responsible for, you need to add her to the list—and right at the damn top."

"He doesn't need to—" Penny started to protest.

"Yeah, he does. Though you can hit a target and inflict a fair amount of damage, you're *green*. You've never been on this kind of an op. Hell, even Ortega hasn't."

But no fucking pressure. Dealing with Taliban leaders in the middle of the desert had nothing on the expectant stare

Penny slid his way. On the exterior, she looked the poster
girl for calm and cool. Direct gaze. Back straight. But the
subtle bite to her lower lip identified it as a carefully controlled ruse.

He wanted to say what his team expected him to—*no
fucking way*. But the words wouldn't come.

Though he didn't have family in the true sense of the
word, everyone associated with Alpha *was* his family—
even their ball-buster analyst, Charlie. If he were in Penny's
shoes, he'd turn over every rock in the Afghan desert, search
every damn block of ice in the Arctic, and make a deal
with the devil if it meant the safe return of his family. That
same brand of loyalty was etched on every feminine curve
of Penny's face.

Lives counted on their success, and not just their own, but
Rachel's and the countless others being subjected to Freedom and God only knew what other nasty drugs Fuentes
peddled around the globe.

Meeting Penny's gaze, Rafe mentally relived the last
week—Penny sparring in the training room, the too-close-
for-comfort scuffle in the alley, and the professional ease
with which she handled the meeting with Fuentes. Hell,
she'd been the one who remained casually aloof while he
nearly reached across the table and throttled the sick fuck
with his bare hands.

He couldn't believe he was going to fucking say it. "Don't
make me regret agreeing to this, Red."

With no questions, no hesitation, the team sprang into action. Logan fired up the laptop while waiting for Charlie to
answer stateside. Stone and Chase talked schematics and logistics with Trey. Backup plans were only good if you knew
where the hell you were, but some kind of contingencies
needed to be made—and a hell of a lot of them. Plans A, B,

and C wouldn't hack it this time around. Their ducks needed to be lined up straight to fucking Z.

Penny's presence hovered behind Rafe's shoulder. "What is it, Red?"

"Thank you," she murmured softly.

He stole a glance and mentally cursed with the sudden urge to yank her onto his lap and tell her everything would be fine. Instead, he gave a slight nod and prayed he hadn't made a mistake. "You can thank me if we manage to get out of this in one piece."

* * *

In her mind, Penny envisioned Alpha's tech guru as a tall, lanky brunet with a built-in pocket protector in every shirt. And the way the guys talked about Charlie Sparks also had her anticipating him to be…well, a *him*.

Not only was Charlie *not* a him, but she sported shaggily bobbed blonde hair adorned with pink highlights—and an English accent Penny couldn't get enough of.

"It isn't a bloody windup toy, Ortega. Stop playing around with the bloody thing." Charlie glared at Rafe from over the video link like she wanted to reach through the screen and strangle him.

"No. It's a watch." Rafe smirked, obviously having a good time teasing the other woman. "But do you really think this looks like something Rafael Manuel, self-made millionaire and professional ladies' man, would be caught wearing?"

"He'd be bloody lucky to wear that baby. And it's quite a bit more than a watch. What you have in your hot, callused hands is my pride and joy. It'll detect any surveillance device that's within a hundred-foot distance—audio or visual.

Because let's face it, Fuentes is going to have his place
bugged like a New York City hotel room. Before either of
you decide to talk *any* kind of shop, you scan. If you move
an inch to the left while in a heated discussion, you scan.
It wouldn't even hurt if you ran a scan after breathing too
deeply."

"I get it," Rafe interrupted. "I scan and scan again."

"Scan until your bloody finger is well...*bloody*. I know I
don't need to remind you that one slipup could mean the two
of you coming back or becoming cheetah bait."

"Are there cheetahs in Honduras?" Penny asked absently.

A grin spread across Charlie's face as she shrugged. "Do
I look like an animal rustler? Although, I have to admit that I
sometimes feel like I am when I'm surrounded by those five.
You have no idea how thrilled I was to actually stay behind
this time around. Too much sweat takes the pink out of my
hair."

Penny chuckled and took a good look at the blonde's surroundings. It didn't look like an office space or have the
stark, cool lines seen in most military bases. Framed photographs decorated a cherry wood-panel wall, and to the far
right over the other woman's shoulder, Penny glimpsed the
edge of an ornate plate-glass window. The way the browns
and golds swirled together into the form of an old-fashioned
beer mug looked...familiar.

"Charlie, where did you say you're stationed stateside?"
Penny asked, her gaze narrowing on the wall behind the
pink-haired dynamo.

"At our new headquarters. And I say new, but we've
really been here six months. Renovating a bar to fit our
needs takes a hell of a lot of time. And as it turns out, you
can't really hire just anyone to build secret bunkers into the
mountainside."

Penny's gaze drifted to one of the photos over Charlie's left shoulder. Two smiling women with arms tossed over each other's shoulders stared back at her. Penny didn't need to see it closer to know the one on the left wore a white tank and blue skirt, and the other wore the exact opposite: a blue top and white shorts.

She knew because she was the one wearing the jean skirt.

CHAPTER EIGHT

Penny stared at the photo, the one she knew for a fact hung on the wall of her hometown's neighborhood bar, Hot Shots. Thousands of miles away. In another time zone. *In Pennsylvania.*

Around her, the room went silent. No one moved. No one spoke. No one even appeared to breathe as she registered the fact that Alpha Security's headquarters wasn't as secret as they thought.

When she turned her gaze on Trey, Penny felt as if the floor slid out from under her. Regret flooded his eyes. He took a small step forward before stopping. "Penn—"

"Your headquarters," she said, cutting him off. "Your headquarters is in *Frederick*?"

"It's not what it looks like."

"No? Because it looks like despite having been back home, you couldn't be bothered to make an appearance, much less dial the damn phone. There was talk about new owners when it was closed down but—"

"We've only been there—"

"Six months. Six. Freaking. Months." Penny couldn't listen to any more. With a hasty good-bye to Charlie, she pushed her chair back, refusing to wait around and listen to Trey's excuses.

Tears threatened to fall, more with every second it took for her to reach the penthouse balcony. She welcomed the warm, stagnant air of San Pedro Sula, taking a deep breath and closing her eyes.

She should be used to this by now. Evasion. Disregard. Disappointment.

Her father had started her off in thinking those three things were the norm with families, but living in the Hanson house had shown her that it wasn't like that at all. At least until Trey left for boot camp and the e-mails became more and more infrequent, first separated by weeks, then months. Although she knew he occasionally sent his mother a quick check-in, the last one Penny had gotten herself had been about two years ago.

Behind her, the sliding glass door opened and closed.

"Can we talk?" came Trey's voice.

"*Now* you want to talk? Or do you just want to make sure that I don't tell Sophie you've been skulking around the neighborhood for half a year without so much as a drop-in? Your secret's safe. I won't tell her, but only because I don't want to break her heart."

"Will you hear me out? Please?"

She was on the verge of saying no when her gaze drifted through the window. Four sets of curious gazes watched them through the balcony door, but Rafe's was the one that snagged her attention. His expression was impossible to read: lips pressed tightly together, blue eyes narrowed on Trey.

As if sensing he was being watched, Rafe looked her way. Her head pounded, too overwhelmed with questions and feelings to add Rafael Ortega to the mix. Penny pulled her attention back to the street below.

"We have a lot of work to do before tomorrow," she pointed out to Trey.

"I know." He came up next to her by the railing. "Penn, I'm sorry. Christ, I know that sounds lame, but I fucked up. I fucked up when I left. I fucked up six months ago. Hell, I'm fucking up right the hell now."

"If you're waiting for me to disagree with you, you're going to be waiting a really long time."

"I wasn't planning on keeping our move a secret. Why would I have done that when I was the one who suggested we use Frederick as our home base? I just wanted to give things time to settle. And before..." Trey scrubbed his whiskered face with the palms of his hands and sighed. "I actually have no excuse for my eighteen-year-old self except that he was a punk-ass kid who didn't realize what he had and focused too much on the things he didn't—and wanted. By the time I made it into the Rangers, I knew it would be awkward to try and make amends. And when I made Delta, I didn't think it would be fair."

"Fair?" Trey's wording caught her by surprise. "What do you mean?"

"I mean that any soldier takes risks. We know it before we even walk into the recruitment center. But *Delta*?" Trey's throat worked to swallow. "Belonging to Delta requires a different breed. It's dangerous. It's secretive. I couldn't imagine making things right with you, Mom, and Rachel when I'd have to lie about ninety percent of my life."

Trey slid her a sideways glance. "Don't look at me like that...Jesus Christ."

"I don't think Jesus wore black camo and carried an Uzi," Penny quipped.

Trey chuckled, and for a minute Penny saw the boy she'd once cared about. He was buried way beneath the buzzed blond hair and tattoos, but he was there. And he was the reason she stood on the balcony and collected her thoughts. "Can I ask you something and get a truthful answer, not some negotiator response meant to keep people happy?"

"You can ask me anything." He looked like he meant it.

"Do you anticipate acting stupid again? Or are you up for trying to make things right?"

A relieved smile bloomed on Trey's face. "No to the first question, though I probably will. And hell yes to the second. Setting things right is the reason I fought so hard to bring Alpha to Pennsylvania."

"I'm not going to make it easy on you," she warned. "I'm still the girl who put cayenne pepper in your strawberry lemonade for ruining my date with Scooter Williams."

Trey laughed. "He deserved that itching powder more than anyone I've ever known. I mean, his name's fucking Scooter."

"It's his name." Penny couldn't help but chuckle.

"It was a *nickname*—one that he chose himself. He's lucky he *only* got the fucking powder."

Trey surprised Penny by tugging her into a hug. Cocooned in his massive arms, she felt warm and comfortable, just like the time he'd hugged her when she was eight and had fallen off her bicycle for the tenth time in as many minutes. Penny burrowed closer, holding on to the back of his shirt. A few breaths later and the teasing moment started shifting.

"Shit," he murmured into her hair. "Mom's going to kill me for letting you do this. I'm a fucking dead man."

"Maybe eventually." Penny gave him a firm squeeze before pulling back. "But at first she'll be too thankful to have us all back at home."

"You need to be careful, okay? I'd do anything for Rachel, too, but I know you have an aversion to people telling you what to do. You have to listen to Rafe every single second that you're out there. Every. Damn. Second. He's the best of the best, and even more, he knows I'll kick his ass if anything happens to you."

Like a magnet pulled their gazes together, Penny met Rafe's blue eyes through the sliding glass door. He'd taken a chance on her. They all had. Now that she'd convinced them all that she was up for this assignment, it was time to convince herself.

* * *

More holes littered their plans than the jeans of a nineties teenybopper boy band. Hours of research wasn't enough. Hell, Rafe could spend a week reading maps and forming contingencies for every contrived scenario and it still wouldn't be sufficient to make him feel fucking prepared.

Around one in the morning, the guys started leaving the suite one by one. Trey lagged behind, hands shoved deep in his pockets as he casually glanced around the room. He looked the most uneasy Rafe had ever seen him, and considering they'd both been sent to some hellish locations during their stint with Delta, that was saying a damn lot.

"Whatever's on your mind, unload it. We have a big day tomorrow." Rafe crossed his arms and waited.

Trey leaned against the doorjamb. "You know I own up to

my mistakes...when I make them. Cutting Penny out of my life the way I did was one of the largest. And it's one I'm not going to repeat."

The sumo-sized weight that settled on Rafe's chest was unnerving as hell, and most definitely unwelcome. Ever since the hugfest on the balcony, he'd barely been able to keep his foul mood to himself, wondering if Trey and Penny's relationship had been as platonic as each claimed.

"What's your point?" Rafe asked, unsure if he wanted the answer.

"My point's that I have a lot of ass kissing to do, and I can't do it if she's dead. She's important to me, man."

"I'll keep her safe and sound so the two of you can kiss and make up the proper way. Don't worry."

Rafe sounded catty even to his own ears. Trey's also picked it up, his face blank for a moment before realization turned shock into humor and the bastard laughed so hard tears sprang to his eyes.

"Glad you find this so funny," Rafe practically growled, his nails biting into his palms as Trey fought to take a deep breath.

"Yeah, well, when one of my best friends looks like a green volcano ready to blow his top, I can't help it. Jesus, Rafe, you think I *want* her, *want* her? Hell no! I mean, yeah, I love her, but like a sister! Christ!" Trey wiped tears of laughter from his eyes. "My mother practically raised her from the moment her asshole father dumped her and Rachel off on our doorstep. Even during my crazed hormone years, I've never seen her as anything more than a sister."

The tightness in Rafe's chest loosened a fraction. "Then what the hell was the bit about making amends and shit?"

"I meant that I've been a raging jerk to Penny through the

years. I took my entire family for fucking granted. It's done. I can't rewind back through the years and start over, but the very least I can do is start looking out for her. That begins by making sure she doesn't get put into a bad fucking situation. You hear what I'm saying?"

"Are you talking about Fuentes now, or *me*?" Rafe's voice chilled significantly.

Trey lifted his hands in mock surrender. "Look, I don't blame you for being interested. She's fucking amazing. All I'm saying is that the two of us are men of the same combat cloth. We constantly put ourselves in these shit storms, disappear for months at a time. Long-term for us is thinking toward the weekend, or hell, the next few hours. I don't care if she's with Bail Enforcement, Central Intelligence, the Federal Bureau, or any combo of the government alphabet. She doesn't fit in this ass-backward life. She deserves better. She deserves more than the half-assed attention that Admiral Kline gave her. And *that's* all I'm going to say on the subject."

About to leave, Trey turned. "Oh, and one more thing. If you hurt her, or if she comes out of this op with so much as a split end, you're going to be pissing in a bag through your belly button. You feeling me?"

"The only way anything would happen to her is if I was already dead." *And it was the damn truth.* He'd jump in front of a bullet or scale a building using nothing but his teeth to keep her safe.

Trey slapped him on the shoulder, the tension instantly forgotten. "Yeah, well, let's not aim for that either. Be safe, brother. Watch your ass."

"I'll watch Penny's, too," Rafe joked, straight-faced until Trey shook his head on a laugh.

"Don't push your luck, man—or you're going to be

investing in a hell of a lot of plastic bags." Trey chuckled before closing the door.

Now alone with only his thoughts and the sound of Penny's running shower for company, Rafe paced the length of the room. When he started making himself dizzy, he sat down in front of one of the Honduran maps, and then got up again a few seconds later. Each lap around the room intensified the ache in his clenched jaw.

His ability to keep Penny safe from harm wasn't bothering him. It wasn't fear that they'd fail this op. Hell, it wasn't even Trey's blatant threat to his manhood. The closer Rafe got to the answer, the more his control inched from his grasp. And then it hit him.

That sumo-sized weight sitting on his chest was gone. It disappeared. Now that he knew where Trey's head—and heart—was at, each breath didn't feel like it was being squeezed out of his lungs.

What the hell was that about?

Nothing had changed. He didn't do relationships. He *couldn't* do them. Getting jerked from one fucked-up foster home to another, he'd never learned much about love and devotion, or reliability. That was what a woman like Penny deserved.

Knowing he and Penny could never work didn't make ignoring the stir in his pants easier, especially when the water shut off. Mental images of her warm, damp body had him planting his ass in the chair. He curled his fingers around the arms and worked on convincing his body to stay seated instead of heading to the room where she was probably standing wet and naked.

Five minutes later, her voice brushed over his skin like a soft touch. "More maps? I thought we'd gone over everything."

"I'm taking another look for my own peace of mind."

Before he glanced over his shoulder, she was taking a seat next to him, her compact body covered head to toe in a terry-cloth robe. The bulky layers of fabric didn't deter his cock's awakening. He went from half-hard to full-scale flagpole in less than a few seconds, his massive erection practically pleading with him to take action.

"It was either the hotel robe or...well, you don't want to know," Penny chuckled, mistaking his drooling attention for curiosity. "Let's just say that between the dress tonight and the clothing Maria so graciously packed for me, you'd think I'd raided a naughty nighties boutique with a limitless credit card."

"Are naughty boutiques something you visit with regularity?" He loved the pink hue that stained her cheeks when he teased.

"A girl needs a few of the basics," she tossed back.

The growing tightness in his pants was a not-so-gentle reminder to put his focus back on the maps and not the mental image of a just-ravished Penny in a dark emerald-green scrap of lace—or better yet, nothing at all.

With a subtle shift in his chair, he yanked the conversation back to her initial question. "A man like Fuentes likes privacy. He's worked too long and hard to take a chance on blowing it to high hell. Not only is he not going to point out the landmarks as we fly over them, but there's a pretty good chance he's going to require us to be blindfolded."

"So how's memorizing maps going to do any good?"

"Because I'm hoping you can hone your inner actress and make a stink about being blindfolded. If we play it right, they'll leave yours off and then you can become our eyes. Don't look so panicked," he added when his meaning registered. "I don't expect you to memorize the maps. I've got that covered. *Your* job is to point out or remember things that might make it easier for me to pin down our location."

"Like rivers and lakes, open fields, and villages. That sort of thing?"

"Exactly. And you need to do it without drawing attention."

"I can do that. If there was one thing being a Navy officer's daughter taught me, it was excellent memory recall. Those military socials are no joke." Their shoulders touched as she huddled over the maps. "We really have no idea where Fuentes's compound is located?"

"Ancient civilizations are easier to find than this bastard's hideout." The subtle sound of flesh being nibbled drew his attention to her mouth. He reached out, freeing her lower lip with a soft swipe of his thumb. "It's not too late to change your mind. I can go to the airfield tomorrow alone."

"Do me a favor, Rafe." Penny's voice was so quiet he had to lean close to hear it.

"Anything, Red. Name it." *And damn it all if he didn't mean it.*

"Stop offering to do this without me. All you're doing by offering a way out is pissing me off and making it harder to act like your brainless bimbo."

"Are you going to be able to handle that?"

"You pissing me off, or acting like your bimbo?"

Rafe smirked. "The moment we hit that airfield tomorrow, you'll have been upgraded from bimbo to lover. Lovers are…affectionate. *Openly* affectionate."

"Is this your way of telling me you're going to be touching my ass, Rafael Ortega? If it is, I should warn you that that perk better go both ways." Penny's voice dropped, the low husk making Rafe nearly come in his pants.

Her breasts rose and fell with each heavy breath as he

slid one finger into the crease of her robe. "What was the longest you had to go undercover to snare a target, Red? An hour? Two?"

"Three." She failed to contain a gentle shiver as he brushed the top mound of her right breast.

"We don't know how long we're going to be at the compound. We won't be in charge of surveillance. That means we're going to have to be *on* twenty-four hours a day. No second-guessing. No hesitancy." Keeping his heated gaze on her, he lowered his mouth to her skin. "And lovers don't look uncomfortable when the other touches them."

"Is that what you're trying to do right now? Make me uncomfortable?"

"Is it working?"

"Not in the way you mean."

Rafe eased down one side of her robe, exposing the curve of her shoulder. The second his lips touched her skin again, she closed her eyes on a soft sigh. She needed to get used to him touching her. To maintain their cover. At least that's what he told himself as he dragged his mouth up to just below her ear where her vanilla scent seemed strongest.

In reality, he just needed the feel of her beneath his hands...and mouth.

With a painful groan, Rafe forced himself to pull way. He didn't get far. Penny's hands slid into his hair and directed his wandering lips straight to hers. This was what nirvana must feel like. She nipped his bottom lip, ratcheting up his desire a thousand and one degrees before slipping her tongue into his mouth.

All good intentions to maintain any kind of distance fell away. Fucking instantly. No way in hell was Rafe stopping her. Trey's threat to his dick be damned, he guided her off her chair and onto his lap. Her legs spread automatically, widening the gap of her terry-cloth robe. She was still damp from her shower, and the warmth of her skin seeped through his clothes.

He let his mouth feast, tangling his tongue with hers as his hands roamed over her curves. Beneath his palms, her body arched, undulating against his jean-covered erection. If she felt this fucking fantastic with a barrier between them, he could only imagine how she'd feel without.

Rafe didn't want to stop her, but he also needed to make sure they were heading in the same direction, and for the same reasons. "Before we do this, Red, I need to make sure we understand each other. This isn't some kind of test, or an initiation. This is you. Me. And this crazy-ass need I have to be inside you."

"Mm. A threesome." Her voice rumbled against his neck before she gave it a playful nip. "I've never been into that kind of thing before."

Rafe nearly went up in flames right then. A threesome? *Fuck no*. He didn't share—*period*. And he sure as hell didn't share her. "I need to hear you say it, Red."

"This is just you, me, and this." An evil smirk lifted her lips as she gave his cock a firm rub. "You're not going to get any complaints from me...unless you take too much longer."

"This may not be the job, but that doesn't mean—"

"A proposal. Trust me, I've seen how that road ends and I have no desire to travel down it. I'm a big girl, Rafe. I know exactly what this is and what it isn't, and there's no chance of me confusing the two. So you may continue, un-worried that I'm going to engrave wedding invitations next week."

She met his gaze, unflinching. She was telling him the truth. He didn't know what irritated him more: her easy dismissal of what was happening between them or that he was the one who didn't have high hopes for it being that fucking simple.

After three seconds of internal debate, Rafe flipped his doubts the bird and deftly untied the robe with one hand while guiding it away from the rest of her body with the other. Every inch of skin he unwrapped, his mouth savored.

Her pink nipples stood at attention, begging to be tasted. And he did. First one, then the other. Penny arched her back, pushing them more securely into his touch. Only when she trembled did he slide the robe the rest of the way to the floor.

"Jesus Christ, you're gorgeous." And she was. Every curvy inch of her.

Women in Rafe's life had always come and gone, leaving no real lasting impact, and that had always been fine with him. But with Penny he found himself needing to mentally record every fucking second.

"Ticktock, Rafe." She rolled her hips.

He lost it, whatever *it* was, and ignored his throbbing cock as he slowly slid one finger along her wet folds. With a keening groan, she pushed her pussy into his hand. He rubbed in slow circles, getting close but never quite touching her hardened clit.

"You. Are. Evil," she complained in a half moan.

"I'm the worst, baby." He simultaneously sucked her nipple into his mouth and slid two fingers into her pussy. One thrust. Two. Releasing her breast after the third stroke, he pulled away far enough for him to see her face when she came apart.

Penny rocked her hips, fingers digging into his shoulders. "Please, Rafe. More."

Fuck, he wanted that, too.

Holding her closer, he thrust his fingers deeper, curling

them to hit the magic spot that would have her coming in no time. With each glide of his hand, he caressed his thumb over her clit—again and again.

Her eyes, half-mast and darkened with desire, closed on a moan.

"Eyes on me, Red." Rafe slid a hand into her hair and dragged her attention down to his. "I want to watch you let go. And then we're both going to watch as I slide all the way into your body. Fuck, sweetheart. I bet you're going to wrap around me so damn tight."

Around his fingers, Penny's body started to quiver. She threw her head back and muttered a soft "Oh God."

Rafe kept going, thrusting and rubbing, bending his head to taste her skin before pulling slowly away to watch her eyes lose all focus. Finally, her inner walls convulsed around him, one pulse following another. When they finally slowed, he brushed her clit with his thumb and skyrocketed her into another, stronger climax.

Only immense control had him waiting until the last quiver left her body, and the second it did, he was fishing for the foil packet in his pocket. Penny had his zipper down and cock out by the time he ripped into the packaging.

He'd barely sheathed himself when she began lowering herself onto his engorged cock. "Fuck, you're really fucking tight, sweetheart."

"I think it may be that you're too big," she teased with a low groan as he pulled her hips down the rest of the way.

CHAPTER NINE

Possession was her only defense. There was nothing else to explain why she couldn't stop and why she, more importantly, didn't want to. It was like there were two Pennys floating beneath the surface of her body, and the one Rafe always coaxed out was the vivacious, brazen, and, judging by the way her hips ground down onto his, horny one.

Maybe it was Rafe. Maybe it was the dawning realization of how dangerous a situation they were stepping into. Suddenly, the woman who'd made it her life's mission not to get emotionally involved with a bleeding-hero type didn't give a snivel about what lay ahead of them as long as she was able to savor *this* moment. And the fact that she acknowledged it and still didn't want to stop made it even worse.

Rafe's mouth and roaming hands temporarily banished all thoughts that didn't involve him and sweaty, bare skin. She let him guide her body into a circular motion, the friction making her entire body begin to pulse with pent-up need.

"More," she whispered breathlessly. Tightening her grip on his shoulders, she ground her bottom harder against his lap. "Please, Rafe, I'm not going to break."

His fingers dug into her hips. "Hold on, sweetheart."

Penny squealed as he stood, but before she could protest the sexual pause, her back hit the wall and Rafe plowed into her with a powerful thrust.

"I don't think we're going to make it to a bed," Rafe growled out, thrusting again.

In this position, she could feel everything—him inside her, him rubbing against her. She rolled her hips and double-fisted her hands in his hair, hungrily bringing her mouth down onto his. "Beds are highly overrated."

"Fuck yeah they are." Rafe murmured against her mouth, "I need to feel you grab onto me, sweetheart. Let me have it. Let go."

Penny moved her hips faster, matching each of Rafe's thrusts with one of her own. He slipped his hand between their sweat-slickened bodies, expertly finding her already throbbing clit. Soft and gentle, he rubbed at her until every muscle in her body tensed.

And then she was falling off a virtual cliff of pure bliss. Her body pulsed around him, pulling out a groan from his throat. Thrust after thrust, it intensified until she felt like she'd burst in a million different directions. When she gently bit into the fleshy part of his shoulder, he followed her over that edge, and she thanked God she wasn't expected to do anything but drape her sated body over his.

"Wow." Penny panted, her body pleasantly limp. "Well, I can honestly say I didn't see that on the agenda for tonight."

"That should be on the agenda every damn night." Breathless, Rafe skated his lips from her neck to her mouth.

"And beds may be overrated, but I can't wait to do that again lying down in one."

She chuckled. "I'm game if you are, but you're going to have to be in charge of relocation because I don't think the feeling's going to return to my legs for at least a week or two."

"I'll make your recovery my top priority." Rafe devoured her with his mouth as he walked them down the short hall to the back bedroom, and he did it without faltering a step or pulling out from her already reawakening body.

Two seconds ago Penny didn't think she could move. Now her body was raring to go for another round despite the nagging voice in her head muttering that she had lied.

Big-time.

Rafael Ortega couldn't just break her. He could crush her.

* * *

Penny's stomach somersaulted a few dozen times, and she wished it was because of Rafe's magical hands. And his talented mouth. And every inch of his lethal-to-her-senses body. Last night, as corny as it sounded, had been a life changer. And she couldn't imagine anyone but Rafe being the one capable of doing it.

Of course, that meant she didn't know what was going to come at any given moment—except her with him. Maybe. Hopefully. But not right now.

Now she was mentally cursing the fact his hissy-fit plan worked too well. Between her earsplitting cries and the fervent stomping of her high heels, Diego's men would've done almost anything to get her to shut up. Hoisting her into the back of a helicopter without a blindfold had been a small price to pay for her cooperation. For them.

Penny glanced at Rafe sitting next to her, a blindfold secured tight over his eyes, and contemplated stealing it for herself.

Through deep breaths, she studied the panoramic view beneath the chopper. For all its drawbacks, poverty and crime to name two, the Honduran countryside was exquisite. Lush green treetops blanketed the untamed jungles. Jagged mountains blended seamlessly into the occasional open plain, and interspersed amongst the terrain rose the sporadic groupings of small villages, villages that looked no larger than a few ant-sized structures.

There wasn't an inch of land lacking beauty, but what *was* noticeably absent were conspicuous landmarks. There were no street signs or roads, and for most of the expedition, no civilization. That meant there was nothing to memorize.

The chopper pitched left. With a gasp, Penny's grip on Rafe's knee tightened. She closed her eyes and focused on making each breath deeper than the last.

Though they were the only ones without communication headphones, Rafe still made certain to keep his concerned voice low as his lips brushed against her ear. "You doing okay?"

"Peachy," she lied.

"The nail marks in my knee say otherwise." Rafe caressed the inside of her leg in soothing circles.

"Sorry." She made an effort to lighten her hold, but the second the chopper shuddered beneath them in a loud grind of metal on metal, she resuctioned her hand back onto his leg. "Okay, maybe I'm not so peachy. We're football fields above a tree-topped wilderness in a flying contraption that looks as if it should've been laid to rest about four wars ago. Your blindfold looks really good right now."

"Would you like me to take your mind off it, *Roja*?"

Murmured seductively into the curve of her neck, in Spanish, his nickname for her never sounded better.

Rafe chuckled, no doubt feeling the surge of her heart rate against his mouth. A promise like that from him was probably the only thing that could take her mind off dropping to the ground in a blazing inferno.

When they landed ten minutes later, Penny would've dropped to her knees and kissed the jungle floor if Rafe hadn't secured an arm around her waist.

"You're looking a little peaked, *Roja*." He grinned.

"I think the color you're searching for is green," she joked dryly.

"But even green tinged, you're still fucking gorgeous, sweetheart."

"Welcome!" Diego's voice turned them both around. Looking very much like a general in front of his camouflaged fortress, Fuentes marched toward them, quickly eating up the distance with his long strides.

And it *was* a fortress. Trees hugged the large stucco mansion on all sides, effectively melding it into the surrounding jungle. Macaws in vivid shades of greens and reds squawked from the red clay rooftop while white-faced capuchins swung on low-hanging limbs.

An over-the-shoulder glance confirmed that Fuentes's men had covered the chopper with camo netting and jungle life. Operation No Backup had officially started.

"Keep it cool, Red." Rafe's lips grazed against her temple, missing nothing.

"Señorita Hanlan. Rafael." Diego placed another gag-invoking kiss on Penny's hand. "I am ecstatic that you could make the trip. One of my men will show you to your room, and after you have had a chance to refresh, we will sit down to dinner."

"I'd rather get down to business," Rafe added. "Not that I don't appreciate your hospitality, but I do have a company to run and eventually get back to."

"All in due time, *mi amigo*. Due time. Think of your time here as a little business vacation."

Diego ushered them into the house, which was no less impressive on the inside than the outside. Expensive pieces of art lined the walls. Antique tables were adorned with statues in a vast array of mediums. And the opulence continued in their room, where four large circulating fans hung delicately from the vaulted ceiling, one of which hovered over a king-sized bed. Everything looked lavish and rich—and Penny fought like crazy not to smash every valuable in sight.

It wasn't until she and Rafe were left alone that she opened her mouth, and turned straight into a kiss that curled her toes. Oh, the man could kiss.

Rafe took full advantage of her impending rant. His tongue brushed against her bottom lip before slipping into her mouth. In zero point two seconds she went from stomach-twisting sick to panty-melting hot. Her arms linked around his neck while his large hands gripped her hips and pulled her between his muscular thighs.

Her gelatin legs no longer mattered when he walked her backward and pinned her body against the wall. Vertical was her new favorite position, at least with Rafe. With unhurried strokes, his tongue mimicked the slow grind of his hips, tormenting every inch of her body until she emitted a husky, feminine groan.

Until last night, she'd never been kissed like this—like the very existence of the earth depended on this one single meeting of mouths. If this was what it was like to be ravished, she'd been missing out on a hell of a lot. His callused hands bit into the silky fabric of her sundress and lifted both the hem and her leg to his waist.

It felt animalistic, primal—fitting since they were in the middle of the jungle. Control obliterated, she tossed her reservations into metaphorical *Yucca* trees and chased after the hot, burning need ripping its way through her body.

She no longer received, but gave. She matched the thrust of his hips with her own, lured his tongue farther into her mouth before invading his. She slipped her hands beneath the cotton of his button-down shirt and relished the feel of hard, flat abs. One strong tug and buttons flew, leaving his chest exposed to her touch. Someone, or both of them, trembled.

With a soft curse, Rafe spun them into the bathroom, never once taking his mouth from hers as he kicked the door closed behind them.

"Keep your arms raised." He clasped her fingers around the mounted towel hook and continued to run his hands down her body. When he got to the hem of her dress, he sifted it up and bunched it around her waist. Her knees buckled as his thumb brushed over the dampened lace of her thong. And when he followed the caress with a slow nuzzle of his mouth, she whimpered, one hand falling to the top of his head.

"Hands up, *Roja*, or this is all you're going to get."

No. Freaking. Way.

Rafe waited until she obeyed to pull her thong to the side and take a long, slow swipe with his tongue. Her body tensed as he skated it back through her wet slit. Up and down. Around. He took his time, making her body quiver beneath his mouth before daring to give her engorged clit a gentle suck.

"Oh my God," she murmured at the exact time the pleasure turned to carnal bliss.

He hummed against her mound, the vibrations tightening her hold on the towel hook to avoid falling. The mix of his rough, stubbled jaw against her thigh and the smooth glide of his tongue made her come so hard that her legs went limp.

Rafe continued to lick her until she was breathless and panting. She lost track of time, watching him beneath half-hooded eyes as he kissed his way to her waiting mouth. Tasting herself on his lips felt so wrong, and yet made her so damn hot.

Not letting go of her, Rafe reached into the shower and turned the nozzle to full blast. With a lazy smile, he dropped his forehead to hers. "Holy hell, Red."

She flashed him a tremulous grin. "You took the words out of my mouth. And not that I didn't enjoy that because I obviously did, but what was that about?"

"Bugs."

With the still-pulsing rush of pheromones, it took a minute to realize he meant microphones and not hand-sized cockroaches. "How did you—?"

He gestured to Charlie's creation strapped to his wrist. "Charlie wasn't kidding. This thing works like a fucking charm. That room out there's filled to the brim with them, and it looks like there's a video signature out there, too."

"So you're telling me that your choices were either giving me a mind-numbing orgasm or having me blow our cover?"

He flashed her a wicked grin that made his eyes twinkle. "What can I say? I've been thinking about tasting you ever since we woke up this morning."

Penny couldn't argue with his chosen option, because she'd been thinking about the same thing. She just hadn't pictured it happening against the door in Diego Fuentes's bathroom.

"I'll scope out the mics and deliver them to our host with

an ultimatum, but I think it best we leave the camera." Rafe got them back on track. "It doesn't appear to have sound capabilities. This way, Fuentes can feel as though he has an eye on us. Of course, that means no breaking character. At least physically."

"Then let's go round up some bugs."

"Not right this second." He propped his arm against the door, blocking her exit.

"Can I ask why not?" She challenged his naughty grin with a lift of her eyebrows.

"It doesn't take a sex therapist to see where things were heading out there. We were going at it pretty hot and heavy. I may be undercover, but I still have a reputation to consider. There's no way in hell I'd be done with you after only a few minutes."

Heat came roaring back to both their eyes with his brutal honesty. Rafe had made her shed her reservations regarding commando types once already, twice if you factored in the kiss at the safe house, and it was clearly going to become a habit.

Her rules hadn't factored him into the equation, because he was more than the ruggedly gorgeous outside package. It was his brief moments of humor, of compassion...and yeah, ridiculous sex appeal. When he dropped his cool exterior and looked at her like he wanted to eat her whole, she shivered. A man like him didn't do anything half-assed. He was thorough and attentive, woefully unselfish. Jealousy over an unknown woman who would one day be lucky enough to call him hers made Penny give herself a mental slap.

His gaze drifted toward the running water. "I can think of one way to pass the time."

Her eyes rounded as she fought not to misinterpret his meaning, but the upward curl of his lip and the matching glint in his eyes said she hadn't misread a damn thing. "Seriously? You want to take a shower? *Now?*"

"It's as good a distraction as any. Water conservation is the eco-friendly thing to do. What do you say, Red? Do you want to help me save the planet?"

CHAPTER TEN

Showers would never be the same for Rafe again, not after lathering Penny in soapy suds and running his hands over every square inch of her gorgeous body. Watching her eyes light up with arousal as she came was a damn addictive sight to behold, which is why he made her come on his hand a second time in the shower before letting her drop to her knees.

And Jesus. He was glad he did. If being inside her warm pussy was the ultimate heaven, having her tongue wrapped around his cock took a damn close second. His strut had a spring to it as he inconspicuously scanned the room for bugs, pocketed them, and then located the camera in their room's unused fireplace. He gave Penny a heads-up and then left her to prepare for dinner.

As he navigated the halls of the mansion, he drew a mental blueprint of points of entry and exit, of every door and corridor and security detail. The entire time, one of Fuentes's homegrown militia shadows followed, but he didn't care.

The howl of curses brought Rafe straight to Diego's door.

"I do not fucking care if it has become difficult for you," Diego snarled into a phone. "Take care of it or I will take the fuck care of you, you arrogant son of a bitch! *Comprende?* Fix this. *Now*. Or I'll have your body parts spread over the entire southern hemisphere. Try spending my money then!"

Fuentes hurled the phone against the wall, making it splinter into a dozen pieces.

"Breaking up with your service provider?" Rafe joked dryly, announcing his presence.

The older man ventured over to his wet bar, his face back to an eerie calm. "It is an unfortunate case of entitlement issues, I am afraid. But I do believe I made my stance on the matter clear. And if I have not, I will soon enough. I trust that you and your beautiful *señorita* have found your accommodations to your liking?"

"The bathroom's quite roomy."

Diego's twisted smirk tested Rafe's control. Yeah, the bastard had seen the show in the bedroom. Rafe was suddenly very glad he'd moved them into the bathroom.

He dropped the mics onto the mahogany desk and let his displeasure be known. "I could've done without these. The kind of business relationship you're proposing requires trust, Señor Fuentes. *This* isn't what I call trust."

"You must pardon me, Rafael, but I do not trust so easily." Diego slipped a drink in Rafe's direction. "Nor, does it seem, do you. However, I do apologize for the necessity, and for the invasion of your privacy."

"And I have your word that no more will be put in their place?" *Not like he'd believe the man for a minute.*

"*Sí. Sí.* Of course!" Diego gestured to one of the plush leather seats. "Come. Join me for a predinner drink and then I will allow you to fetch your beautiful lady friend. You must tell me how a man from your rather humble background has acquired so much success."

* * *

It was Vince, Penny's friend and mentor, who told her that using the attributes given to her by God and genetics sometimes couldn't be helped. It was the way of the world, and the men they often sought after in bail enforcement didn't expect a curvy vixen in fishnets and a micromini to tote around a shiny Glock 19 and an arrest warrant beneath her garters.

It was a tactic she'd never felt truly comfortable executing, and it wasn't any different now than it was then. Except for the fact that Fuentes wasn't a parole jumper with a penchant for beating on prostitutes...and she wasn't armed. It wouldn't have mattered if they had been able to sneak in their handguns. Although it covered her body from neck to knee, the snug fit of her blue Asian-style dress couldn't have hidden the outline of a matchbook, much less a weapon.

The sleek material hugged her every curve as if it were airbrushed onto her skin. All the clothes she'd brought on this op fit the same way, as if they were designed and made just for her. It made Penny wonder if Maria had somehow managed to take her measurements while she was sleeping.

Penny turned sideways, looking into the bathroom mirror from different angles. No matter which way she turned or how much smoky-eyed makeup and lip balm she applied, the woman staring back at her looked uncomfortable.

The click of the bedroom door followed by the complete lack of footsteps broadcasted Rafe's arrival. "Our host is waiting for us, *Roja*," his voice echoed from the bedroom.

She peeked around the corner and watched him act casual as he did another electronic scan of the room with his Hot-and-Cold watch. "I'll come out, but you're not allowed to judge. Also, don't make me bend, laugh, or expect me to breathe too deeply. In other words, anything physical is pretty much off the table. But if we need one of those living statues, I'm your girl."

Pulse pounding, she showed herself in the doorway and felt her heart plummet to her stomach at the sight of Rafe's wilting smile. "Oh God. It's bad, isn't it? I look ridiculous? I knew it." She turned, prepared to hide her head in the nearest hole.

"Don't move a muscle." His soft order brought her feet to an automatic stop. But it wasn't until his presence warmed the front of her body that she hesitantly met his gaze. She watched in fascination as his blue eyes changed to stormy gray.

Though she was covered, she couldn't have been more exposed if she stood in front of him naked. His eyes scanned her from the toes of her peekaboo stilettos to the curves of her breasts. By the time he reached her eyes, every inch of her body hummed.

"And here I thought it couldn't get better than the dress from the club. You love proving me wrong, don't you?" Rafe's low voice gave her goose bumps.

Her lips stretched into a tremulous smile. "When this is over, I'm going back to jeans, cotton T-shirts, and tennis shoes. I may even go the crazy extra mile and toss on a hoodie...but there will be no dresses and sure as hell no heels. Or thongs."

Not that she was wearing one now.

When this Fuentes nightmare ended, she also needed to deliberate a plan on what she'd do with her attraction to the man in front of her. If Alpha really had set up shop right in her backyard, it wasn't like she could enjoy now and never see him again. Frederick was a small town, and despite the fact their paths hadn't crossed yet, Rafe wasn't on assignments year-round. The chances of bumping into him at the one and only gas station or the grocery mart were more than likely. It was a given. Eventually.

She was working on her acting skills for the bail enforcement job, but she wasn't about to win any awards. And when it came to Rafe—forget about it. His many layers made her head spin and feel like the newest recipient of a Razzie Award.

He was bravery, loyalty, and a kick-ass attitude wrapped up in a six-and-a-half-foot mass of hard muscle. For years he put his life on the line for his country, and even though the ink had long dried on his discharge papers, he was doing it still. Alpha wasn't a job to him. It was a way of life, as much a part of him as the heart beating in his chest.

Her father had been like that. Trey was like that, too. But what neither had done that Rafe did in the little time they'd known each other was take a chance on her. It both humbled her and fired her up. And it also rumbled the walls of her carefully constructed boundaries.

She pasted a smile to her face as Rafe stepped forward, careful to keep his wide back blocking the camera. He was close, *so* close that the front of his shirt brushed against her breasts.

"What are you thinking about that's got your brow furrowed like that?" He gently rubbed a finger over the wrinkle that had formed on her forehead.

Her eyes closed automatically as she savored the gentle touch. "Oh, you know...my to-do list. Groceries. Errands. The fact that the longer it takes us to crack Fuentes, the longer Rachel's subjected to Freedom and God only knows what other nasty drug the man's invented."

The moment he cupped her cheek, Penny didn't hesitate to move into Rafe's warmth. Solid and unwavering, his arms surrounded her like a protective shield. With a heavy sigh, she braced her forehead against his chest.

This open, wilted person she became in his embrace unnerved her. She hadn't invited her, and she sure as hell wasn't comfortable with her. But that didn't seem to matter when Rafe's hand slipped into her hair and gently kneaded the tight muscles at the base of her neck.

Her voice shook as the admission slipped too easily from her lips. "I know we need to keep our guard up, to not rush this, but I keep picturing Rachel in a dark, dank dungeon, scared out of her mind, and the harder I try to change my focus, the worse the images get. How can I not let them affect me?"

"I'm not going to pretend to know what you're feeling." Rafe's breath brushed intimately against her ear, his words weighted with sincerity. "And I can't say your concerns aren't warranted, because Fuentes is one sick fuck. But one thing that helped me back in Delta and with Alpha now is focusing on the end result. Rachel's already *in* this situation. It's done. We can't change that. But we're going to do our damned best to get her *out* of it. In other words, focus on the things you can change, not the things you can't. Rachel's lucky to have you in her corner."

"She's been in mine long enough. It was never a question of *if* I'd try to find her, but whether I could actually do it. Thanks to you and the others, we're close. I never would've gotten this far without all of you."

"The same could be said about you. We've been after this bastard for close to a year—three months in San

Pedro Sula alone. Before you, we only had suspicions and hearsay about where Fuentes was getting his guinea pigs. And if you hadn't overheard that conversation between those two drug peddlers, we wouldn't have known that Fuentes kicked up his timeline, much less known where to score a face to face."

Her gaze flickered down to his mouth, mere inches away. "So you're saying the moment I kicked you between the legs is the moment your luck changed?"

"The moment I met you, *a lot* of things started to change." A charged silence thickened between them until he stepped back, trailing his fingers down her bare arm until their fingers entwined.

Penny was still looking down at their linked hands when he started leading the way out of their room. Hand holding was a simple, innocent gesture, but that nagging little jump in her stomach told her that there was nothing innocent about the intimate contact.

And there was nothing simple about the way it made her feel.

* * *

Dinner tasted like ash in Penny's mouth, and on a few occasions, she battled back her gag reflex. The woman from the club, Carlotta—Diego finally introduced her—had joined them, but she didn't so much as look in their direction, her big brown eyes as sightless as they'd been the other night at the club.

It didn't take long to realize the poor woman was nothing more than a puppet. She stood when Diego told her to fetch drinks, sat when she finished the task. Never once did she make eye contact or smile. She reminded Penny of the other women who had been in *El Sótano* with the exception that Carlotta appeared better fed.

But that little tidbit didn't stop Penny from imagining lunging across the table and gouging fuertes's eyes out with a dinner fork—for Carlotta. For Rachel. For everyone his cruelty threatened or harmed.

Men like Fuentes had a reserved seat in hell.

She'd mentally vowed to take Carlotta out of this nightmare when the weight of Rafe's hand settled on her thigh.

A quick glance around the table had her realizing that she'd become the focus of both men's attentions. She slid a forced smile onto her face. "I'm sorry, sweetheart. You must have caught me in a daydream."

"Which shows my hunch is correct." Rafe's eyes narrowed in concern as he gave her leg another gentle squeeze. "Let Carlotta escort you back to the room, *Roja*. It's been a long day and I know you must be tired. I'll be along in a bit."

"I don't mind waiting for you."

If looks could've pushed her out the door, Rafe's would've tossed her on her ass. "Señor Fuentes and I have some business to discuss," he said calmly. "Go. Get comfortable, and maybe you can take a soak in that Jacuzzi tub you were eyeing earlier."

"Or perhaps you'd like to take a stroll around the grounds," Diego surprised them both by suggesting. "I take much pride in my gardens. You will find plants and flowers that are unable to be viewed even in the most renowned horticultural centers. Even in the moonlight, their beauty is awe-inspiring. I often take midnight strolls myself."

Penny's gaze flickered to Rafe, hoping for some kind of sign as to what to do, but his face was a mask. "I wouldn't want to get lost. My mother always said that I could get lost trying to get out of a paper bag."

"You must stay on the path and within the perimeter of the compound, but if you were to get turned around, you'd only need to call out for assistance. My security team will *always* be nearby to assist you."

Calling Diego's group of thick-necked mercenaries security guards was like referring to the bubonic plague as a bad case of the sniffles. Penny opened her mouth to decline, but Diego stood, his arm outstretched in her direction.

"Come, Señorita Hanlan," Diego beckoned. "Carlotta will see you to your room so that you may change into something more suitable to enjoying an evening walk."

The brunette waited by the doorway for Penny to follow orders. And they *were* orders. Diego Fuentes was obviously not a man who heard the word *no* often. She kissed Rafe good-bye, feeling his gaze on her until she left the room. It was one thing to be apart, but an entirely different feeling being separated at the suggestion of Fuentes.

"I wouldn't suppose you'd like to go with me for a walk?" Penny asked Carlotta when they reached the bedroom door. After a five-second blank stare, the other woman turned on her high heels and click-clacked in the direction from which they came. "Guess not," Penny muttered to herself as she entered the room.

Nothing looked amiss, but remembering what Rafe said about the likelihood of Fuentes reinstalling the mics, she made certain not to do anything that could be considered suspicious. She nearly forgot about the walk altogether, but then common sense and cabin fever took over.

While Rafe was busy making nice, the very least she could do was scope out their surroundings. She slipped into the bathroom and changed into a tank and shorts. Then after sliding into her sneakers and grabbing a mini flashlight, she headed out the room's patio doors.

There was dark, and then there was black-abyss, fall-to-your-death dark. The surrounding jungle most definitely fell into the second category, but between the dim lanterns illuminating the stone path and the occasional streak of moonlight breaking through the trees, her chances of falling flat on her face were relatively low.

The cold slither of watching eyes followed her as she turned each corner. She ignored it, her forward movement fueled by the mental images of Rachel's frightened face. She'd meant it when she told Rafe she'd do anything to get Rachel back.

Being only three years younger, Rachel had felt more like a sister than Penny's late older sibling had. They were each other's best friends, accomplices, and therapists. Everyone from the crotchety old bartender at Hot Shots to the doe-eyed children at the after-school program adored her.

The more Penny thought about Rachel, the tighter her hand reflexively gripped the flashlight. Before she realized it, she'd nearly circled the entire compound.

It wasn't like she didn't know she wasn't alone. With every inch of her walk, she'd felt the eyes of Fuentes's men. But the shadow standing by the pool was smaller and about a foot shorter than the six-foot he-men she'd seen earlier. Penny squinted into the darkness until Carlotta's narrow frame came into view.

She was talking to herself, incoherent rambling that didn't make sense. At least not until Penny heard the words *prisoners* and *bunker* muttered in the same unintelligible sentence.

In English... and with the hint of a Midwestern American accent.

Penny's sneakers hit a patch of loose pebbles, making Carlotta jump. Eyes wide, she spun around.

"It's okay." Penny lifted her hands. "It's just Nell. You remember me, right? From dinner? And the club?"

Carlotta's gaze flickered back and forth between her and the jungle.

"I was just taking a walk," Penny said in an attempt to sound casual. "It's beautiful out here. So open and yet tucked away. I bet it must get a little lonely sometimes though. Do you get many visitors? Family who comes to visit you? Or any other people who come around?"

The mention of people set Carlotta off again. This time her words flowed too fast to catch more than a word or two for every twenty syllables. Carlotta paced frantically, edging to where the stone walk met rough jungle only to turn around and do it again and again. Her gaze kept slipping away from the mansion and into the thick foliage to the east.

"Are there people out there, Carlotta?" Penny murmured, keeping her voice low as she took another step toward the woman.

"No. No." She shook her head frantically as she spoke to an unseen entity. "No. I can't. I can't do it. I-I have to st-stop, or I can't help them."

"Help who, Carlotta? Is someone in danger? Where are they?"

"No!" Carlotta's shout startled the birds in the trees, sending them into flight. "I can't! Leave me alone!"

Carlotta's scream created an eruption of chaos. Loud shouts came from the mansion, and seconds later, the running pound of footsteps echoed up the trail. The closer Fuentes's men got, the more agitated the young woman became. Three guards barreled around the corner, lethal-looking guns pointed in Penny's direction, while a fourth physically dragged away a now hysterical Carlotta.

"Leave her alone!" Penny shouted. She stepped forward

to intervene and got the muzzle of a gun jammed into her side. "You're going to hurt her!"

After another jab between the ribs, the guard nearest Penny started spewing an elaborate list of orders, none of which she intended to follow. His fingers bit into her arm hard enough that she didn't have to fake a wince.

"Ow! Hey! Get your mitts off me! Please, *no hablo...* your language," she said, pretending not to understand. "I didn't do anything wrong. She looked really upset. I just wanted to make sure she was okay. Do you understand me?"

Either they didn't, or they didn't care. Gun still aimed in her direction, one of the other guards lifted a radio from his hip. "*Get Fuentes. We have a problem...with one of our guests.*"

Penny's throat went dry. Hell, dry would've been preferable. Rafe was definitely going to do his fair share of growling now, and this time, she would deserve it.

CHAPTER ELEVEN

Y our Señorita Hanlan…she is a wild spirit, is she not?"
Diego offered Rafe a freshly cut cigar and then took a seat,
the leather creaking as he leaned back. "I sense a fire in her
that one doesn't often see."

"She's headstrong," Rafe stated simply. "But then again,
I'm a man who likes to be kept on my toes."

"Carlotta also used to be very…willful, but there are
times when such traits can become a detriment to busi-
nessmen such as ourselves. It can be distracting, cause an
undesirable shift in focus. I say this only out of a desire to
see our partnership flourish."

"So far, we haven't spoken much about a partnership."
Rafe didn't bother hiding the bite behind his words as he pictured dragging Fuentes across his desk and in direct line of
his fist. His simmering violence had little to do with *business*
and everything to do with concern for Penny's safety. Ever
since she'd left the room, Fuentes had spoken of little else.

"I'm wealthy in my own right, Diego," Rafe reminded him. "I can leave your home and return to any of my own. As I said before, I won't risk my comfort, my company, or my name for a product that isn't worth it. Likewise if I'm being sent in as a cleanup crew for misguided procedures."

"I assure you that Freedom is worth it. It is cheaper to manufacture than cocaine and more addictive than heroin and meth *combined*." Diego's dark eyes narrowed in thought as he took the first long puff on his Cuban. "I don't pretend to understand all of the chemical components and the bindings of molecules. I'm the visionary, not the scientist. But my doctors have proven that the effects of Freedom are plentiful and, most importantly, long lasting. The second it hits the bloodstream, a person's body *needs* it to function. I have seen even the most willful individuals become obedient simply so they are gifted another taste."

Rafe's internal warning bell started to chime as Diego's oil-slicked smile slid onto his face. "Obedient to whom?"

"To whoever is in control of distributing the drug. In our case, we sell to men and women looking to put their stamp on the world for whichever reason they choose. If they wish to lure a government official into their power, so be it. If they choose a more personal avenue to keep that ex-lover by their side, well wishes go with them. The opportunities for which Freedom can be used are quite endless... if they have the monetary funds, of course."

Rafe swallowed his own bile. Only the sickest of bastards would name a drug the exact opposite of its intended side effect. "That's a pretty big claim, my friend. I'm assuming that you have the testing to back up all of your ideas."

Diego's eyes widened with insult. "*Of course.* Any laboratory tests that are performed by the much American-loved FDA are performed by my scientists. We follow the same testing measures—with a bit more flexibility and expedition, of course. We have recently completed trials on our male volunteers with great success and have been undergoing a second round of female trials for the last two months. Everything looks very, very promising."

"I can't believe you have people volunteering to become drug addicted."

"The Honduran countryside can be very unforgiving. With starvation and disease running rampant, many villagers would do anything if it meant a better life for their family— or one less mouth to feed."

"You use locals." *And anyone else who's threatened to throw a chink in his plans.*

"To a varying degree, yes. And as for production and distribution, a few well-placed connections grant me relative free rein to do with Freedom as I please. And now with your involvement, Freedom could span across the four ends of the globe as soon as spring."

Rafe snorted. "While I'm flattered that you think so highly of me, you'd have to have a significant degree more than *well-placed* connections. You'd have to have inside men or women in every continent and from every government agency out there."

"I am a man of many talents, Rafael. And I also happen to be very persuasive. Even the once-feared American DEA has been relegated to nothing more than a nuisance to my general plan."

Despite having been the agency to have contracted them to track Diego's movements, the DEA being compromised wasn't without possibility. It would explain how Fuentes kept his operation from authorities for so long.

"You have someone on the inside helping you." Rafe chuckled, feigning an impressed look. At Diego's slow smile, Rafe's stomach curdled. "From what I heard, the DEA was your biggest obstacle, so why do you need me if you already have someone paving your way?"

"Do the Americans not have a saying about not putting all your eggs in one basket? My contacts remain beneficial for as long as they remain discreet. When there is nothing to lose but money, discretion can be compromised. As you've said, you would be putting your name, your company, and your reputation on the line. You have a vested interest in remaining discreet and efficient."

"I admit I'm intrigued, but as I said, I don't do a damn thing without physical proof," Rafe stated firmly.

"As you wish," Diego finally conceded. "But it will take a few days to secure a flight and to make certain everything is prepared for your arrival."

"You don't perform any of the testing here?"

"What I have on location is nothing but a decoy, something that if found, would distract authorities long enough to protect my other assets. But you will get your wish, and then we can start this new venture. Together."

"*Señor Fuentes.*" Diego's head guard appeared at the mouth of the office, a grim look hardening his face. "*We have a situation—with Señor Manuel's friend.*"

Diego smiled as if unconcerned. "Then let's go see her, shall we?"

Rafe schooled his expression to show nothing but the faintest bit of curiosity as Diego's man led the way toward the back of the mansion. Penny's voice reached him before he laid eyes on her. Two of Diego's men clenched each of her arms in a grip that would more than likely leave behind handprints.

"What do we have here?" Diego asked calmly as they approached.

"Oh, thank God," Penny cried out. "I was just explaining to these *gentlemen*—and I call them that very loosely—that I was simply out for a walk when I bumped into Carlotta. She was upset and I was just trying to make her feel better. They're acting as if I tried to shove her into my suitcase and kidnap her or something."

Though her performance made the explanation sound feasible, Rafe still took a step forward when Diego did the same. Cover or not, he wouldn't tolerate anyone threatening her in any capacity.

"It is thoughtful of you to want to help someone in distress, *señorita*." Diego kept his voice low as he brushed a strand of hair from her cheek. "But I assure you that Carlotta wants for nothing. She has been my constant companion for many years now. Your concerns are best turned in your own direction."

Despite Penny's supreme efforts to hide it, Rafe saw the flinch. Hell, the double meaning nearly made *him* cringe. He brushed by Fuentes before tossing a lethal glare to the two men restraining her. Only his Delta-taught control kept him from ripping their arms from their fucking sockets.

At Diego's slight nod, they released their holds. The second she flew into his outspread arms, Rafe cupped the back of her head and pulled her close. He shot Diego's thugs another death glare before leveling the man himself with a fixed stare.

"Nell's misguided attempt at assistance or not"—Rafe's voice went flat—"I will not tolerate anyone putting their hands on what's mine. The next time your men do more than give her a passing glance, they'll be wiping their asses with their noses. If you want this business arrangement as bad as you say, then you'll make sure they remember that."

Diego stayed silent for a beat before nodding. "Consider them warned."

With their first night in the compound at an official end, Rafe twined his fingers through Penny's and led the way back to their room. By the time the door closed, his teeth ached and his jaw twitched. A wave of the hand silenced her explanation as he inconspicuously scanned the room for replacement bugs.

Furious couldn't begin to describe the anger coursing through his veins. A man like Diego Fuentes didn't need a good reason to put a bullet in someone's head. And now she was on his fucking radar.

He counted to ten—twice. Only when his heart fell back into his chest did he let words slip from his lips, ice cool and level. Penny flinched as if he'd screamed them in her ear. "What the hell did you think you were doing?"

"We're being eyeballed, remember?" she reminded him needlessly.

He kept his back turned toward the camera. "The only thing Fuentes is going to see is that I'm pissed off, and that's pretty damn close to the truth. What the *hell*, Red? I didn't bring you along so you can fly off, half-cocked."

"There was no flying—half-cocked or otherwise. Do you not remember that I was practically *ordered* to go for a walk in the gardens so the manly types could talk business?"

"Were you told to go snooping? Or to cross-examine Fuentes's resident pet?"

"She's not a resident, Rafe. She's *American*—at least I think she is from what I could tell of her accent. And I wasn't snooping, *or* cross-examining. I stumbled across her and she was honest-to-God upset, mumbling and muttering incoherently." Penny lowered her voice to a near whisper. "Gazing toward the east, she said something about prisoners and a bunker. How was I to know that she was going to go apeshit crazy?"

"That is exactly my point—you *don't know*. Which means you do nothing without my knowledge, and that includes approaching anyone on this compound. You may not be helpless, but you're still *my* responsibility. Your actions affect my ability to do my job, and more importantly, they directly influence our chances of getting to Rachel. Diego's now going to be watching us closer than ever, and that's if he doesn't decide to get rid of us entirely."

"I didn't realize—"

"No, you didn't realize," Rafe growled, hauling her onto her toes.

She flinched, more from his words than his firm grip, and he almost apologized. Then the thought of her at Diego's mercy fired him up all over again.

"I was a few minutes from getting the 'in' we needed. Unless the man is sampling his own drug, Fuentes seems to think Freedom is going to make him the ruler of the world and everyone in it. He's not planning on this being a run-of-the-mill street drug, Red. He's going to sell stashes of it to the highest bidders, and *those* people, who could be anyone with a fat wallet and a fucking twisted disposition, will intentionally addict people so they have no choice but to come back to *them* for more."

"Instant obedience." Penny's face paled.

"Exactly. I know I don't have to tell you the litany of fucked-up ways that can be used. Mass distribution means that—"

"Rachel's already gone."

Rafe witnessed the heartbreak in her eyes. Goddamn, he wanted to chase that look on her face away as if he were the fucking Grim Reaper of Bad Thoughts. Instead, the replayed mental image of her in the hands of Fuentes's thugs turned him into ten different degrees of asshole.

"Let's hope your little stunt hasn't blown our chances of finding her before it's too late. Now, if you'll excuse me, I have to go suction my lips to the man's ass and see if we can get them back."

* * *

Rafe's words echoed in Penny's ears long after he'd left the room. They gnarled her insides, souring the contents of her stomach to the point she barely made it to the bathroom before bringing it all up. When the dry heaves finally dissipated, her throat was raw and her body ached. A hot shower did little to relieve the tension of her sore muscles, but she didn't really deserve to feel better.

At some point, she must have closed her eyes and fallen asleep, because the soft rustle of clothes hitting the floor snapped them open. Facing the wall, she waited for the dip of the mattress. Rafe's scent beckoned her to slide backward into his warmth. Instead, she burrowed her face into the pillow and denied herself the comfort.

He'd been right. Any misstep, slight or huge, could blow their chances of finding Rachel, and there'd be no one to blame but herself. The bucket of tears she'd cried earlier had nothing on the ones that rose fresh to the surface the moment Rafe's arms wrapped around her.

"It's okay." His mouth brushed against the shell of her ear, his embrace tightening.

"No, it's not." She squeezed her eyes closed on a hiccup. An anvil bore down on her chest, making each breath more difficult than the last. "You were right. I could've seriously ruined everything—our chances of finding Rachel, of bringing down the Fuentes cartel. *All of it*. You have every right to be mad at me. *I'm* mad at me. I can't even tell you how sorry I am."

"*I'm* the one who should be apologizing, Red. Not you."

He must have heard her snort of derision. With gentle hands, he rolled her over and captured her chin between his fingers until she had no choice but to look him in the eye. Even in the darkened room, his eyes glittered, homed in on her face. "Other than Fuentes thinking you're a Grade A pain in the ass, we're fine. One thing you should know about me is that I don't give false assurances. If this is the only problem we run into on this op, we're in good shape."

"But you were so—"

"Angry?" Rafe's brow lifted. "Funny how I've always been able to control my temper—until you."

"Are you trying to tell me that I have a knack for pissing you off?"

Rafe's thumb brushed over her bottom lip. When his gaze dropped to her mouth, breathing became an issue all over again. "I'm saying that I was angrier at the thought of you putting yourself in harm's way than with you possibly blowing the mission."

He stilled, watching as she traced the wings of his bald eagle tattoo strategically placed over his heart.

"You were worried because I'm your responsibility?" she asked, using Sean's words from the hotel.

"Yeah. And a hell of a lot more."

Rafe slowly slid the tips of his fingers up the length of her arm, her shoulder, her neck. There was no alpha-man stoic mask in place at the moment. His gaze held hers, open and curious and just as confused as her own.

"I don't know how you managed to do it, Red," Rafe murmured. "I've never felt unsteady a day in my life, but worrying Fuentes would get rid of you before I could react...I nearly tumbled right to my damn knees."

Tense silence hovered over their heads, and Penny didn't want to be the one responsible for breaking it. Silence was safety. It deepened, had the potential to develop into a bottomless pit, but as long as everything stayed unspoken, it was relatively harmless.

Rafe shattered that safety net the moment his gaze dropped to where his thumb brushed against her lower lip. She saw the kiss coming, yet when he touched his mouth to hers, she startled. It started as gentle exploration, sweet and more tender than anything she'd ever felt before. Rafe was hard in so many ways but this.

When he gradually began to slide away, she slipped her fingers through his hair and brought him back.

Hot and languorous, this wasn't a savage attack of mouths and limbs. Rafe came over her, careful not to crush her with his weight as he braced his forearms on either side of her head. The warmth emanating off his skin sent her hands into motion.

His chest, all hard muscle and smoothness, was velvet-covered steel beneath her palms. She traced down the width of his torso and around his defined abs. Slipping beneath the band of his boxers, she found his cock, already hard and pulsing.

"What the hell do you do to me, Red?" Rafe murmured against her neck as he slowly rolled his hips and thrust his erection into her hand.

"If you don't know, then I'm doing it wrong," she whispered, her bravery encouraged by the dark.

With a low groan, Rafe slipped his hands beneath her body. Over her behind and down her thighs, he lifted her legs around his waist. Penny arched into his touch. The instant her already sensitized breasts caressed the heat of his skin, her satin slip of a nightgown may as well have been nonexistent.

Her body burned. Craved. *Needed*. It needed *him* and the impenetrable comfort that came along with his arms. Being with Rafe, it was easy to pretend nothing existed except for the two of them. No operation. No danger. Just them and the warm glow that started forming in the center of her chest.

From somewhere in the mansion, a door slammed. This time, it was Penny who broke the kiss with a painstaking groan.

Rafe tucked his nose into the curve of her shoulder. "Hell, Red. You see what I mean? *Unsteady*. This isn't the time or place to ravish you head to toe, and yet I'm one hip roll away from not giving a hot damn about either and taking you right here."

Penny completely agreed. Fighting the temptation to spread her legs and rub against the hardness pressed against her upper thigh probably wouldn't have been a battle she'd have won. Rafe unknowingly tested every set of limits she'd ever drawn for herself and probably a few more she should've made up.

Taking a deep breath, she slowly slid her hands over Rafe's bare back. "I guess we should change the subject before we end up starring in our own adult film. Any suggestions?"

"Grandmas and puppies?"

She almost smiled, right until a torrent of guilt nearly swallowed her whole. Flashes of Rachel's face, dirtied and frightened, tightened Penny's chest. Each image was worse than the last until her heart pounded in her ears. She struggled, tried to squirm out from beneath Rafe, but he kept her still, his body still pressed into hers as he tried to gain her attention.

"Breathe," he ordered gently. When she didn't obey, he cupped her face in his hands and forced her to hold his gaze. Calm and steady, he ordered again, "Take a slow breath, Red. Breathe. Relax." He ran a hand up and down the length of her arm. "It's okay."

"No. No, it's not." She fought against a surge of tears. "How horrible a person am I to be doing *this*...with *you*...while Rachel is being subjected to God only knows what?"

"It doesn't make you horrible. It makes you human."

Penny waited for him to tuck tail and run from the emotional display, but he didn't. As a matter of fact, he never did what she expected. The corners of his eyes softened as he brushed away the moisture dampening her cheeks.

"Even the biggest badass needs a release valve." He sounded so adamant, she almost believed him. "Why the hell do you think soldiers are scheduled R and R in cities close to where they're stationed? Constant stress and danger weighs down even the most dedicated."

"But—"

"It's *not* wrong." Rafe silenced her words by gently brushing his mouth over hers. "And it's not selfish if it's what helps you to move forward. We *will* find Rachel."

"What if she's a carbon copy of Carlotta by the time we find her?"

"Then she'll have you to help remind her who she is. She'll have you to help her through it." He curled her into his side, the move so natural she nestled her bare cheek against his chest. Callused fingers caressed her arm from the back of her hand to the bend of her elbow.

Lingering sexual tension made every inch of her body

tingle, but it wasn't alone. Something infinitely more dangerous huddled beneath the hum of their bodies. Warm and cozy, it settled in the center of her chest, branching out until she didn't give it a second thought when her hand absently stroked down the length of his torso and back up.

It was *intimacy*.

Beneath her ear, the quick thumping of his heart matched her own.

Rafe murmured softly. "Get some sleep. Tomorrow we'll start mapping out the lay of the land, look for things that may be hidden beneath the pretty surface—like why Carlotta was so preoccupied with what was toward the east."

"And if it's more nothing?"

Rafe tugged her gaze upward. "Then we'll deal with that just like we'll deal with anything else that happens to come along. And we'll deal with it together."

Penny didn't have the strength to ask him what that meant. She was too preoccupied with his use of the term *we*.

And *together*.

CHAPTER TWELVE

Quick and easy. That's how this was supposed to go. With Penny keeping the eyes of Fuentes's men turned in her direction, this would be a piece of cake. Of course, that meant Rafe had to keep his head from wandering to Penny keeping the eyes of Fuentes's men turned in her direction.

He hadn't liked the plan when she'd suggested it, but he'd had to admit that it made the most sense. Keeping the focus away from him, he'd be able to slip away undetected and find the main source of the compound's power. Now that he had, he cursed.

Fucking solar.

"Where's Charlie when you need her?" Rafe muttered.

Give him a Glock, a KA-BAR, or a fucking pair of boxing gloves and he was golden, but don't expect him to pull out the science. Knowing he didn't have time to nap on the job, Rafe got down to work.

Luckily for him, there was no way in hell Fuentes had the

compound on-grid, not this far away from civilization. And sure enough, he found the battery bank that kept the system running off-hours. Once he took away the backup, it would be lights out at sundown.

Rafe couldn't just pluck a wire or snip it in half, because even the dense security Fuentes had on staff would be able to tell the difference between sabotage and a furry critter. So he pulled out his toys and got creative, quick. The longer it took him to disrupt the compound's solar grid, the longer Penny was out there alone.

* * *

Eyes closed but not the least bit sleepy, Penny pretended to enjoy a lazy morning at the pool. Jungle life surrounded her with the cackles of mischievous monkeys and chirping birds, but it wasn't a symphony fit for the masters. Each sharp trill drilled through her temple like an ice pick and reminded her that she wasn't here on vacation. She had a job to do, and this morning it was to keep the eyes of Fuentes's guards on her so Rafe could sabotage the compound's power.

Her plan had seemed like a good idea at the time. A cup of ice and a bathing suit didn't really leave room for errors. But that was before she remembered the suit Maria packed was less suit and more like brightly colored dental floss.

Penny picked up another ice cube and forced her mind away from the watching gazes. Neck. Collarbone. Arm. Occasionally, she threw in the slope of her leg or alternated the order. But every time she ran a piece of ice over the bruises circling each bicep like a black-and-blue version of a tribal tattoo, she was reminded how close she came to screwing up every inch of progress they'd made.

Rafe had been sweet telling her it wasn't as big a deal as she thought, but they both knew that had been a fib. Well, *she* knew it.

Mistakes and failure hadn't been tolerated in the Kline house—at least when she'd lived there. Her father's pep talks went something like: Fell off a bike? *Get back on it.* Got pummeled by a bully at school? *Hit them back harder.* When she'd fallen off the school monkey bars and dislocated her shoulder, her father's reply to the nurse's phone call? *Slip it back in and send her back to class.*

At seven years old.

Rafe and her father were sculpted from the same kind of clay. He did his job without apology, put his life on the line for what was right. Fearless may as well be his middle name. Yet last night, he'd held her close, offered reassurances instead of anecdotes, soft caresses instead of shrug-it-off pats on the ass—and all the while he pretended not to notice the subtle shake of her shoulders.

Each day, Rafe showed her that he wasn't the typical red-blooded male. It was a good thing, but it wasn't enough for a storybook ending. One look at Carlotta, back in her drug-induced stupor this morning, confirmed it. Happily ever afters weren't possible as long as sick men like Fuentes roamed free, and as long as they did, men like Rafe would feel inclined to put a stop to them.

Penny had just grabbed another ice cube when the man himself strutted onto the patio. Behind her sunglasses, she let her eyes feast. He was too sexy for both his own good and hers. His shirt, half unbuttoned and hanging loose, show-cased muscles that had been chiseled from years of hard work and extreme circumstances. And the dark strip of hair that bisected his tanned chest and sculpted abs trailed provocatively beneath the waist of his pants. Picturing its ending destination would've made her stumble in her six-inch platform sandals if she hadn't been lying down.

Rafe's mouth twitched with a smirk. "Undressing me with your eyes, *Roja*?"

"Are you here to stop me?"

"Absolutely not. You look to be enjoying yourself."

"I'd be enjoying myself a lot more if you were here with me, baby." Rafe's eyes darkened, telling Penny that her words had their desired effect. "Are you sure you have time to spend with me? I wouldn't want to take you away from your work."

"Right now all I want to work on is you, *Roja*."

It was the phrase they'd come up with to signal that things were on track, but it still spread a liquid warmth straight to her nonexistent bikini bottoms. All they needed now was to wait for sundown, and Rafe would be able to go all dark-wing commando without being seen by the many layers of Fuentes's security.

Rafe grabbed the tube of sun block from her bag and with a gentle tap on her hip, he ordered her to flip. The butterflies in her stomach turned prehistoric in size, but she turned, pretending that waiting for his touch wasn't the excitement equivalent of national All-You-Can-Eat Ice Cream Day.

Oh, who the hell was she kidding? It surpassed it—by *miles*.

Rafe worked the warm lotion into his palms, then turned his strong hands onto the knots in her shoulders. Down her spine and around her torso, with every inch he touched, goose bumps that had nothing to do with wind-induced chills peppered her skin. There was a whole lot of something to be said for a man with callus-roughened hands.

When his hands slid back up beneath the string holding her top in place, her breath quickened. Her breasts, crushed beneath her weight, grew sensitive and heavy. "Rafe," she croaked, his name sounding more like a moan.

"Go on and turn over, *Roja*."

She obeyed without question. Even if she'd been able to form a cohesive thought, the sight of his erection straining against his linen pants would've cleared it from her mind. Fuentes's men watched their every move, but when Rafe sat on the edge of her lounge and took her leg in his hand, there was no way she was going to tell him to stop.

Hot tingles followed the path of his hands, from the delicate arch of her foot to the sensitive spot behind her knee.

"When it's just the two of us, you're going to give me a private showing," Rafe murmured. His eyes followed the path of hands.

"A showing?"

"You. Me. And that damn cup of ice. You have no idea how much I want to take you back to our room right the hell now." Rafe's voice grew rougher the higher his hands went. "I want to taste every inch of you. Touch you. Make you scream so hard your throat goes raw. And all before I finally bury myself into this lush little body." Rafe let out a long, low groan. "This bathing suit is just fucking cruel, sweetheart."

He skated his hands just below the swells of her breasts. Penny sucked in a sharp breath as the backs of his knuckles brushed over her tightened cloth-covered nipples. Her reaction brought a smug smile to his lips.

"So is what you're doing to me right now," Penny panted breathlessly.

His smile made her heart skip a beat. For Penny, the lines of reality quickly started blurring together. Add in her own swelling feelings, and her mucked-up head didn't know which way was right or left, real or for the sake of their cover.

With Diego's men across the patio, there was no reason to mutter such words—unless he meant them—which was dangerous in its own right. It was way too close to what she desperately hoped would happen, and would keep happening.

She pulled her legs from his grasp, needing to put some distance between them before she did something so embarrassing there was no returning from it. She stood too fast, the epic heels catching on the lip of the patio. Graceful, she wasn't. Her arms flailed as she pitched forward... right into the cavern of Rafe's waiting arms.

Penny didn't have the chance to voice her complaint aloud when his hand brushed over her cheek and into her hair. Gentle yet guiding, he held her in place as he brought his lips down against hers. One nip to her lower lip and she went boneless.

"No running, *Roja*," Rafe murmured his order, his voice low and rough. "Not from *me*. Not ever."

He brought his mouth back to hers in a kiss that sucked the air straight from her lungs. It wasn't a hesitant meeting. It was a full-scale invasion as his tongue slid past her lips and into her mouth. Between the hand entwined in her hair and the one settled proprietarily on her ass, she couldn't move. She didn't *want* to move. She gripped his shoulders and let herself be plundered.

The kiss rode waves of change: soft and steady, hot and needful. All devastating. *This* was the dangerous part of their operation, because it didn't take long before it wasn't Nell Hanlan kissing Rafael Manuel. It was Penny kissing Rafe.

About the time she started giving back what he demanded of her, Rafe's body stiffened beneath her palms.

Penny stopped, noting that her leg had coiled itself behind his knee. Good God. She'd been about to climb the man like a tree. No wonder he'd frozen. They were in public, for God's sake, with not only Fuentes's guards surrounding them, but dozens of cameras probably hiding in every nook and cranny and filming the entire show.

Embarrassment coated her cheeks pink as she uncoiled her body from around Rafe. Two seconds from apologizing, she noticed his attention focused over her shoulder.

"What's wrong?" she asked. His sudden spike of tension told her that she probably didn't want to know. "Rafe?"

"It looks like Fuentes invited another guest. Show *nothing* when you turn around, Red. I mean it. Absolutely *nothing*. And if I tell you to run, you run."

The urgency in his voice made her want to run right then—and hide. "You're making me nervous."

"Then you're not alone."

And that made her *really* nervous.

"Rafael!" Diego's voice boomed, demanding attention.

Penny turned, attention focused in the direction of Rafe's gaze. Standing next to Fuentes was a much younger man.

"I'd like to introduce my nephew, Marco." Diego brought the young man closer. "He has been overseeing the production aspect of our product and will be the one to guide your tour of our facilities. I'd been expecting his arrival sooner, but he had been unexpectedly detained. The matter has now been cleared, and he will be joining us for our discussions."

Rafe's fingers dug into Penny's waist in a supportive hold. To the untrained eye, Rafe looked relaxed, but every muscle was prepped to move fast. "How nice. A family business."

"And I aim to keep it that way," the nephew stated matter-of-factly.

When the nephew's eyes shifted her way, both Penny's heart and breath lodged in her throat.

"Breathe, baby," Rafe whispered. His lips brushed against her ear with a soft kiss.

It was the jolt needed to push the air from her lungs before she passed out cold.

Because standing in front of her was the abusive bastard from the alley.

* * *

Concern for Penny clawed at Rafe's gut like a wild animal. Though she'd tried to hide her fear back at the pool, he'd seen her cheeks pale as she'd laid eyes on the thug from the alley—except he wasn't a thug.

A fucking nephew. There'd never been a shred of information on any living relatives—no sisters, brothers, or even childhood-fucking-pets. But he couldn't ignore the possibility. Everything from the forty-year age gap to the twin glares they now fed one another across the desk made the resemblance between them uncanny.

But unlike the alleyway thug, Marco exuded a self-appointed superiority his broken nose hadn't managed to stifle. He'd even had the audacity to eye-fuck Penny while Rafe stood at her side. It was a sheer miracle he hadn't put his fist through the bastard's face. The only reason he hadn't—besides Penny's fist bunched into the fabric of his shirt—was that there wasn't a hint of familiarity coming from Marco's eyes. *Nothing.* Either he was a damn good actor, or he didn't recognize her as the woman who'd broken his nose and knocked him unconscious.

Despite their good fortune, Rafe still didn't like her being out of his sight, but he'd had little choice when Diego suggested the three men retire to his office to talk business. He and Penny needed more info if they were to find Rachel and take down the operation. If that meant spending more time with Sick Fuck Numbers One and Two, so be it.

"What we have in place is enough. We don't need the likes of *him*." Marco's glare flipped toward Rafe the second the office door closed.

"*He* has a name," Rafe commented evenly.

"*You* are what we call an efficiency sucker, *Rafael*," Marco snarled. "An efficiency sucker and a waste of time. Everything has already been set into motion. Another player will only further complicate matters."

The younger Fuentes waited for Rafe to jump to the defensive. He did the opposite as he took a seat and leaned back, propping his leg on his knee. The lackadaisical response had Junior tightening his jaw.

Diego spun toward his nephew. "What do you mean everything has already been set into motion? The final declaration was to go through *me*!"

"And you put me in charge of production. It's ready. There's no reason to wait longer than necessary. We've waited too long as it is, and we lose money each day we delay the first shipment."

"Which is why Señor Manuel is here to discuss the use of his company."

"*Fuck* his company."

Diego's eyes went wild. He moved damn fast for a man in his sixties. Coming out from behind his desk and into Marco's face in seconds, the older Fuentes drilled the muzzle of a Beretta into the kid's left nostril.

"You have already made personal messes that I have been forced to clean up, and I refuse to let *my* business become yet another of your blunders. As long as there is life left in this body, you will make no choices without my permission. Is that clear?" Diego snarled. When Marco didn't answer right away, Diego cocked the gun. "I asked you if that was clear."

"*Claro*." Marco didn't even blink.

Diego continued glaring at his nephew before pulling the gun away and turning to Rafe with an apology. "This *will* be cleared up. Immediately. I promise you."

Rafe casually draped an arm along the back of his chair. "Unless Junior's actions start impeding on *my* business, personal or otherwise, it's of no concern to me. The first time it's attempted will be the last."

"A man who doesn't accept challenge is weak," Marco growled.

"I didn't say I wouldn't accept challenge." Rafe hardened his gaze on the other man. "But it would be the last time that person would be capable of voluntary physical movement."

Diego focused his demand on his nephew and pointed toward the door. "Undo what you have already set in motion. And for your sake, nephew, I hope no damage has been done. Or I will not hesitate to feed you to the circling sharks at the DEA. You risk what is not yours."

Marco stood, throwing a severe scowl in Fuentes's direction before muttering a soft, "We'll see," and slamming the door closed.

* * *

Penny fought against the return of last night's dinner as shock curled her stomach into knots. She clutched the counter and willed the shake out of her hands. Even an ounce of Rafe's cool stoicism would be good right about now. He hadn't so much as batted an eye at Marco's appearance. He'd been calm and level-headed, not a sign of unease anywhere on his face.

Damn it. She really needed to learn how to summon his nerves of steel, especially when the chill in the air told her Marco had entered the kitchen.

"Aren't you missing the meeting?" she asked. Unwilling to let him linger at her back, she turned.

"I think I'd be missing more by staying." Marco's gaze flashed down to her breasts. "How do you like my uncle's home?"

"Honestly, I'd much prefer a beach. All these trees make tanning impossible."

"Our view here *is* quite limited to the wilds of the jungle, but the treetops serve our purposes well. Besides, the sun is much too harsh for the delicate skin of a woman such as yourself. We wouldn't want anything to mar this perfect flesh."

Smirking, Marco bracketed his hands on either side of her hips. In a matter of seconds, she became trapped between the edge of the counter and his body. Shivers of revulsion scoured their way along her nerve endings as the back of his hand brushed across the dip of her collarbone. He leaned forward, his breath scraping across her cheek. Rancid bile rose to her throat as he pushed the evidence of his arousal against her belly.

"Maybe you should worry about your own skin, Señor Fuentes," she warned. "My Rafael is a very jealous man. I can't promise you that it would be the only thing at risk."

"A jealous man is an insecure man. And I don't scare easily, *mi bonita.* You shouldn't bother yourself with someone who would prefer to busy himself with business rather than the pleasure of your company."

"And you're that type of man?" she asked dryly.

"I'm a man of many surprises." Marco's hands slipped back to her hips, the bite of his fingers making her wince.

"And I would love to show you all of them—starting with the way a man takes care of his woman. Properly."

"Remove your hands. *Now*." Rafe stood in the doorway, his gaze fixed on Marco like a missile targeting its drop. His hands clenched and unclenched at his side. Face hard, and eyes harder, this wasn't Rafael the businessman. This was Rafael the commando, the highly skilled soldier with the ability to make grown men pee their pants. "I wasn't kidding earlier about losing voluntary movement, Junior. If I have to move your hands for you, you'll regret it."

The younger Fuentes smiled as he turned unashamedly in Rafe's direction. The second he dropped his arms, Penny skirted past and let Rafe tuck her at his back.

"I'm okay," she muttered.

"Well, I'm not," he returned softly before focusing his attention back on Marco. "You don't like that I'm here, and I don't really give a flying fuck. But while I'm working with your uncle, you damn well better keep your hands to yourself or you'll have to learn how to jack off with stumps."

Marco stepped forward until he was only inches away from Rafe's face. "You. Cannot. Threaten. Me!"

"I didn't threaten. I *promised*. And once I make a promise, I keep it no matter the cost. Learn your place before I show you one you're not likely to enjoy."

Marco ran a predatory glance over Penny's body. "You can hardly fault a man for enjoying the artwork when you thrust him in front of a masterpiece. I wonder if she fucks as good as she looks. Perhaps you'd care to share, *Rafael*?"

Penny grabbed Rafe's arm just as he was about to lunge. "No. It's not worth it."

Marco chuckled, turning from the room. Before he left, he flashed Penny a brazen wink that nearly had her releasing her hold on Rafe and telling him to go to town. "I look forward to our next meeting, *mi bonita*. Perhaps I'll be able to show you I'm a man of my word as well."

Tension poured through the kitchen even in Marco's absence. Penny let out a trembling breath. "Would it be terribly unprofessional of me to wish I could break his nose a second time?"

She slipped in front of Rafe, who'd gone eerily still. His jaw flexed wildly with the hint of barely controlled anger.

"Hey. It's okay." She soothingly stroked the hard lines of his jaw and mouth, and when that didn't work, she stood on tiptoe and covered his face in feather-soft kisses. "Tone down the caveman. I'm okay. See?" She unclenched his fists and brought them to her cheeks. "You need to breathe and focus, because I'm pretty sure we've gone over how much I need you right now."

"He touched you."

"Yeah, he did," she said carefully. "But it's nothing a hot shower won't cure, okay? Promise."

Rafe blinked. Once. Twice. And then he pulled her into a kiss, his hands holding her snugly against the front of his body as if trying to erase every bit of revulsion Marco's touch had conjured. It worked. It wasn't long before her whole body hummed pleasantly, Marco almost entirely forgotten.

"I can't stand the thought of him touching you...not even a strand of fucking hair," Rafe growled softly against her lips. Throat convulsing in hard swallows, he pulled back and studied her carefully as his hands continued their soft, caressing journey over her body. "Please tell me he didn't—"

"I'm okay, Rafe. Promise. But..."

"But?" His worried gaze snapped to hers.

"If you're worried about my fragile sensibilities, why don't you take me back to our room and help me shower off all this sun block? It's probably going to take a few good rounds—at least two if not more. I'm a redhead after all. I put on *a lot*."

CHAPTER THIRTEEN

A freaking compass had nothing on Rafe's gut. It always instructed him on which way to go, whether he needed to fight or lay low. Right now, it screamed that this mission had turned into a level of FUBAR that a truckload of fucking pixie dust couldn't fix. Fucked up beyond all recognition. He needed to get Penny the hell out of this damn jungle. The sooner, the better.

Anyone could tell that the junior Fuentes was a branch off the sick-bastard family tree, and Rafe didn't want the sick fuck anywhere near Penny when the entire tree snapped in half and came crashing the hell down.

He needed quiet. He needed to think. And the sight of Penny biting her lip raw the second they walked into their room told him he also needed to calm his shit down. It was easier said than done, something that had never been an issue until she kicked him in the balls that first time. Now, it took all his focus and then some to keep his head on the grand finale.

The second he blurted out his plan, Penny stopped biting her lip and gaped at him. "You're insane."

"It's what we need to do," he clarified. "It's time."

"Aren't you the one who said we have to think about every single move we make? You're not thinking about this, Rafe. You're reacting."

"Damn fucking straight I am, Red," he growled out.

He closed the distance between them, already knowing he couldn't be this close and not touch her. His hands slid over her hips and brought her flush against his body. Like a slow-moving storm, the wariness in her eyes turned to arousal. Every breath she took brushed her breasts against his chest.

With her warmth saturating his body, he felt as though he could do anything. "There is no way in hell we're staying here a moment longer, not if it jeopardizes your safety." He silenced her opening mouth with a finger. "No. Way. It's non-negotiable, Red."

"He doesn't recognize me."

"Yeah, and how long is that going to last?"

"What if you get caught? And I'm not talking about what Fuentes would do to us. But what would happen to all those other women...Carlotta...Rachel. If we disappear off the face of the planet, who's going to fight for them?"

He gently trapped her face between the palms of his hands. "Nothing's going to happen to us. And on the far, *far-off* chance we can't make it to Rachel, the team *will*. Alpha doesn't stop until we get the job done."

"Rachel isn't your job; Fuentes is."

Fuck it all. He hated seeing the doubt on her face. The lack of trust hurt a hell of a lot more than he anticipated. Ducking to eye level, he forced her gaze to meet his.

"*Rachel* is our top priority," he stated adamantly. "And you're mine."

Rafe could see in her eyes that she didn't believe it, not entirely. If the great Admiral Kline wasn't already gone, Rafe would be on the asshole's front steps with a specially delivered package—*his fist*. Because of her father, Penny saw herself differently than Rafe did. Knowing he couldn't stand her in front of a mirror and point out each and every one of her kick-ass qualities frustrated him to hell and back.

"We'll get to Rachel," Rafe heard himself promise. "And we won't get caught."

"You're not a freaking superhero, Rafe. What if the power never goes out? Have you thought about that? No doubt Fuentes has this entire compound outfitted with surveillance, and if they don't catch you in the act, what about the dozens of armed guards? Despite that hard body of yours, I doubt it's bulletproof."

He took her mouth in a fierce kiss. "It'll work."

And it wasn't entirely because he knew his job and did it well. It was because there was no way in hell he'd put her into the position of having to fend for herself. Penny may not need it. Or want it. But she had his protection, and he couldn't provide it if he was dead.

* * *

After Rafe accompanied Fuentes on a hunting expedition later in the day, the hours had trudged by as slow as molasses. Now that they were back and the sun was close to sinking behind the tree line, time zipped by way too fast for her jagged nerves.

When she botched a sixth attempt at a pedicure, she

couldn't take it anymore. She slipped into the steam-filled bathroom and ogled the nude outline of Rafe's body.

Water rolled down his broad shoulders, landing in large splats as they fell off his tall frame. He hummed an unfamiliar tune as he scrubbed himself from head to toe, working up a lather and increasing the smell of spice and pine that started permeating the small space.

He hadn't seen her yet.

Before thinking about it too much, Penny shed her clothes and slid back the door. The man was built like a god, a slightly roughened god with long-ago-healed battle wounds. And the naughty smirk on his face as he turned toward her, cock in hand, told her that he was a very observant one, too.

"About damn time you decided to join me."

* * *

Rafe tugged Penny close, swallowing her soft squeal with his mouth.

When he'd stepped into the shower, he'd pictured a scene close to this and thoughts of her watching him had instantly brought him to half-mast. After realizing his daydream had come to life and the woman herself stood on the other side of the shower door, there hadn't been anything half-mast about his cock.

"This is going to be quick, Red. I don't think I have it in me to do anything else." He dragged his mouth down her neck, tweaking one rosebud nipple with one hand while laving the other with his tongue. A hand slipped into his hair, giving it a smarting tug that made his dick jump.

He chuckled against her breast, loving the way she let him know that she wasn't quite done with his exploration just yet. That was fine with him. He took his time tasting, touching, tugging. When she was a quivering mess in his arms and he was about to explode, he turned her around and gently pressed her cheek-first into the cold tile.

Her heavy breaths matched his own as he slipped his hand between her legs, pushing first one finger into her dripping pussy and then a second. "Jesus. You're so wet and ready."

"Rafe," she panted heavily. "Oh God. Now."

Yes, now. Rafe couldn't take too much more. He twisted his fingers, curving them until they hit her sweet spot. In and out, he pistoned his hand, giving an occasional caress to her enlarged clit. He kissed and nibbled the back of her neck, his days' worth of stubble abrading her sensitive skin. And he loved it. He loved seeing and feeling the affect he had on her—each breath, each pant, each faint moan spurred him further.

"Rafe," Penny's husky voice groaned when, after three more thrusts, she came undone on his hand. Not letting her ride it out completely, he flung the shower door open and quickly grabbed a foil packet from his bag. He'd barely turned around when Penny tore the package from his fingers and glided the condom onto his thickened cock.

"I need to be inside you," Rafe warned. "Right the fuck now."

"Trust me—that's what I'm working toward." She grinned in response to his low growl.

Penny wrapped her legs around his waist. Pinning their hips against the wall, he thrust into her body as if their lives depended on it. There was no soft coupling. No holding back. He pounded her until it felt as if their bodies were joined as one solid form.

Her fingers clutched his shoulders. Head thrown back and looking fucking beautiful, she bucked into the movements that brought them closer. He fisted a hand into her damp hair, gently demanding her attention. "Eyes on me, Red. Don't take them off for one damn second."

"Rafe."

"With me, baby. Right now."

Her body began to pulse around him, dragging a groan from his lips and moving his hips even faster, and all the while, her gaze remained locked firmly on his. They came together, her pussy milking him in tandem with each one of his strong throbs. Intense. All consuming. And mind-numbing. Even when the last of the trembles subsided and he'd emptied himself into the condom, Rafe wanted to do it again. Christ, he never wanted to stop.

His watch beeped out a reminder. Sunset.

"Fuck," Rafe cursed, dropping his forehead to hers as arousal slowly turned to wariness. Penny unraveled her legs from around his waist and slid her slick body down his.

He didn't need to tell her what that alarm meant. He kissed her again, this time savoring the tangle of their tongues until his head began backstroking through an oxygen-deprived fog.

They dried and redressed in strained silence. The pensive look on her face nearly stripped him raw. Before she fully shut him out, he dragged her back into his arms for another hot melding of mouths.

"You better be really damned careful," Penny whispered against his lips.

"Always," Rafe promised.

And then the lights went out.

* * *

Penny paced the room, keeping track of time by the shortening of a candlewick. On each pass, nerves ate more of her stomach lining. Rafe had been gone far too long. Maybe he hadn't cut off the power to the security system like he thought. Maybe after one step off the path, the place lit up like a prison yard. Every single *maybe* scenario attacked her thoughts so brutally that when the knock on the door came, she let out a faint squeak.

"Who is it?" she called through the door.

"Señorita Hanlan." Marco's voice chafed her nerves like knees on asphalt. "We're checking to make certain you and Señor Manuel are *muy bien*."

And still locked away in your rooms was the half of the sentence he didn't say aloud. "We're perfectly fine. Thank you."

"*Por favor, señorita*. Please. I insist you open the door." Two heartbeats passed before he added, "Now."

She forced her face neutral as she tugged open the door. For all the chills his gaze elicited—and not the good ones—she may as well have been wearing the dental-floss bikini instead of a tank top and shorts.

"As you can see, I'm fine." She let her voice drip with cool annoyance.

"Very fine indeed, *señorita*." His overt attention slid over her shoulder and into the darkened room. "You're alone."

"Well, yeah. When the lights didn't come back on, Rafael went looking for someone to find out what happened. Do you know when they're going to come back on? Because I was in the middle of giving myself a pedicure. As it is, I'm probably going to have to start the whole thing over again."

"It'll be just a matter of time."

"The sooner, the better."

Marco's eyes took a lazy stroll toward her cleavage before finally looking her square in the face. Seconds felt like hours as she held her breath. He narrowed his eyes, gave her another head-to-toe scan, then nodded. "Good night, *señorita.*"

Penny didn't wait to hear anything else. She closed the door, using it as a crutch to keep herself on her feet. Her heart hammered as she counted to ten and then pushed her ear to the door.

"Raúl!" Marco's voice barked.

"*Sir.*"

"*Find that bastard Rafael and bring him to me.*"

"*And your uncle?*" Raúl asked. "*What would you like me to do with him?*"

"*He stays where he is for the time being, as does the girl. Once I give her boyfriend a lesson about interfering in Fuentes business, I'll see to her myself.*" Marco's voice lost all pretense of civility. It was the same tone from the alley, harsh and cruel. "*No one makes a fool of me—especially some street-rat puta. Oh, and Raúl? I don't really give a fuck what kind of shape Rafael is in when you haul him back. If it suits your needs, drag him in piece by piece and stuffed in a fucking barrel.*"

Penny's heart rate skyrocketed, and not because he called her a whore, or even because he appeared to recognize her from the alley after all. It was the fear of them getting to Rafe that made her feet move faster than she thought herself capable.

The shit had officially hit the rotating ceiling fan.

With one hard yank, she flipped open their suitcase. On packing, she'd made fun of Logan for slipping a mini-sized bug-out bag into the inside flap. As she shoved the meager clutch into her front pocket and silently shimmied out the patio door, she was no longer laughing.

* * *

Penny's gut and Carlotta's ramblings had been right on the money. About a half mile off the compound's boundary, Rafe stumbled onto the bunker. But the inch of dust and cluttered debris hinted that it hadn't been used in a damn long time.

With every step, broken vials crunched beneath his feet. Trash and paper littered the floor, and empty cots were pushed up against each wall, making an eerie aisle toward a purged medicine cabinet. It was a ghost clinic, and as disturbing as it was in its own right, it was nothing compared to the four sets of steel cuffs that adorned each of the twelve beds.

Sick fucking bastards.

Praising his luck that Penny hadn't been with him to see the evidence of Fuentes's warped disposition, Rafe stepped out of the bunker, no sooner covering the vines back over the front door, when the sound of voices drifted through the trees. He flicked off his Maglite and pushed his back flat against a rock.

Two of Diego's men stalked through the jungle, guns raised as they bitched about the rich American bastard they'd been ordered to haul in at the barrel of a gun—or in pieces. It didn't take much to figure out that he was the bastard in question.

Too bad for those men that he had no intention of going along with either plan.

But if Fuentes sent his goons looking for him, he worried what they'd already done to Penny. Anger burned a gaping hole through his chest at the thought of anyone touching a hair on her head. Anyone who did would meet an untimely—and painful—end. Hell, he'd take a page out of their own twisted torture handbook and bring them back to Fuentes in the form of a jigsaw puzzle.

He needed to get back to her, and may the devil help the bastards who got in his way.

Footsteps circled the perimeter. The men bitched, their voices slowly fading as they distanced themselves from Rafe's hiding niche. He anxiously waited for his opening and, when he saw it, dropped low and took his first step toward the mansion.

A second set of footsteps froze him to the spot.

Much lighter than the heavy footfalls from the security staff, this one was buoyant and quick. As if speed were a matter of life and death.

Penny.

Crouched, he moved slow, listening and judging, tracking her route. More than once, she came within close proximity of Diego's men and had to bunker down into the brush. Rafe used the faint trace of vanilla shampoo to guide him to the imprint trail her tennis shoes left behind.

In a matter of minutes, he found her half-hidden in a cluster of drooping vines as she watched Fuentes's brood less than ten feet away.

Careful not to make a noise, he slipped one hand over her mouth. Her body arched, prepped to fight him off before he murmured in her ear, "It's me."

Instantly, her body melted into his hold.

Six feet away, one of Diego's men stopped. Rafe reflexively pulled Penny closer as the man's gaze passed directly where they were crouched, hidden. Her back to his front, they waited until the guard drifted out of sight before breathing a sigh of relief. And then Rafe's body used that moment to physically express how happy it was to have her safe in his arms.

"*Seriously*, Rafe?" she whispered, obviously having felt the bulge of his erection tucked against her ass.

"Like a man can help it around you."

"He can if he has even one functioning brain cell. In case you haven't noticed, we're up the jungle creek without a tour guide."

"I noticed, but a Penny-induced erection takes more precedence." Rafe could practically hear the roll of her eyes. "I'm guessing there's no going back to get our luggage," he joked dryly. "What happened?"

"What happened was that I'm pretty sure Diego's clone recognized me from the alley, and you he just doesn't like. What are we going to do?"

"There's only one thing for us *to* do." Like the snap of a finger, the compound lit up like the Vegas Strip. *So much for the cover of darkness.* "*Fuck.*"

"Rafe." Eyes wide, Penny looked to him for directions.

"Let's go." He grabbed her hand, bursting through the cover of vines at Mach speed. He ran, dodging trees and limbs while Penny held on and followed like a track star. A moving target was a harder target, or so he hoped.

Nearby shouts echoed through the jungle and urged them to go faster. On their left, a faint beam of moonlight flashed off the barrel of a rifle. Their options deteriorated by the second. He gave Penny a small shove forward and directed her north. "You gotta run for it."

"What? No!" Her eyes widened into bright green orbs. She latched back onto his hand and tugged. "I'm not going out there without you!"

"The hell you won't! *Go!*" A bullet whizzed past his ear, cutting off his harsh demand. *Goddamned mothersuckin'*—

A guard popped out from behind a tree like a twisted version of a jack-in-the-box. Penny ducked, allowing Rafe's fist to smash into his nose with a sickening crunch. It went steadily downhill. They needed to get the hell out of there. Yesterday.

One man turned into two, two into three. Rafe landed an elbow strike in one assailant's throat that was immediately followed by a quick disarming kick to his friend's left flank. And frustratingly, Penny's feet remained planted two feet away as she dealt with her own opponent.

"Damn it, *go*!" Rafe barked.

"And where the hell would you like me to go? In case you haven't noticed, there's not a freaking metro stop!" she yelled over her shoulder, a moment before she slammed her foot directly across her attacker's kneecap. Birds scattered at the man's yelp, their wild calls a homing beacon for anything carrying a submachine and a bad attitude. With one man down, Penny efficiently turned to a second.

Her red hair, hanging in loose waves, swung around her face as she pivoted. A punch, a kick, a quick sidestep. She never stopped moving. With each second, her eyes glittered with both concentration and confidence. She looked like an Irish warrior princess, not even flinching when her new opponent landed a solid punch to her jaw. Instead, it slid off her. She reached out for a handful of the man's danglies and let the momentum take her down into a quick roll.

The man screamed like a toddler and dropped to the ground while Penny quickly returned to her feet. *Fucking beautiful.*

Rafe reluctantly pulled his gaze away. Two more guards stood in front of him. A hasty rush brought fool number one into a headlock. Rafe squeezed, cutting off the man's oxygen long enough to weaken his body before cannonballing him into his waiting friend.

A snap of a twig spun Rafe around just as Penny brought

a rock down on the final sneak attacker's head. The man dropped like a lead weight and took her attention with him.

Breathing ragged, face pale. She looked a second away from throwing up or passing out. Rafe took the rock from her shaking hands. His own hands were steady, but inside, his gut clinched with the fierce need to get her out of there. And safe.

In the distance, more shouts and directives could be heard.

Rafe cupped her jaw and forced her gaze upward. "You have to go. *Now*. No arguments."

"But—"

"The more of Diego's men we put down now, the fewer that will be after us later."

"I can stay and help."

Rafe shook his head. "I can handle the rest on my own, and quicker if I'm not worried about you, too. Go north." He prayed she wouldn't argue. "I swear: I. Will. Find. You."

In an abrupt move he didn't anticipate, she captured his face between her soft hands and planted a kiss on him that rocked him straight to his core. He savored what she gave him and took a bit for himself. The sweetness of her lips made it too damn easy to get lost, which would've been what happened if she hadn't pulled away first.

Breathless, she murmured, "If you don't, I'm going to kick your ass."

"Sounds kinky." Rafe's mouth kicked up in a mischievous smirk that Penny's frustrated growl quickly evaporated. He dropped his forehead to hers and breathed in her flowery scent. "I need you to trust me right now, Red. Believe me when I say that nothing is going to keep me from finding you."

Heavy footfalls broke the tense moment. She pulled away, anxiety etched on her face in the form of a frown. "I do."

Rafe reeled her in for another quick kiss and whispered against her lips, "Then *go*."

She hesitated and then took off in the direction he pointed to. Once he was certain she was safely gone, he cracked his neck and turned around as a second set of camo-covered vultures skulked out from behind a set of trees. "Let's finish this, gentlemen. I've got places to be and bigger heads to knock together."

CHAPTER FOURTEEN

Penny ran as if her life depended on it. And it did. Her chest ached with the effort of pulling fresh oxygen into her lungs, and her eyes, unaccustomed to the darkness of the surrounding jungle, missed uprooted trees and hidden rocks. She stumbled. Fell. Then she picked herself up and kept running although she had no idea to where. Putting distance between herself, the armed men, and the compound became her only goal.

After another near face-plant to the jungle floor, the tears threatened. Each step and stumble not only increased the distance between her and Fuentes's thugs, but Rafe, too. Lethal didn't even begin to describe the man, especially when he was pissed. He'd single-handedly taken down at least six of Diego's henchmen without breaking a sweat. But how the hell would he *find* her?

Every inch of the jungle looked like the next, each tree like the one before. If it weren't for quick sneak peeks of the moon, she wouldn't even know if she'd gone in a straight line or in circles.

Self-doubt hijacked what remained of her concentration and, with the aid of a tree root, literally brought her down to her hands and knees. This time getting up wasn't as easy.

A lightning bolt pierced through her upper thigh. *Jesus, it hurt like hell.*

Penny pushed herself to her feet with a strangled cry before feeling around for the source of the white-hot pain. Her fingers bumped against a two-inch-long branch impaled into the fleshy part of her outer thigh.

"This is *so* not the time to summon your inner klutz, Kline," Penny muttered. Closing her eyes and taking a deep breath, she wrapped her fingers around the offending twig. "You can do this. Easy-peasy."

Not giving herself any more time to anticipate the pain, she gave it a yank and only half swallowed a whimper. "Holy hell. Okay. It's all good. No more stick. No more pain."

She deep breathed for ten long seconds to try and convince herself of the latter, when the sound of faraway shouts echoed through the trees. Time up. Ten seconds would have to do. Sucking in a keening wail, she started running again. One hundred yards in, her lungs seized.

There was a reason why she relegated herself to the cheering section during all of Rachel's marathons, and it wasn't because she got to wave her little pom-poms. Hand braced on a tree, she focused on easing the tightness in her chest. A wet warmth slid down the outside of her leg. She probed the area where the tree branch had been and winced at the metallic-scented stickiness it left behind on her fingers. It was too dark to see the damage, and when Rafe burst through the foliage like a tornado with legs, there wasn't time to either.

He grabbed her hand without missing a beat and dragged her along for another sprint. "Gotta keep moving, sweetheart."

"Do I even want to know why?" She nearly stumbled again before getting her feet back under her.

"No."

They ran, faster than she'd ever run in her life, throbbing leg be damned. Bark flew, becoming flying missiles as bullets whizzed past their heads. Rafe pulled her along as if he knew exactly where they headed. A leap and dodge later, he screeched to a sudden stop, her body bouncing off his back.

"Why did we...?" Penny followed the direction of Rafe's gaze.

Her stomach plummeted. A cliff. An honest-to-God drop that ended either into the roiling river below or the ominous rock formations that lined its shore.

"Please tell me we're not going to do what I think we are," she pleaded. Behind them, the shouts of Diego's men got louder. But Penny's gaze was too focused on Rafe's apologetic look to care that they were running out of time.

"You do realize I have a fear of heights, right? If I had a problem with a chopper that supposedly receives regular maintenance, what makes you think I'd be okay with free-falling off the face of a cliff?" Her throat dried as she glanced over the edge at the churning water. "What if we hit a rock?"

"Actually, I'd be more concerned with what's living in that water."

Before she could yell at him, he pulled her in for a hard kiss. "We're doing this together, Red. Side by side."

"We really have no other choice?" A bullet zinged into the tree to their left. "I guess not."

Penny squeezed his hand with everything she was worth

and got into position. If it had been anyone else telling her
to jump, she would've gladly pushed them over herself and
watched their descent. But this was Rafe. With him by her
side, she felt as if she could do anything...maybe screaming
like a banshee while she did it, but anything nonetheless. "If
we die, I'm still kicking your ass."

"That's one beating I'll enjoy, sweetheart. On three."
Rafe smirked, the damn-crazy fool of a man. "One. Two."
He squeezed her hand, flashing her a wink. "Three."

* * *

From far away, the sound of Penny's name echoed in her
head. She groaned, burrowing her face into her hard pillow
as her sleep-addled brain slowly connected a trail of
dots...the smell of earth, of sweat...of cold, rushing water.

Penny sat up with a start. Her head cracked against something solid, making her wince.

"Damn, sweetheart." At the sound of Rafe's low curse,
she lunged in his direction. He caught her and pulled her
into his lap, still rubbing the spot where her head connected with his jaw. "If I didn't already guess it, now I
know you have a hard head."

"Where are we?" She blinked repeatedly, squinting into
the darkness. "Oh God. Are we dead? Did something eat us
when we dove into the water?"

"If we're dead, someone should really talk to the Big Guy
Upstairs about his accommodations." Rafe brushed his hand
over her cheek, pushing a strand of wet hair off her face.
"We jumped. We lived. We're fine."

Everything slowly started coming back to her. The bullets. The kiss. The damn freaking cliff. When they'd managed to swim their way to the bank of the river God only

knew how many miles from where they had jumped, Penny had been ready to pass out from exhaustion. And it looks like she had.

"You're fine?" she asked. "No bullet holes? No missing limbs?"

"I'm whole and intact. Right as fucking rain."

Good. Because she'd hate to hit an injured man. She swatted his chest, making him chuckle. She went to smack him a second time, but he grabbed her wrist and pulled her into a kiss. As far as methods went for silencing someone, she favored this one. By a lot.

Anger at being forced to leave him behind evaporated, or maybe it washed away in the river, because with one brush of his tongue, she kissed him back with everything she had. Tongue. Teeth. The shift of her body. The embrace was short but loaded with so much electrically charged heat that it took a while to register that she was still drenched from head to toe.

The kiss turned salty. She tried to pull back, but Rafe slipped a hand into her hair, ensuring she didn't go far as his thumb wiped away the errant moisture on her cheeks. Lip to lip, his mouth brushed against hers as he said, "Please tell me you're okay."

Now that he held her, she was hunky-dory. As the fear that she'd never see him again slowly poured from her body, her heart rate leveled. Penny was in more trouble than just being stranded in the middle of the jungle with no charted way out. Because if she hadn't thought it before, she knew it now. Her risk of falling hard for Rafael Ortega had grown exponentially.

"Red?" Rafe asked again, pulling her from her own thoughts.

"What was it you said? Right as fucking rain?" She

forced a quivering smile. When compared to the possibility of future heartbreak, the persistent throb in her leg was nothing. "But what about you? Are you sure you're okay?"

With Rafe's body as her guide, she ran her palms over his shoulders and down his chest. She'd worked her way toward his abdomen and waist when he caught her roving hands.

"Keep doing that and you're going to see just how okay all my limbs are, sweetheart."

"Oh." Warmth flooded into her cheeks. "Sorry. I didn't mean to do... *that*."

"You do *that* a lot without meaning to. It's become my permanent physical state when I'm around you."

"I'm sorry."

"I'm not."

She closed her eyes on a mental whimper. *No touching!* "What are we going to do now? And what about Carlotta? We can't just leave her there to fend for herself."

"I'm sorry, but that's exactly what we have to do. At least for now. We'll be no good to anyone if we're caught and hooked up to intravenous drips of Freedom. That cliff was our saving grace. It's going to take Fuentes's men time to scale down or go around, and before that happens, I want to make sure we're long gone. Something tells me Senior has nothing on his mini-me in the psycho department. You good to move?"

"I may need a little nudge," Penny admitted.

With gentle hands, he helped ease her out of their makeshift hidey-hole. The cave was no more than a dent built into the face of the cliff, but it served its purpose and had kept them hidden from Diego's searching men for the last...

"How long have I been sleeping?" Penny asked, absently

stretching her sore muscles. A zap of pain zipped through her thigh, making her wince.

"Not long. A half-hour at most. You needed a rest and I needed to re-group. Hopefully Fuentes's men will think we're dead and will stop looking for us and turn the hell around, but I wouldn't place all my money on it."

The shift of moonlight confirmed that at some point while she'd been sleeping, Rafe had channeled his inner jungle mercenary. A combat vest stretched over his broad chest. It was adorned with a collection of ammo clips for the AK-47 draped over his shoulder and the Glock strapped to his thigh.

From head to toe, he looked mouthwateringly good—and dangerous. He tossed a black bag she hadn't seen before on a nearby rock and began pulling out its contents. Camo pants. Boots. The last thing to come out was a knife with a seriously lethal-looking blade.

"Was there a department store around here that we passed? Or a hunter's lodge?" she asked.

"It would make it easier for us if there were, but no. Both the clothes and the bag"—he tossed her the pants—"are courtesy of one of Diego's men who is nearly buck-ass naked and trying to explain why to his boss. It's no runway material, and the bag isn't exactly a survivalist's wet dream, but it's better than nothing. And by some stroke of luck, everything inside managed to stay dry."

Penny held up the pilfered pants and lifted a skeptical eyebrow. "I'll need a good amount of luck to keep these pants around my waist. Tell me you have a belt in your magic bag of tricks."

"Actually, I do." Rafe produced a utility belt from the bag. With a flick of his hand, he had it hooked around her waist and tugged her body—and her mouth—straight to his. "But you won't hear me complaining if your pants happen to fall down. Not one damn bit."

"I'm sure I won't, but I think I'll use the belt anyway."

"Killjoy." His mouth twitched with a faint smirk. Way too soon, he pulled away, back to business as he nodded toward the clothes. "You need to change out of those wet things and into something more travel friendly. And make sure you tuck the bottom of the pants into the boots and tie the string up nice and tight."

"Why?"

"Because otherwise, you'll become a taxi service to creepy critters. Trust me. A few of them bring an entire different meaning to the phrase *ants in the pants*. And let me tell you, rain-forest leeches are a bitch—and don't need water to creep into warm crevices."

When Rafe redirected his attention to his magic sack, Penny shimmied out of her running shorts and smothered a groan. Her leg burned as if someone had shoved a branding iron through her upper thigh, but using a flashlight would risk broadcasting their position. She made a mental note to check it when there was not only some natural light, but a few solid miles between them and the compound.

She slipped into her new clothes, rigging the oversized pants as best as she could with the belt so they didn't drop down to her ankles. Next were the boots—the very large, oversized ones that would fit easily if her feet were four inches longer. "I've never been a fan of clowns and now I get to play one while running for my life."

Rafe looked her way, his attention dropping to the "borrowed" boots and her noticeably smaller tennis shoes. "That's not going to work."

Penny snorted. "You think? I already have a problem

staying on my feet but you can forget any chance of it if I have to stumble around in these clod-hoppers."

The visual of her stumbling through the jungle brought a smirk to his lips, too. "Keep your sneakers on. We'll just have to make sure we dry them out every time we make a stop. Still, try and tuck the pants into your socks as best as you can."

She nodded and tried to fix the hem as best as she could. "You said we need to get gone, but to where? Were Diego's men kind enough to draw you a map with a big you-are-here X?"

"No such luck, but Diego confirmed he used local villagers for Freedom's testing. He wouldn't want something like that done in his own backyard, but he also wouldn't want to go too far from outside his reach either. And you said Rachel mentioned him dropping into her village often, right?"

"Often enough to raise her alarms." Penny grabbed the emergency clutch from her wet shorts and stuffed it into one of her now many pants pockets.

"Then we can bet we'll run into a village sooner or later." Rafe rechecked the magazines on the confiscated guns before turning around.

She could have stood in the middle of a war zone, surrounded by the stench of smoke and death, and one look from Rafe would make her feel as though she were draped in silk and lying seductively on a mound of rose petals.

This moment was no exception. The longer his gaze lingered on her, the more the soft flutter of stomach butterflies transformed to pterodactyls. She cleared her throat and tried to direct her attention to their situation rather than the stir of awareness. "So, how do we find a village?"

"One thing you can rely on no matter the continent or country is that the people will be where the water is."

"Well, we obviously found that." She felt her lips pull up into a faint smirk and was rewarded with a chuckle from Rafe.

"We can't stay too close. The area around the river is going to be the first route Fuentes's men search, but since this one flows north"—he nudged his eyes up to the brightly glowing stars beyond the canopy of trees—"I'm almost one hundred percent certain that this is the *Río Patuca*. It arches up until it reaches the coast—and, most importantly, reaches civilization. Wherever there are villages, there's food and supplies. We can barter for what we need to get us to the nearest established town, and from there, get in touch with Stone and the others. Fuentes may have an inside man in the DEA, and the sooner we get that info to the team, the sooner this'll end."

Temporarily distracted by his use of the word *we* again, Penny took a moment to realize what he'd said. "Wait. What? Who? Why?"

Rafe shrugged. "The *who* is what I don't know. But he made it clear his connections make his job a hell of a lot easier, and we've been after him too damn long for it not to be a possibility."

"Why would anyone want to help a monster like him?"

"Money. Power. Greed—in all its forms—is a powerful motivator. We'll find a village, get someplace where we can contact Sean and the team, and then we'll work on flushing out the turncoat. Right now, we need to create some distance. Once daylight hits, we'll start cycling in sleep. We'll be less easily tracked if we move at night and sleep during the day."

Trekking through the dark jungle turned out to be a lot less precarious when not hurdling sprawling shadows, but it wasn't a cakewalk either. Especially at the insane pace Rafe set. By the time daylight peeked through the treetops, hours had felt like weeks.

There was nothing special about the place where they finally stopped—no holes in the ground, no caverns. She watched as he circled the base of a particularly high tree as if he were a lumberjack estimating a trajectory.

"We're stopping here?" she asked curiously.

"To rest and recharge. Once the sun sets, we'll get on the move again."

"Do you have a tent in your little bag of tricks?"

"Unfortunately, Diego's man didn't pack a tent...but we do have this." From his procured bag, Rafe pulled out a long segment of climbing rope—and shot her a boyish smirk. "Ever sleep in a tree?"

Penny blinked. Nope, the mischievous grin still twisted up his lips. "Are you kidding me right now?"

Not even Rafe's smile was enough to erase the dread that made her eyes scan up the length of the tall, tall tree. Her gazed swayed from Rafe to the tree, and back again. He wasn't joking.

Feet sore. Leg throbbing. She did the only thing that would get her closer to sleep. She took the rope from his hand. "Give a girl a boost, will ya?"

CHAPTER FIFTEEN

Waking up perched in a tree shouldn't have led to the morning wood from hell, but with Penny tucked firmly between Rafe's outspread thighs, his dick had long since turned from wood to granite. One little shift, a slight nudge, and he'd come in his pants like a randy teenager. They needed to find civilization before he started envisioning ways to use the damn rope that didn't involve tying his ass up in a tree.

His job had always been enough to pull his mind from the sexual gutter. No one could get a hard-on while calculating the amount of C-4 needed to drop a building. If he needed a bit of feel-good stress relief post-mission, he'd work out his sexual frustrations with a blonde or a brunette and get back to work the next day. Hell, a few hours later.

It wouldn't be that simple with Penny. There wasn't a thing about her that didn't mess with his head or other parts of his anatomy. Her death-ray glares created an instant erection. When she got that pain-filled, faraway look in her eyes as she thought about Rachel, he craved to kiss the pain away. And when she ravaged him with a simple glance, he mentally mapped a route to the nearest flat surface—vertical or horizontal.

No woman had ever affected him this way, not on a physical level and most definitely not in a way that made him worry over everything going on in her head. He could no longer deny it when, with a sleepy sigh, she shifted innocently against his crotch. The only thing that kept him from expelling his load was the sight of the viper not four inches from her bare left foot.

He should've seen it, should've realized that as the sun set, day-sleeping creatures would start to rouse. And of all the venomous snakes, it *had* to be an eyelash pit viper.

He swallowed a curse as the small, coiled yellow snake shifted securely on the branch where Penny's sneakers were tied and air drying. One eye on its movement, Rafe nudged his mouth against Penny's ear. "Red, baby. I need you to wake up. And *don't move*."

With a sleepy groan, she shifted. This time, the movement didn't create a single stir in his pants. As a matter of fact, the snake extinguished his hard-on completely.

"Penny." He gave her ear a gentle nip. "We have a bit of an issue here, and I need you to wake up. *Slowly*."

"Is there ever a time when you're not raring to go?" Slow to rouse, her words sounded sluggishly amused.

"Around you? No. But right now I'm more concerned with creating a little distance between us and the snake."

"The what?"

He knew the instant she saw it because her body stiffened like a flagpole. "Oh God," she whispered breathlessly.

"Please tell me that thing isn't venomous and that it's more afraid of us than we are of it."

"Wish I could. It may look small and dainty, but the eyelash viper suffers from a continual streak of general bitchiness. We must've invaded its home turf."

"You mean it *lives* in trees?" The tight squeak of her voice made the viper lift its triangular head.

"If it's any consolation, there's a whole hell of a lot more poisonous things on the ground. Trust me—you don't want a dart frog jumping into your pants."

"Oh yeah. That's much more comforting. Any idea how we're going to get out of this?"

"Can you get to the knife strapped to my left thigh? Just move slow. Be careful. And if the snake moves, you freeze. Immediately."

"We really need to talk about this reassurance thing you seem to lack." Penny inched her trembling hand slowly onto his thigh.

"That's it. Slow and steady. Easy. You're doing great, Red." The second her fingertips made contact with the knife's handle, the damn snake tightened its body into an offensive position. Rafe urged her still with a touch. "Don't move."

Every muscle in Penny's body froze. The staccato huffs of her breathing were the only thing he could hear above the pounding of his heart.

"Where's that commando s-superhero cape?" she joked in a stutter.

"I must've left it in my other tree."

"Too bad you didn't leave your snake there, too." Her voice shook. Hell, he was scared, too. A venomous bite was one thing they didn't need tallied onto their list of fucking obstacles.

Rafe slid his leg over hers, ignoring the ten names of stupid she mumbled at him from under her breath. The viper rose, body tensed. Rafe swung his booted foot just as it struck. Both speed and luck knocked it off course before a second well-aimed kick dropped it fifteen feet to the jungle floor.

He felt the hitch in Penny's breathing before he heard the first quiet sob. Damn if his own hands didn't shake as he wrapped his arms around her trembling body. "It's okay. It's over. Where's my badass bail enforcement agent, huh? The woman who can wear six-inch stilettos and still kick a man's ass to the curb?"

From out of nowhere, a string of soft giggles shook her shoulders. Laughter definitely wasn't the response he'd been expecting, but the sound of it pulled a smile to his lips.

With a deep sigh, she dropped her head back onto his shoulder. "Yeah, I left that woman somewhere in the helicopter, or in that dark alley. She may have even stayed in the States, because she sure as hell isn't here."

Sarcasm laced Penny's words, making Rafe frown. This beautiful, courageous, force of a woman thinking she wasn't the epitome of bravery didn't make the least damn bit of sense. He knew grown men who didn't have the balls to go through everything she'd dealt with over the last week.

Hell, traveling to a foreign country would've deterred most people. She'd not only navigated the streets of one of the most notorious South American cities, but had had no intention of leaving even when they'd threatened to put her ass on a plane. And there hadn't been the slightest bit of hesitation when Fuentes suggested their little trip into seclusion.

Fuckin' A. *She jumped off a goddamned cliff!*

Penny doubting herself pissed him off. But what

infuriated him even more was knowing that she wouldn't believe him even if he listed off each of her accomplishments in a fucking PowerPoint presentation.

* * *

Six hours, four blisters, and a precarious hike later, each breath took more effort than Penny would've liked. The stagnant jungle air invited insects to buzz around her body as if she were a walking buffet, and the cloud of bugs worsened the closer they got to the river.

She didn't care. Let them eat her alive. She'd suffer through a lot worse if it meant feeling even a degree cleaner.

They stepped through the edge of the tree line, and there it was. The river. Murky brown jungle water never looked so damn good. Rafe's hand landed on her arm before she could dive in face-first. After twenty-four hours without a drop to drink, she seriously contemplated pushing him in.

He chuckled when she shot him a murderous glare. "Just let me take a look around the area. We wouldn't want any surprises popping out, okay?"

"Yeah, I've had about all the popping and dangling I can handle for a while." She shooed him away. "Go. Inspect. And then I'm diving into that river like an Olympian."

Penny understood his caution. Even though the river meant they were on the right track, it also made them more vulnerable. It didn't stop her from giving the water a longing look as Rafe disappeared back into the jungle.

Her leg was bouncing like a pogo stick by the time he reemerged from the trees after what felt like eons. "We're all clear. If you want to wash up, now's the time." Rafe gave the river a side eye. "Only wish our Fuentes buddy had been hospitable enough to pack us some iodine tabs."

About to slurp a handful of water, Penny stopped. "Iodine tabs?"

"A survivalist's friend for staving off a parasitic invasion, because chances are that if the water didn't immediately fall from the sky, it'll make us sick. But I guess that's the least of our worries right now."

Penny could've smacked herself as she dug out Logan's bug-out bag from her pocket. "And I suppose that would be something a commando type would make sure to pack in one of these things?"

Rafe's mouth formed into a dimple-inducing grin as he reached for the clutch. Wrapping one palm around her nape, he hauled her in for a fierce kiss. "Goddamn, Red. You're a fucking beautiful genius."

"It was Logan who stuck it into our things. I just thought to grab it. Does that mean you're going to kiss him when we get back, too?" Penny teased.

Rafe chuckled. "I just damn well might."

Penny accepted his hand as they navigated the slick rocks. River water sprayed up, misting any inch of skin that wasn't already damp with sweat. She took a seat and watched him pull out two brown pills from the bug-out bag and drop them into their procured canteen.

He caught her watching him and winked. "It'll have a metallic taste, but it's a hell of a lot better than the other option. Looks like Logan also thought to load us up with the necessities, because there's dried jerky and antibiotic ointment in there, too."

"Looking more and more like that kiss is going to happen," Penny joked.

"Jealous, Red?" Rafe's mouth twitched into a forming smirk.

"Maybe."

He handed her the canteen. "Bottoms up."

Penny wrinkled her nose as the first drop of water hit her tongue, but she chugged it eagerly. Microscopic parasites or not, it was the best damn thing she'd ever tasted. She downed her share and passed the canteen back to Rafe, their fingers brushing.

Maybe it was the luminescent glow of the moon, or the wild call of jungle animals protesting their presence, but she half expected a melodic, hidden voice to break into a love song and cartoon lions to roll their way down the riverbank.

After meeting Rafe, she understood what women meant when they said a man possessed the ability to undress a woman with his eyes. Even dusted in the grime of nature, Rafe's intense gaze made her feel flat-out sexy. *Wanted*. And it had been a long, long time since anyone had made her feel that way. If ever.

She hoped he'd act on that look, but he tore his gaze away and spread his weapons out on a nearby rock. "I don't like being out in the open, so let's make this a quick scrub-down."

"So we're conserving that water again, huh?" she teased.

His cool mask quickly reverted to all heat. *Okay*. Maybe joking with him wasn't the best course of action if they needed to make this a quick pit stop, but she couldn't help it. She secretly hoped he'd take her up on the offer, which was ridiculous because they were in the middle of a jungle with God only knew how many men after them.

That's how potent Rafael Ortega was. He'd lured her in at the first glimpse of his sea-blue eyes, but it was the man himself who kept her coming back for more.

She'd quickly learned he was a bit more than a solider— a lot more. He'd taken a chance on her, believed in her when she didn't entirely believe in herself. He pushed aside his own Fuentes agenda to help her focus on hers...on Rachel. And she had no doubt that whether for one of his friends or a perfect stranger, he'd step straight into a bullet and not think twice.

That was *Rafe*. Not soldier Rafe. Or Alpha Rafe. But the *man* Rafe.

He was the kind of man she could fall easily in love with...the kind that could break her heart to smithereens simply by living his life the way he was meant to. Love—in general—was a land mine. Falling in love with a man whose sense of duty was etched into his DNA was like walking through that land mine blindfolded with explosives strapped to your chest.

Realizing she could very much be approaching the point of no return, Penny closed her eyes and took a shuddering breath. When she opened them again, her gaze clashed with Rafe's. She forgot it all—except the sweltering pull she felt to be close to him.

"Oh boy," she murmured.

Never once breaking eye contact, Rafe shed his shirt and tugged off his boots. By the time the pants followed, Penny was a raging hot mess of mixed emotions. The fabric of her bra chafed against her sensitized nipples, and a dampness coated her body, which had nothing to do with humidity. Modesty definitely wasn't an issue with the man, and why would it be?

Beneath the glow of Honduran moonlight, he looked like a warrior god. Every chiseled muscle flexed and rippled with fluidity. His broad chest melted into the taut angles of his abs.

The only imperfection marring his granite-hard body was a six-inch jagged scar to the right of his navel. Raised and rough, it contrasted the smooth perfection of his skin.

Penny blamed pheromones for not having seen it before. It looked vicious, as was the method by which it was probably obtained.

"That looks like it really hurt." Her whisper sounded like a shout against the low drone of jungle wildlife.

"It didn't tickle."

Rafe's muscles twitched as she gently ran her fingers over the serrated line. No, it wouldn't have tickled. Even without a medical degree, she could recognize a mortal wound. An injury like that would've required life-saving efforts and a grueling recuperation. Her chest ached at the thought of him dealing with it alone, then throbbed with the realization that he'd dealt with it at all. In his line of work, injuries like this were collateral damage. And it didn't stop him in the least.

Her pathetic handful of haul-ins in rural Pennsylvania didn't qualify her to buff his combat boots, much less assist him on an operation. They sure as hell didn't equate to a relationship where he didn't pull out all his hair from boredom and run in the other direction.

"I was in a remote region near Kandahar—with my Delta unit." His rough voice pulled her eyes up to his. As he spoke, his hand slipped on top of hers until their fingers entwined over the scar. "Villages were being pillaged for food and supplies. Residents lived in constant fear, too afraid to stick their heads out of their doors. From one day to the next, they never knew which travelers were friends and who wanted to blow them to kingdom come. Any assistance offered by US troops was always refused because they feared retaliation."

"I can't imagine living that way." Penny shook her head, horrified.

"Neither can I, and eventually the village elder realized he wanted more for his people. My unit was sent to babysit a government official who wanted to broker a deal for intelligence-collection in exchange for protection from the insurgents. One of the elder's sons wasn't as receptive to the coalition. All he saw was the threat of danger to his family."

When she got his meaning, her mouth dropped. "And he stabbed you because of it?"

He gave her fingers a gentle squeeze. "Fear and desperation sometimes make people do things they wouldn't normally do. Kind of like a social worker turned bail enforcement agent boarding a plane to the murder capital of Central America and hunting down an international drug lord."

Penny wanted to tuck this moment in her pocket and save it for later. Men like Rafe were a rare breed. Time and training could make a Sunday school teacher a trained sniper. What set him apart was that he genuinely cared. The growls and glares and conceited innuendos were a Band-Aid covering the vulnerable parts. Even if it was only for a split second, he'd taken that bandage off and exposed himself—to her.

It made her happy and sad, jumbled her emotions until she couldn't figure out which one dominated her thoughts more. He was so much more than he even knew. He was so much more than *she* could have ever known.

Until now.

Her damn rules. No soldiers. No hero types. No men who sought to save the world one mission at a time. For years she'd lived by them without any second guesses or what-ifs. And then Rafe Ortega walked into her life and made her start to think maybe—just maybe—she'd been wrong.

Maybe there were exceptions to the rules.

And maybe one of those exceptions was Rafe.

CHAPTER SIXTEEN

One minute Rafe had been purging his soul, and the next, his arms were empty. He watched Penny pull away, both figuratively and literally, and felt the stab far deeper than the knife that nearly gutted him in that Afghan desert.

Not even his team knew about his time overseas. The only one who did was Trey, and that was because he'd been the one who'd kept his insides from spilling to the ground. But Rafe had told Penny when she hadn't even asked.

Sharing it with her hadn't just come easy—it had felt right. At least until he'd watched a mental suit of armor drop into place right before his damn eyes. She thought he couldn't see through it, but she was wrong. He invented the damn tactic to keep people at arm's length, and he couldn't blame her for being wary.

Hell, she'd practically painted the picture for him in permanent fucking markers. No soldiers—current or former. And after getting that glimpse of what her father had put her

through, he understood. She deserved to be someone's *first*.
Not an afterthought, or someone's second tier. And Rafe
didn't do anything half-assed. If he couldn't be the man she
needed, that she deserved, then it was best that he took a
step back.

Later.

Right at that moment he needed to hold her in his arms—
for however long they had—and use the time to make her
realize that she was a hell of a lot more than she knew. Her
words from the tree had been a dark shadow lurking in the
back of his mind since she'd uttered them.

*She'd left that badass bail enforcement agent in the heli-
copter, or back in the States.*

Like fucking hell.

The fact that she doubted herself even now chafed him
raw. When they'd first faced one another on that San Pedro
Sula street, she'd been a force of nature. Her gritty determination flowed through an interrogation, the training. Grown
men pissed their pants dealing with Diego Fuentes, and
she'd willingly, if not eagerly, stepped into the man's domain
without a care for her own safety. The possibility that she
didn't see that in herself pissed him the hell off.

"What the hell did you mean earlier about leaving *that
woman* back in the States?" he heard himself ask.

Penny pulled her gaze from his as she attempted to
step away.

He grabbed her arm as she tried to pass. "Red."

"It meant nothing."

"I call bullshit."

"You can call whatever you want, but that doesn't make
it any less true." Red faced, she tugged her arm away.

"Do you want to hear what an incredible fucking job
you're doing? Because sweetheart, you are. I don't know

a woman—and trust me, I've known a lot of them—who would even consider a stunt like this, much less be able to pull it off."

"I don't want praise, damn it. And I'm *not* doing well."

"You could've fooled me."

"Maybe *that's* my calling. I bluff a good game."

"That's a bunch of fucking shit and you know it!"

Eyes bright with anger, Penny stepped forward until the warmth of her body suffused his. But there was something in the droop to her shoulders. Disappointment? Doubt? He remained rooted to the spot and let her vent. *Finally*.

"What I *know* is that I was scared shitless in that alley and would've gotten myself killed if it hadn't been you and the guys who found me. I *know* Logan pulled punches during our hand-to-hand demo. And you were right... I *was* lucky that night with Marco," Penny said, undercutting herself.

"You're a fucking bounty hunter, Red. You're not exactly an ivory-tower princess."

"Yeah, I work bail enforcement," Penny scoffed. "But did I ever mention that my mentor hasn't even allowed me to go out in the field on my own yet? In case you didn't notice before, I have a keen ability to stick my nose where it doesn't belong. All I am is a good bluffer. But the longer I act as though I have a clue about what I'm doing, the more lives I put in danger."

"This isn't your fault."

"Of course not." She flipped up her hands and let out an irritated sigh. "I only screwed up the *first* day at the compound. I brought suspicion on us for absolutely *nothing*."

Rafe ached to kiss away all her self-doubts and infuse into her the images the way *he* remembered them. Instead, he caught her attention with an upward hook of his finger.

Moisture clung to her dark lashes, the sight of it walloping him more than one of Logan's beefy-handed right hooks.

"*You're* the reason we know without a doubt that we're on the right track." He tugged her chin back when she attempted to look away. "So what if you were scared in the alley? *You didn't back down.* Just like you stuck with it when you faced Logan *and* Marco. And seeing you stand your ground back at the compound when those goons were gunning for us was fucking incredible."

"What's your point?" she asked softly.

"My point is that despite being scared, you still went through with this—*all* of it. *That* is the definition of courage, and you have it by the fistful. Stop selling yourself short. Alpha would've never let you get this far if we didn't believe you capable. Hell, *I* wouldn't have let you get this far."

"But none of this is getting us any closer to finding Rachel. I can't lose her, Rafe. She's the only family I have." Penny's throat visibly seized.

Rafe brought her mouth within an inch of his own. "Wrong on both fronts. We *are* closer. And she's not your only family, Red. I barely remember my mother. But I sure as hell remember being shipped from one foster home to another, sometimes not staying in one place long enough to unpack my fucking knapsack. In that time, I learned something pretty damn quick. And that's that family is who you *want* them to be. Blood is blood. It's a fluid. *Family* are those who help you go through life with a purpose. For you, Rachel's both, but that doesn't mean you don't have family elsewhere. You may not have a commando cape of your own, but you're an honorary member of Alpha now. And sweetheart, we *are* a family. In every way that counts."

Her lips twitched with the threat of a watery smile. "I thought you weren't a man with speeches."

Until her, he also hadn't been a man to envision himself with one woman, but damn if he wasn't starting to like the idea... if that woman was her.

Sucker-punched by the wayward thought, Rafe forced his lips into a smirk. "What can I say? I'm a cheerleader."

She glanced down his body, her hot gaze damn near bringing him to his knees. Like clockwork, his cock began to rise for the occasion. With it pushing against the fabric of his briefs, there was no way for her to miss it.

He couldn't hold back if he tried. Pulling her into his arms, he kissed her.

He meant it to be a show of innocent affection, but there was nothing innocent about his feelings. Hot and needful, he slipped his tongue into her mouth and felt her go liquid in his arms. Bodies flush, he quivered on contact. It wasn't long before her hands ran up the length of his chest.

As always happened when she was in his arms, Rafe lost track of time, forgetting all about where they were and that they needed to make this a quick stop. He ripped her shirt from the waist of her pants, pulling it off in one fluid movement before lowering his mouth to her lace-covered breast.

Penny's hands locked onto his shoulders, her fingers gripping his muscles and holding him close... like he'd pull away. Never in a million fucking years. He needed this too much, needed *her* too much to even contemplate letting her go so soon.

Eager to dive into the wonderland that was her warm, damp pussy, he unsnapped her cargos with the flick of his fingers. Her breathless gasps spurred him on, and the slow spreading of her legs gave him easy access as he slipped his hand beneath the back of her panties and dipped his fingers into the wetness between her legs.

"Rafe." Penny's knees buckled.

He caught her before she dropped into the water. "Whoa there, sweetheart. You fainting on me now? I know I pack one hell of a punch, but . . . " He scanned her face and what he saw erased the cocky smirk from his face. Her cheeks, usually pink and lively, looked pale. Worry superseded horniness as he gently shifted her in his arms. "It kills me to say this, but I think we need to press pause for a bit. Breathe. Drink. *Rest*."

"I'm okay." She shook her head as if clearing cobwebs from her mind. "But I won't turn away more water."

He held the canteen to her lips, tipping it back up when she'd dared slow down. Only when he was satisfied that she'd drunk enough did she let him escort her to an inlet that wouldn't knock her down with the force of the churning water.

She rolled her eyes at him when she noted his hesitancy to leave her there. "Go. Finish. Seriously, Rafe. You said it yourself. You pack quite the punch. It's probably best if you stay far, far away when you slip out of your skivvies."

He wanted to argue with her, but the jut of her jaw told him there was no point. "Fine. But you damn well better holler if you need me. We haven't come this far for you to drown in three feet of water."

* * *

Penny took a deep breath when Rafe finally turned his back. Fighting against a woozy head, she managed to shed her sneakers and clothes, and she imagined each scrub of her hands washed away more than jungle grime.

Rafe was one of the reasons she wouldn't—*or couldn't*—quit. Even if his belief in her had been nothing but a prettily wrapped speech, it was a damn good one. She loved the way he could make her feel like she was capable of anything.

Her heart told her to hang onto that feeling, take whatever Rafe could give her, for however long, and run with it. Her head told her to be rational. Both options had perks and drawbacks. Neither took into consideration how addictive he was—not just his touch, or even his smile. It was *him*.

Penny trudged back to her clothes. With the help of the faint moonlight, she could now see the quarter-sized gash on her thigh. It wasn't *too* bad. But it wasn't pretty either. Up to a half inch of redness circled around the darkened edges of the wound. Dried blood had already crusted over, creating a rough scab, but she didn't want to leave anything to chance.

She patted it dry before slathering it with a generous amount of antibiotic ointment from the bug-out bag and then covered it with a piece of gauze and a bit of first-aid tape. Penny finished tucking her shirt into her pants when Rafe finally turned around.

He nodded toward the starlit sky. "We have another hour or so until daybreak. Do you want to stop for the day?"

"As excited as I am about tying ourselves to another tree, I say we keep going."

Ignoring the burn in her thigh, Penny accepted his offered hand. She slipped her fingers through his and let him lead the way back into the jungle.

* * *

Another day came and went, and when evening returned, it was back to hiking. They'd made good time, the land around them slowly changing from jagged mountain peaks to wooded jungle plains. Flat and level was a good thing, because with every hour that passed, the more Rafe expected Penny to do a face-plant into the jungle floor.

Worried, his gaze drifted over his shoulder to where she clumped through the heavy brush. Every gentle curve of her face had long glazed over in a haze of exhaustion. Sweat glistened over her forehead, and her mouth was tight in a permanent, white-tinged grimace.

He'd ask her if she was okay or wanted to take a quick break, but he knew he'd get the same answer as he had the dozen other times he'd asked: a terse *I'm fine; let's keep going*.

Fine. That damn word now topped his pet-peeve list right up there along with reality television and those damn commercials with photoshopped infants speaking like adults. Anyone with fucking eyes could see it for the lie it was—both the commercials and Penny's continued insistence that she was *fine*.

Eventually, Rafe had enough. He threw the backpack to the ground and leveled her with a stern look. "We're bunking down. I'll keep first watch while you get some rest."

He waited for her wrath, or at the very least, a death glare. Instead, her shoulders slumped as she gazed up the length of a nearby tree. "Up there?"

Every protective cell in Rafe's body wanted to wipe away the defeated look on her face. He gentled his voice, for once at a loss as to what to do. "No. No tree climbing this time around, Red. I'll make sure nothing crawls into your unmentionables."

Penny folded her legs to the ground, plumped the backpack into a pillow, and lost consciousness in a flat three seconds, shifting Rafe's concern straight to stratospheric levels. He'd been pushing them hard, hoping to get the maximum distance between them and Fuentes's compound that they could. Now two days out, he was finally starting to feel like there wasn't a thick-necked goon about to pop out from behind a tree.

Rafe sat next to her, unwilling to be more than an arm's length away, and watched her sleep. It definitely wasn't a restful one. Her murmurs, mostly indecipherable mumbles, ran through cycles of unease and agitation.

"It's all right, Red," he murmured, stroking her back in slow, soothing circles. "Rest. Sleep."

None of his friends would call him a nurturer. When things didn't go as planned, he sucked it up and soldiered on, and he expected anyone in his company to do the same. Failure wasn't an option, and neither was exposing or admitting weakness.

Penny wasn't a soldier. She hadn't been trained to endure extreme situations. Half the men in his first Delta unit would've at least made a grumble or two in their time hauling themselves through the jungle. But Penny...nothing. She still claimed to be *fine*.

He wanted her to show a little weakness...just so he could become her support...feel fucking useful.

He brushed his knuckle over her warm cheek, pushing a strand of damp hair behind her ear. She bolted upright, back ramrod straight, nearly knocking him off his perch as she jumped unsteadily to her feet.

Rafe stood up and caught her shoulders as she swayed. "Whoa. Slow it down there, speed demon."

"I'm fine." She brushed his hands away and took a wobbly step back.

He didn't like the distance she put between them one damn bit. "I think our definitions of fine are seriously different, Red. And yours is the one that's ass-backward."

"I didn't say that I'm about-to-break-into-song-and-dance

happy." *There* was the death glare Rafe had been waiting for. "I'm *fine*. Okay. Hunky-freaking-dory. Don't worry—I'll try my best not to slow us down."

"If you need to take it slow, we'll drop it down a notch."

"Stop," Penny ordered through gritted teeth. "Just... *stop*."

"Stop what?" he asked, genuinely perplexed by her sudden rush of annoyance.

Her hands flailed in his general direction as she stalked closer to him. "This. *You*."

"Me?"

"Yes—you!" She stumbled but quickly righted herself and pointed at the hand that had been poised to catch her. "And that! Being...*nice*. And thoughtful. And just...so... freaking...*perfect*."

He snorted. "I'm far from perfect, sweetheart."

"Yeah, that's what you say, but I know better. It's not fair. You swagger around all sexy and alpha and growly...but men like that...like *you*...are supposed to be jerks. You're supposed to be aloof and programmed to get the job done no matter what you have to do or who you have to hurt. Why do you have to make things ten times more difficult by being thoughtful and caring and...supportive?"

She looked seconds away from blowing steam out her ears. Rafe was lost, completely. "Let me make sure I'm following you here. You're pissed off at me for being nice...and for caring about you? Is that right?"

"Yes!"

"And it would make you feel better if I started acting like a sexist asshole?" *What the actual hell?*

"Now we're getting somewhere." Penny's hands fisted his shirt. "Be an asshole, Rafe. Be a sexist, selfish, one-track-mind asshole."

She gave him a hard shove that pushed his back against a nearby tree, and then she followed, putting her mouth over his and kissing him like it was the cure to end the apocalypse. And hell, maybe it was the end of the fucking world, because he sure as hell didn't know what the fuck was going on—except that Penny was devouring him whole.

And fuck…he was already the worst kind of asshole, because he knew something wasn't right. In the last few hours, she'd gone from sweet and tender to a walking, mouthy supernova. And he couldn't tear himself away from her lips long enough to find out what the problem actually was. He took advantage, her touch stoking a fire in his veins that couldn't be extinguished except by taking her here against this damn tree.

Like his head and his mouth weren't connected by a brain, he kissed her back in the ultimate of sparring matches. Give and take, slow and deep. Twin hands tugged his shirt until he leaned forward, helping her pull it over his head. Penny didn't miss an inch of skin as she dragged her hands over his chest and stomach, scouring his skin with her nails, then with her mouth.

Rafe's groan caught in his throat before he efficiently whipped her shirt off, too. He needed more. He needed to touch her. He needed to *feel* her with every primal part of his being. In a quick spin, he reversed their positions, his arm tucked behind her to protect her back from the rough tree bark. Not letting the fabric of her bra get in his way, he tugged the thin straps to her elbows, and at the sight of her cherry-red nipples peeking above the lacy trim, he dove in like a man starved. He nibbled and teased, pulling the tip of her left breast into his mouth with a tug that made her body quiver.

She moaned breathlessly, her hands fumbling with his belt. "God, I want you. I *need* you. *Now*."

"You're about to have me, sweetheart." Ten seconds after the hiss of his zipper, she did. In her hand. She gripped his erection so tight he nearly came right then. With a growl, he pushed himself deeper into her grasp and was rewarded with another maddening squeeze. "Ease up, baby, or this is going to be over before it begins. We have to talk condoms and the fact that I don't have any on hand."

"Don't care. Don't need them. I'm clean and protected."

Fuckin' A, that was a goddamn symphony to Rafe's ears. It was a testament to just how far-gone he was, because ever since the ripe young age of fifteen, he'd never once considered going bareback, much less gone through with it. Feeling Penny wrapped around him without a single barrier sounded like fucking heaven.

She pumped his cock again, making him hiss. "God-damn, sweetheart. I'm clean, too. Alpha makes sure we get triannual checkups, and I've never once gone bare."

"Then what are you waiting for?" Penny rolled her hips against his aching erection.

At this point, he had no clue. With the flick of his fingers, he unsnapped her pants and followed them as they dropped to the ground.

Bringing his mouth to just below her mound, he nibbled and tasted, locking his gaze on hers from his vantage point on his knees. Her gorgeous green eyes watched him, clouded over in a haze of desire that only made his cock harden more. Standing up and slipping into her hot body would be too damn easy, but he wanted to give her more.

"Rafe. Please," Penny begged in a whisper. Her hand dropped to his head, urging him closer.

With her damp pussy his goal, he skated his mouth over the inside of her thigh. She spread for him on trembling legs, making him suck down a curse. Her mound was right there, damp and ready and practically begging for his tongue. He coaxed her stance wider and was about to take his first eager swipe with his tongue when her pain-filled cry made his blood run cold.

Rafe's muscles froze him in place. Penny shifted away from his touch, but not before he saw the piece of gauze halfheartedly taped to her thigh.

"What's this?" he asked, gently peeling it off the rest of the way. "Fuck, baby. What the hell did you do?"

He didn't need a flashlight to tell the gnarly gash on her leg was an unsightly shade of red. It was puffy and puckered.

And infected.

"It's nothing. It's just a scratch." She tried tugging away.

"It's not nothing. It's fucking infected!" Rafe pulled the Maglite from their pack and inspected the wound.

He fought off a string of curses. It looked ten times worse than he thought. Not only was the cut itself infected, but the redness looked to be spreading to the tender tissue of her thigh. He'd seen two-hundred-pound hard-asses get taken down by a single scratch while in the middle of a jungle. The heat and conditions helped the infection seep into the bloodstream where it could wreak havoc on the body.

Ignoring her protests, Rafe pinched her chin and aimed the small beam of light into her eyes. Unfocused and dilated, her gaze skirted around his face in a haze that had nothing to do with arousal and everything to do with a fever. Her out-of-norm behavior all made painful fucking sense. *Now*.

"How long, Red?" Rafe asked, pushing the panic from his voice.

"How long what?"

"How long have you had that gash on your leg?"

She rubbed her temples as if trying to remember. "A day. Or two."

"Which is it, sweetheart?"

"Since the compound...," Penny said, her words starting to slur, "when you told me to—"

She dropped, unconscious and half-naked, into his arms.

"Red!" Panic tightened Rafe's chest as he shifted his hold on her limp form and recited a silent prayer. He stroked her damp cheek, forcing himself to calm the fuck down. "Baby, wake up. *Penny.* This is one hell of a time to go lights-out on me, sweetheart."

Fuckin' A, this wasn't good, and way beyond his minuscule first-aid training. She needed a doctor, a hospital, and a heavy round of antibiotics, and she needed them right this fucking second.

Rafe centered her body weight and made a halfhearted attempt to pull up his damn pants when he came to an abrupt stop.

Never once could he remember being so outmaneuvered, but the proof was right there in front of them... surrounding them. A dozen men, all armed with homemade weapons and deep scowls, looked a hell of a lot more menacing than he did with his out-of-reach Glock and his pants an inch from falling to his knees.

Holding a half-naked Penny, there wasn't a hell of a lot of options.

"I don't suppose you can direct us to the nearest hospital?" Rafe asked dryly.

CHAPTER SEVENTEEN

Pain surged and ebbed in waves, from the throbbing in her head to the cascading sensation of needles ricocheting down her left leg. It was one of two things that kept Penny from falling down the dark well that weighted down her eyelids. Pain... and *Rafe*.

Hazy images drifted through her mind like a cloud. They rolled together, one after another, until memories took the form of his eyes, glittering with an unnamed emotion as he stared down at her in concern; and his arms, strong and warm and cocooned around her, had made her feel safe. At home.

Now there was nothing.

A chill seeped into her already trembling limbs. Each panicked breath spun her dark world and took her stomach along for the ride. She needed air. She needed light. She needed *Rafe*.

A cool drop of water brushed across her forehead right around the time she registered the soft coo of a voice. One painful centimeter at a time, Penny's eyes opened. It took a few blinks and a minute or two for the blurry images surrounding her to come into focus. And when they did, she had no clue as to where she was.

Sheets of roughly cut timber formed four walls, and a thatched roof, inlaid with remnants of jungle brush, allowed for a few scarce rays of sunlight to slip through the gaps. A rotund woman dressed in dingy Western-style clothes stood in front of an open-flame fire pit, her back turned.

A soft giggle redirected Penny's gaze to the source of the cool water and soft touch. No older than three, a curly-haired little girl holding a damp rag excitedly turned to the woman, the words they exchanged sounding similar to Spanish.

"*Go, child.*" The woman ushered the little girl from the hut. "*Fetch him.*"

Penny tried forcing her throat to work. "Where am—"

"Shh," the older woman hushed, brushing the cool rag over her brow. "*Sleep.*"

She must've obeyed, because it felt like only a second had passed when her eyes flew open at the sound of a loud crash. Rafe's broad shoulders filled the width of the doorway, his sapphire gaze locked on hers. He'd shed the clothes from the jungle but looked no less lethal in a basic dark shirt and frayed cargo pants. The circles beneath his eyes made him look haggard and tired, but he was still the best thing she'd seen in forever.

She didn't register the soft sob as hers until in three long strides, Rafe was by her side, palming her face between his hands and drying her tears with his thumbs.

"What's wrong? Are you in pain?" Concern weighted down his every word.

Penny cleared her throat and winced from the trail of fire that zipped down her leg. "I'm okay."

And she was—now that he was here.

Rafe's shoulders dropped their stiffness as he slowly scanned every inch of her face. He brushed a strand of hair from her cheek, making her eyes open again. A healthy dose of worried relief was etched in every line of his face. "*Okay* is right up there with *fine*. Jesus Christ, Red. You scared me shitless."

"I'm sorry."

"You should be. You sure you're feeling—"

"Fine?" Penny teased weakly. Rafe didn't smile. He looked a second away from giving her a gentle throttle with his bare hands. "I'm a little headachy and a whole lot sore, but I've felt worse when I had the flu."

"Good. Because I'd hate to spank your ass if you were still feeling under the weather." Rafe scrubbed his face and released a heavy sigh. "This has officially been the longest three days of my fucking life. I think I aged ten years."

Engrossed by the way his thumb brushed over the curve of her chin, it took her a moment to register his words. "*Three* days?"

Rafe leaned until their faces were less than an inch apart, giving her an up-close view of the exhaustion lurking in his eyes. "Three. Agonizing. Days. And I think we both know how this could've been avoided. You should've told me you were hurt."

"At first there wasn't any time, and then I cleaned it as best as I could and even used the antibiotic ointment from the bug-out bag. I didn't think it was anything serious. It was just a scratch."

"In the jungle, there's no such thing as *just a scratch*. We were lucky Rosita's the medicine woman of the village. She took one look at your leg and sent the men back into the jungle for supplies."

Both she and Rafe watched soberly as Rosita removed a layer of green leaf bandages from her upper thigh. Red and raw, the skin around the gash hurt like hell but looked marginally better to her own untrained eyes. Penny turned her attention to Rafe, his silence unnerving her more than the fierce tightening of his jaw.

He watched the older woman slather the wound with an ointment that stank more than an overused gym sock and rewrapped it with a fresh batch of leaves. When Rosita finished, she gave them both a smile and left them with an "*I'll leave you alone with your wife.*"

It took a moment for Penny to translate the words. At her look of confusion, Rafe explained, "They made the assumption from the way they found us."

"What do you mean the way they found us?"

"Both half-naked and just about to—"

"Oh. My. God." A rush of memories made her cheeks go crimson.

Rafe chuckled, not looking the least bit flustered. "Yeah, you may have said that a few times already."

He easily caught the hand she halfheartedly attempted to smack him with and leveled her with a smile that almost stopped her heart. Her own soft chuckle died as he hooked a chair with his foot and dragged it next to the bed. He sat, staring at her in silence before they both looked down to where his fingers slowly caressed the backs of her knuckles.

The only way to catch even a glimpse of Rafe's thoughts was if he cared to relinquish them. Penny really wished he would. God only knew her own were a jumbled mess. Maybe it was the fever. Maybe it was the entire screwed-up situation. But somehow, Rafe drew out parts of her personality she tried to keep buried, or that she hadn't known she had.

A few moments ago she'd cried—with no shame, no hiding. She hadn't felt like she needed to explain the appearance of her tears, because it had felt natural. *She could be herself*—a quirky smartass with a passable roundhouse and an addiction to Rafe Ortega.

As if sensing her thoughts, he tucked their clasped hands beneath his chin. His stoic mask dissolved, leaving behind an unguarded expression that clenched her heart. "You really did scare the fucking hell out of me, Red. If it hadn't been for these people, I don't even want to think about what would've happened."

"You would've figured something out," she said softly.

"I think you're seriously underestimating my panic level. They took you away from me. Wouldn't let me see you until you woke up. I've been in some hellish situations before, but none come even close to the last three days."

Penny blinked fresh moisture away, his words tugging more to the surface. The things she said to him in that jungle...

They'd been true for the most part. It would be easier to keep an emotional distance if he'd just played the part of the misogynist jerk. But that wasn't him. He was perfectly *im*perfect, in all ways except for his choice of occupation.

Her heart ached for purely selfish reasons. "Where are we?"

"In a Miskito village just off the Patuca. Once the people here realized we weren't part of Fuentes's crew, they've been ridiculously helpful." He brushed the back of her hand against his lips. "We'll wait a few more days just to make sure you're fully recovered, and then we'll head out. We're only a day-and-a-half's hike away from the Honduran military base at Mocoron."

The reason why these people should know a man like

Fuentes turned her stomach. Rafe must've read the realization in her eyes, because he gave her hand another kiss, this time keeping it propped against the corner of his mouth.

"All I need is another day and I'm good," Penny stated. "We'll go."

"I already promised the village elders that we'd leave once you were able to get back on your feet and they wouldn't listen. They insist on us staying until you're entirely healed."

"There's no telling what Fuentes will do if he finds out they were helping us. I don't want to chance staying longer than we have to."

"They know the risk, and they're willing to chance his wrath if it means stopping him once and for all," Rafe said somberly, looking more tranquil than worried about a Fuentes appearance. "But there's no reason for him to come back here. He's already ripped apart their families, and they're close enough to the base to make even a cocky bastard like him uncomfortable. So we're staying—at least for the time being."

"But—"

"Don't argue with me, Red." There was no mistaking the gleam of stubbornness in his eyes. "I nearly lost you once already and that was one time too many for my liking. You can glare, pout. I don't give a hot damn. Until you're able to get out of this bed and kick my ass without staggering on your own two feet, we stay right the hell here."

"Then maybe you should go without me." She nearly choked on her words, but she trusted him with her life and with Rachel's. "You wouldn't have me dragging you backward. You could make contact with the team and come back for me when you got the chance."

"I'm not leaving you behind," he growled softly.

"Damn it, Rafe." Her curse held no power. "We've already wasted *three days*."

"And we'll get them back. You can argue with me until you're blue in the face, sweetheart, but I'm not changing my mind. Your energy is better spent getting well."

* * *

After three days of being cooped up, Penny stepped onto the hut's front porch and tilted her face to the sky. Both the warm pound of the sun and the simplistic beauty of the village worked wonders on the soul. It was a dusting of civilization nestled on the edge of the Patuca River, a mixture of minimalism and complexity with clapboard structures housing entire families.

Off to the left, a handful of women gave her a friendly wave, and huddled on the porch of the next hut, two elderly men gave her nearly toothless smiles. No one could tell by the looks on these people's faces that their lives were forever altered by Diego Fuentes.

Penny smiled back with a small wave and let her self-appointed mother hen, Carmencita, gently tug her toward a gaggle of giggling children. With a tiny finger, the three-year-old instructed her to sit beneath the shade of a *Yucca* tree before she toddled off to join the activity. Back and forth, up and down, the children chased after their tallest playmate with a flourish of laughing squeals.

The sight of a tattooed ex-Delta operative playing forward in a miniature-person's soccer game was more entertaining than watching the World Cup. The children shouted eagerly, all calling for Rafe's attention with a cry and wave. Little Carmencita howled in innocent laughter when the ball bumped her bare feet. But Rafe was right there, sweeping the doe-eyed beauty into his arms and tunneling them both toward the goal line.

Easy laughter and slick, loose smiles replaced the hard lines of his whisker-stubbled face as he carefully aimed the ball toward some of the youngest players. At that moment, he wasn't a soldier. He wasn't a seasoned Alpha operator. He was a two-hundred-pound child...and Penny couldn't take her eyes off him.

He claimed to be the type of man to never settle down, but she didn't doubt for a moment that he would excel at it—*all of it*—protector, husband, *and* father. Images of dark-haired children with vivid blue eyes and warm, tan skin chiseled their way into her mind, taking her breath away.

Her heart heavy with what-ifs, the weight of Carmencita climbing into her lap brought her back to reality. She wrapped her arms around the little one and savored the sound of her sweet giggle.

Even from thirty yards, Rafe's eyes missed nothing. Their gazes collided, his scanning her from head to toe, no doubt calculating if she was well enough to be out of bed. She squirmed on the spot, her body growing warm. If her libido could be revved by a cross-country stare and in the presence of screaming children, she was most definitely on the mend.

Emotion flickered across his face, and with each flash, a new one was painted into place. Desire. Need. Concern. And something else that made her heart skip a beat the moment he took his first step in her direction. He only made it three when the pack of children literally brought him to his knees. Carmencita leaped up to join the fray just as he turned on them with a mighty roar that had the kids shouting in glee.

There was no sense in denying it anymore.

Tattooed ex-Delta operators were *exactly* her type. It didn't jibe with what she wanted from life, but it was true.

From beneath a mountain of children, the smile and wink Rafe sent her blasted its way through her walls of resistance.

She loved him, was *in* love with him. And now she needed to figure out what to do about it.

Eight hours later, standing in front of the buffed tin mirror in her newly acquired quarters, she still hadn't figured it out. She stared at her reflection and looked for the change she'd felt happen. A round of nervous nibbling left her bottom lip swollen, and a week's lack of appetite had made her face a bit thinner, but her eyes were still green and her hair shone the same dark shade of red. On the outside, she was the same military brat with a penchant for getting into tough scrapes.

The change was internal, embedded so deeply that extraction was impossible. *She was in love with Rafael Ortega.*

Thoughts of maintaining a physical distance from him made it difficult to breathe. She didn't know if it was worse to love and lose, or to never experience the thrill of love at all.

A heavy knock interrupted her internal debate. There was only one person she was expecting.

"Come in," Penny called.

The door squeaked on its hinges as it opened. Rafe stepped into the hut, eyes scanning the modest interior. "You've been granted your own suite."

She squeezed her eyes closed at the sound of his voice. His presence filled the small room, diffusing his warmth straight into her lower abdomen. She pulled herself together with a few deep breaths and nearly fell apart again when their gazes clashed in the mirror.

His stare raised her heart rate to an unhealthy triple time. They were alone. *Finally.* And she was scared out of her ever-lovin' mind. Her body warred with her head, and her heart was flying off in an entirely different direction.

She shifted on her feet. "I think it was less about giving me my own space and more for preserving Rosita's sanity. I'm pretty sure I heard her muttering about overbearing, oversized American men. Know anything about that?"

"Nope." He remained straight-faced except for the slight twitch of his upper lip. "But it looks as though I've been ousted, too. I'm beginning to think the village elders have given us approval to have a little husband-and-wife time."

Their gazes simultaneously strayed to the leaf-mattress bed tucked into the corner of the room. Minuscule was the term that came to mind. Constructed of roughly cut lumber and with a mattress support made of an intricate lattice-work of rope and vine, the thing would barely contain Penny, much less the two of them.

"Cozy." Rafe half smirked.

Too cozy. Penny could practically touch the palpable tension with her fingertips. God, she'd missed him over the last week. Her body manifested his lack of closeness much like an addict needing a fix, with unsteady hands and racing heart.

She dried her palms on the thin cotton shift Rosita had given her before forcing her thoughts in the exact opposite direction of where her body wanted to go. "Rosita mentioned that the village's hunting party was planning to lead us to Mocoron. I don't like the idea. I mean, what if Fuentes finds out? I don't want him to punish them for helping us."

"I already told the elders we didn't need anything except a finger pointed in the right direction and maybe a few supplies. We'll get to Mocoron. Contact the team. And then we'll take it from there."

"Take it where, exactly? It's not like we know how high up the chain the mole may be. We can't exactly walk up to everyone with a badge and politely ask if they're raking in two separate paychecks—one from the government and one from a psychotically crazed Honduran kingpin."

"No, but we'll have our gut instincts. And no one can find information better than Charlie." He slid his arms around her waist, pushing his front to her back, and tucked his chin onto her shoulder. "We knew this wasn't going to be a cakewalk, but there's *always* a link. *Somewhere.* Charlie's specialty is finding it, and when the fucker makes a stupid mistake— and he or she will eventually—we'll be there. And that much closer to finding Rachel."

"That's almost what Vincent told me—that people make mistakes and the key to catching them is using that to your advantage."

Penny hadn't realized she'd spoken aloud until Rafe's body stilled. His lips brushed against her neck as he spoke. "Who's Vincent?"

"A friend, my mentor at the bail enforcement agency. He's actually a retired SEAL."

"I'm surprised you didn't go to him when you suspected what happened to Rachel. Even as retired old-timers, SEALs eat this kind of shit for breakfast."

"Actually, I did. He was reaching out to his former team."

"Then what happened?" Rafe linked his large hands just below her belly button and held her close.

"I left two days before they were scheduled to leave...because Vincent would've never let me tag along."

It took a moment to interpret the shaking behind her shoulders as laughter. She turned in his embrace and punched his arm. "It's not funny!"

"Honey, if you can strong-arm a brood of Alpha oper- atives, you can sure as hell get your way with a crew of geriatric SEALs."

"Can I have my way with you?" Eyes wide, she slapped

a hand to her mouth, but a string of giggles still escaped through her fingers. "I didn't mean...oh hell. That came out *way* wrong."

"I like the way it came out, and the answer is without a doubt, *yes*." Rafe eased her chin up. One dropped glance to her lips and air became in short supply.

Needful heat ripped through her veins and he'd yet to touch her any more intimately than the brush of fingers sliding into her hair. He held her gaze so long she could've sang the national anthem. And then she saw it—the slight flicker in his eyes, the crease of his frown as his gaze dropped to her mouth and back. *Something* bothered him.

She palmed his cheek, tracing her thumb down the line of his frown. "What is it? What's wrong?"

"I think you were right a few days ago. You should stay here in the village while I head to Mocoron," he finally said. "You can rest, continue to collect your strength. And then when everything's done and over, the team and I will come back and get you."

That wasn't what she expected. Her mouth dropped right before it snapped together with an audible click. One small step and she pulled herself from his embrace, uncaring of the show she was no doubt giving him in her paper-thin cotton pajama dress.

"Are you freaking kidding me? After that whole spiel about not leaving me behind you're now suggesting that you do just that? I don't know what kind of medicinal jungle products you've been smoking while we've been here, but it's made you delusional. You had your chance to go at this alone and you refused, remember? Now that I'm healed, you want me to stay behind? Why?"

"For once, can't you just do as you're asked? I have my reasons."

"No...because your reasons are obviously stupid ones."

Rafe's face reddened to the point Penny expected steam to start spewing from his nose. Instead, he growled out, "You want to know? *Fine.* It's because I don't want you anywhere near the fucking shit storm if Fuentes's mole happens to be holed up in that base. Call me a caveman or a Neanderthal...I don't fucking care. But I'm not willing to take that kind of risk where you're concerned."

She poked a finger into his chest, making him wince. "I am *not* a damsel in distress, Rafael Ortega. I do not need to be sheltered or coddled or protected from anything you deem unpleasant. So any thoughts you have of leaving me behind better get wiped from that hard head of yours right the hell now. If you're going to Mocoron, so am I. This isn't kindergarten. There are no *take-backsies.*"

"You could use the rest to—"

"Go crazy. Because *that's* what would happen. I haven't gotten this far to stop now. If I'm not actively doing something to find Rachel, I'll go out of my mind. And then there's worrying myself sick over you, you big, too-sexy oaf."

"I'm a hardheaded, sexy oaf, am I?"

"I call it like I see it. Look, I *know* I screwed up. I should've told you I was hurt from the start, but—oh, never mind."

Angrier at herself more than anyone, she tossed her hands up with a low growl and turned. Rafe didn't let her go far. He grasped her at the elbow and gently whipped her back around.

Penny shook her head. "I can't do this with you right now."

"Look at me." Keeping his voice soft, he caught her shaking head in his hands. "Look at me. *Please.*"

Oh God. She was *so* not ready for this talk. She made

an attempt to build her own emotionless mask, but instead, her heart trembled the moment she met his gaze. The lines around his mouth relaxed, and instead of steel blue, his eyes transformed to a warm cobalt. "Can we revisit that big-sexy-oaf comment?"

"Rafe," she sighed.

He tipped her face up, all signs of teasing erased from his face. "Yeah. You messed up by not telling me about the damn scratch. And you will *not*, under any circumstances, put your life in jeopardy like that again. And before you accuse me of being a Neanderthal caveman, I'm going to admit to it. I *am*. When it comes to you, I may as well wear a bearskin loincloth and carry around a fucking club."

Nerves ate at her stomach lining as she wondered where this conversation was heading.

"I care about you, Red," Rafe admitted. "I'm not going to apologize for it, and I don't know what the hell to do with it. But my first instinct, regardless of the fact you've already knocked my ass to the ground, is to protect *you*."

Penny's mouth suddenly went very, very dry. She shook her head, afraid she'd be unable to form actual words and make even more of an ass of herself than she already had.

It wasn't a declaration of love, but it elevated her heart as well as her toes. Suddenly, there was no thinking. She *felt*. She slipped her hands into his hair and pulled him down to her waiting lips . . . and she kissed him with everything she had.

CHAPTER EIGHTEEN

Penny was done overthinking everything, done denying herself what she *needed*. And she *needed* Rafe. Every fiber of her body ached for him. Her heart shuddered with the thought of not seeing him. Touching him became nearly as important to her as breathing.

The damage was done. She'd fallen in love with the exact type of man she'd sworn to stay away from since childhood. Whether she lost him now or watched him walk away later, both methods of losing him would be like having her heart ripped from her chest. Turning back time was the only way to ensure a different ending, and even if it were possible, she wasn't sure she'd do it. Not if it meant never having him be a part of her life in the first place.

Their tongues pillaged and plundered, hands gripped and kneaded. Rafe trailed his palms up her torso. By the time his fingers locked into the depths of her hair, hot lava spilled through her veins.

"I want you to be damn sure about this," Rafe growled against her neck. A soft nibble followed by a soothing flick of his tongue made her whimper.

"I've never been more certain about anything in my life. I know what I'm getting myself into, and I'm prepared to deal with the fallout later." Her heart teetered on its side with the half-truth. She wasn't so sure she'd ever be able to deal with the possibility of not having him in her life. Even the idea of it made her heart throb so hard it hurt to breathe. "Make love to me, Rafe. Right here and now."

He pulled back and stared at her so long she thought he'd turn away. Then with renewed fervor, he brought his mouth down with a heated tenderness that buckled her knees. His lips ate at her mouth with the slow deliberateness of a man who wanted to savor every last morsel.

He reached for the hem of her nightdress. Each inch of skin he exposed brought a new eruption of goose bumps. He kissed her neck, leaving a trail of warm tingles as he traveled upward until his tongue teasingly flicked the edge of her ear. In a flash, her nightgown disappeared, and Rafe walked them backward to the bed.

He was everywhere: in her head, in her body. A slow glow of need turned hot when he cupped her breasts in the palms of his hands and caressed both nipples with his thumbs. At the sound of her lusty groan, he did it again, this time giving them a gentle tug.

She was exposed to him, in more than her nakedness. It was as if he could see straight through her shivering flesh to the insecurities beneath. The questions. The doubts. The false bravado she had a nasty habit of conjuring when things got uncomfortable. Rafe didn't let her hide. With a gentle touch, he caught the hands she automatically lifted to cover herself and linked them around his neck.

"Nuh-uh," he admonished her with a soft kiss. "Never hide yourself from me. You're fucking perfect."

"Hardly," she scoffed. "But it's what I've been given."

Rafe kissed her again, making her breathless by the time he pulled away. A mischievous smirk kicked up his mouth. "And you're giving it to me. You have no idea how much I want it, Red. I want to toss you down on that bed and bury my cock into your body and never come out. I want to taste every last inch of you. I want to explore you. *All* of you."

God, she wanted that, too. Her body was on fire for it. She rubbed her breasts against his still-covered chest and smirked at the rolling growl it pulled from his throat. "So what's stopping you?"

"The thrill of the journey." He kissed her down onto the bed before leaving her in its center and getting back to his feet.

There was no way to hide her awed expression as he dragged his pants down in one swift movement. He was the epitome of masculinity. The eagle tattoo on his chest flexed as he tore his shirt over his head. His erection, already thick and proud, made it no secret he was as eager for this to happen as she was.

"Like what you see, sweetheart?" He let her look her fill, and one edge of his mouth twitched into a grin. She didn't think she'd ever get enough of him.

Her voice was lost, her mouth so dry all she could do was nod as he climbed back onto the bed. Both his hands and his mouth glided up her body. She writhed beneath him, loving the scrape of his raspy stubble.

"Jesus. I don't want to rush this with you, baby, but I honest-to-God don't know if I can hold back anymore," Rafe admitted.

"Who said anything about holding back?"

"I don't want to hurt you." A haunted look clouded his eyes as his gaze dropped to her healing wound. He bent, softly trailing his mouth up her leg until he was inches shy of the puckered skin. "Do you have any idea how close I came to losing you a few days ago?"

"Close enough to know I don't want to waste this chance." At the pained look on his face, she cupped his cheek and tilted his gaze toward her. "You're not going to hurt me. And you don't need to hold back. I don't *want* you to hold back."

"I think you're underestimating how much I want you."

"So why don't you come up here and show me?" Penny's lips melted into a naughty grin, the smirk widening when Rafe chuckled. She loved the lightness that glittered from his eyes when he laughed. At least if she couldn't hold onto the man, the memories were hers forever.

He kissed every inch of her in excruciating slowness: the curve of her hip, the indent of her belly. By the time he flicked her hardened nipple with the tip of his tongue, she was already three-quarters into her own blissful little world.

Penny dropped her hand to his granite-hard erection, making it jump on contact. Slow and firm, she stroked it, spreading the bead of moisture leaking from the tip down his thickening shaft. Just when she didn't think he could get any harder, he did.

Rafe pushed himself deeper into her hand. One thrust, then two. She pumped harder and quicker, flying on a sexual high created by his low moans. The second she slipped her other hand toward his tightening balls, Rafe gently pinned both her wrists above her head.

"Fuck, baby." He panted breathlessly. Wide and dilated with arousal, his blue eyes looked nearly black in the dim light. "Those hands should be registered as lethal weapons."

"You never know what other kind of weapons might be hanging around. Maybe you should frisk me."

* * *

Penny's provocative words did nothing to hide the unguarded swell of emotions hovering in her green eyes. Rafe knew the same emotions stirred in his. Sure, lust burned through his body, turned his kisses a bit harder and his touches more brazen. He needed to feel her wrapped around his cock as much as he needed his next fucking breath. But it was his need for *her*, for her concerned gazes and loving caresses, that sent him on a ride like no other.

Never once had he *needed* a woman so bad. She was beautiful inside and out, her insecurities making her as desirable as did her stubborn, Jack Russell determination. To have witnessed both made him one lucky bastard. She was a complication in its truest form—and he didn't give a hundred fucks.

His "The less complicated, the better" motto had smacked into a five-foot-two-inch redheaded roadblock and shattered on impact. It hadn't sent him running in the other direction. He wasn't deterred. He'd dug in his heels and started thinking the kind of what-ifs he had no fucking business thinking.

For the first time in his life, Rafe hadn't been scared out of his mind at the thought of spending the rest of his life with a woman.

No, with *Penny*.

It took seeing her pale and weak, watching her fight demons in her dreams from which he couldn't save her, to realize he had so much more to lose than he ever thought.

"Rafe. *Please*." Her whispered moan ripped him from his

thoughts and straight into her eyes. With a groan, she canted
her hips toward his hand.

He nearly slid into her body right then but knew the
second he did, he'd be a goner. The selfish bastard in him
wanted the sight of her coming carved into his retinas.

With his cock heavy and hard between his legs, Rafe focused on Penny. He slipped his fingers through her drenched
folds and swallowed her soft gasp with his mouth. Careful
to avoid the sensitive nub of her clit, he mapped out the
area with touch alone. The lift of her hips and her hot,
breathy moans encouraged him to slip one finger into her
tight sheath, then two.

She squirmed beneath him, fingers digging into his shoulders as he caught one nipple tightly between his lips and
fucked her with his hand.

He curled his fingers into her body, groaning when he felt
her flex around him. "I need to taste you so goddamned bad."

"God yes." Her breath hitched as she opened her legs to
admit his wide shoulders. Eyes hooded in arousal, she
watched him settle between her thighs. Spread before him,
open and unguarded, she offered herself to him with no
reservations. No barriers. He didn't take his eyes off her as
his tongue took its first slow swipe.

Her taste exploded on his tongue. He couldn't get enough.
The wet walls of her body tightened around his fingers with
each lick. He didn't relent, keeping it up until her body arched
into him and her whispered plea reached his ears.

He *needed* to hear her come.

With a twist and push, he pumped his fingers in and out of
her pussy. He licked, flicked, dragged the tip of his tongue to
her clit. The hands in his hair tightened, holding him close.
He didn't need the help or the encouragement, but the smarting tugs made him ache to be inside her even more.

"I want to hear you come, Red," he whispered against her body. "Let go, baby."

Alternating between soft and firm, slow and fast, he kept up the pace until with a rough tug on his hair, she came. The sweet burst of her arousal flooded his senses, and he rode it with her until the last of the quivers eased through her body.

In the dim light of the hut, her porcelain skin glistened with the pink glow of satisfaction. She looked like a woman thoroughly ravished—and he was nowhere close to being done. He trailed a path of kisses over the slight curve of her abdomen and the peaks of her breasts.

At her mouth, he shared her sweet taste with a slow thrust of his tongue. "I need to verify the whole condom situation."

"I'm safe and protected," she said, verifying what she'd told him in the jungle. "The shot works wonders."

"I'm clean, too. But I'd understand if you don't want to—"

"I *do*," she said quickly.

When she brushed her hand against his jaw, Rafe turned and took the pad of her thumb in a gentle bite. "Say the words aloud, Red. Plain and clear so we have no miscommunication."

"I'm saying I want more. I want *you*. You've already given me one spectacular orgasm; it would be a total shame not to go for another." She slid her hand down to his aching cock and flashed a grin. "And at least one for you, too, of course."

Goddamn, this woman was something else.

Keeping his gaze locked on hers, he pulled her knee to his hip and tested her readiness. She was warm, wet, and completely open to him. With a shift of hips, he slipped into her pliant body as if he was always meant to be there.

This time, they both trembled. There was nothing on

earth that compared to the sweet feel of her body. Flesh on flesh. Heat on heat. In and out, he withdrew and sank back in a series of thrusts that had them both panting in a matter of seconds.

"You're so fucking tight, baby." Afraid of finishing before they even began, Rafe took a deep breath, groaning as her body contracted around him like a pulsing vise. "I don't want to hurt you. Dear God, tell me I'm not fucking hurting you."

Her soft hands settled on the curve of his ass. With a squeeze and an upward thrust of her hips, she urged him deeper. "I'm not as breakable as I look."

Rafe's control snapped. With a caveman growl, he surged in the last few remaining inches. Beneath him, Penny gripped his ass tighter. He brought his mouth down on hers as if he were a man dying of dehydration and she were a bottomless well, and only when his head began to swirl did he come up for air. He kissed a path of kisses over her cheek, her nose, the curve of her slender neck.

Every inch of her was smooth and supple. He couldn't get close enough, feel enough, when it came to this woman. He slipped a hand beneath her hip and braced her body as he plunged in and out. It didn't take long before the bed beneath them creaked and groaned with the force of each thrust.

Her hands touched him everywhere: the muscles of his arms, his back. Their heavy pants fueled the already raging fire until Rafe lost track of where he ended and she began. Need for release warred with a need to never let go. The second her lips met his mouth in a kiss that pushed them both over the edge, Rafe knew.

One more night—fuck, a million nights—would never be enough.

CHAPTER NINETEEN

Penny would never look at sex the same way again, because with Rafe it hadn't felt like *sex*. It was intimacy and total abandon disguised as a marathon of hot touches and hotter kisses. He woke things deep inside her that she never knew existed.

In Rafe's arms, there'd been no walls. She gave herself to him without fear that would've before made her turn the other way and run like hell.

She was in love with him.

And she didn't regret it. Not a kiss. Not a touch. Not the way he made her feel as if she could do anything and still be herself—and it was *enough*. Somehow, he'd managed to make vulnerability feel good.

Until this morning.

At some point after the fourth round of lovemaking, something shifted. A dark cloud of tension followed Rafe as he paced the room, collecting the clothing they'd strewn about. He hadn't spoken to her, hadn't looked in her direction for the last five minutes except for the occasional sneaking glance. At first she'd been confused, then hurt. Now she was angry.

It wasn't as if she expected the coo of sonnets or a devotion of love ever after. Though they'd practically clawed her throat raw, she'd been careful not to mumble those three little words that could make him regret everything they'd shared.

She'd shed her clothes knowing that making love wouldn't change anything, and she hadn't regretted a moment of it—until the first time he refused to glance her way.

"You can stop stomping around like you're on a death march. I don't have any expectations." Her words sounded a hell of a lot steadier than she felt.

Rafe's back went taut before he tugged on his shirt.

"You should," he muttered.

"Excuse me?" Her voice went up in pitch.

Finally, Rafe turned. Jaw tightly clenched, he could've just been told he had one month to live and she wouldn't know it by the steel hardening his eyes. The man staring back at her hadn't been the one who'd made love to her throughout the night, nor the one who was so eager to get inside her that he couldn't wait to get her into a bed. Standing in front of her right now was the stern-faced commando from their first San Pedro Sula encounter.

"I don't *do* relationships, Red," Rafe reminded her, his voice low and even. "I don't do complicated, messy feelings. Hell, it's more than the fact I don't do them. I *can't*. I know absolutely jack shit about being in a relationship in general, much less a healthy one. Disappointment, detachment, and danger—I'm your man. Anything else may as well be a fucking fairy tale."

"You do realize that I was raised by the world's most unaffectionate father, right?"

"But you had Rachel. And you had Trey and his family. You had people in your life who showed you that wasn't the norm. I had foster parents who usually didn't bother memorizing my last name, much less asking me how I felt about things. It's not that I don't wish things were different. It's just reality. Relationships aren't in me to give. Not even to you."

His words were as lethal as a dagger through the ribs. She tore her gaze away and sat to pull on her shoes, battling against the shake of her hands.

He stepped closer. "Let me—"

"No." She stopped him with a shake of her head. "You tell it how it is and you don't apologize, remember?"

"You said you understood," he murmured. "You said you weren't looking for anything permanent with someone like me."

Penny's throat convulsed with the effort to keep her cool. "I did say that, probably numerous times and both aloud and to myself. I guess I'm not as immune to you as I thought. But that's my problem, not yours."

"*Penny.*"

It took strength she didn't know she had not to run into his arms at the sound of her name falling from his lips. Not Red. Not sweetheart. *Penny.* She'd thought she could handle the pain of losing him in whatever way that happened, but she'd been deluding herself. She felt raw and open. And scared out of her mind.

As a defense against the gaping hole forming in her heart, she hiked up her mental walls, closed off her emotional wounds, and summoned the courage to carry on. Dwelling on her loss and the things she couldn't have only did one thing: it hurt. And there was too much riding on them right now to let that happen.

"Trust me, Rafe. I've already done the whole second-place thing when it comes to the military, to *this* kind of life. I have no desire to do that again. You're in the clear. Your soldier-of-fortune lifestyle can remain perfectly intact without you having to worry about the little woman at home."

He looked as if he'd been slapped, an unknown emotion finally dissolving his blank mask. Penny looked away and forced herself to breathe. She thought she'd known what real pain felt like, but it didn't come close to the sensation ripping apart her insides.

This kind of pain—the one brought on by losing the man you love before you ever really had him...

This pain felt like death.

* * *

Instinct made Rafe want to kick the ass of whoever had put that haunted look in Penny's eyes, but what could he do when *he'd* been the bastard to put it there? He wished like hell that he could give her everything she deserved. But longing for the impossible only resulted in more shattered dreams.

Rafe's mouth opened to say something—anything to make her understand. Except he didn't get it himself. Before he could conjure the right words to form some kind of an explanation, the hut door slammed open.

Rafe spun around, his gun coming up on reflex. Instead of the enemy charging into the room, one of the village children pointed toward the eastern line of the rain forest and spoke in rapid-fire Miskito.

Men. *Strangers.*

Rafe rechecked the barrel of the Glock and placed it in Penny's hands before picking up the AK-47 for himself. "Stay here."

Penny stepped into his path. "Are you *insane*? What if it's Diego's men? They'll shoot you on sight!"

"It's not Fuentes's men, but that doesn't mean I want you anywhere near this right now." He grasped her arms in a gentle grip and maneuvered her to the side. "*Stay*," he ordered over his shoulder right before he stepped outside.

It took an entire ten fucking seconds before Penny followed him onto the porch with the Glock still tucked in her hand. He whirled on her, not bothering to dampen his agitation. "Damn it, Red. What the hell did I tell you?"

"You told me to *stay*, but I never went to obedience school, so I still get those commands all confused." Her narrowed eyes dared him to say something.

Rafe's chest rumbled with his growl. She drove him fucking crazy. Short of throwing her over his shoulder and tying her to the damn bed, there was no way to keep her out of this.

Seven figures approached the village, all with badass assault rifles propped on their shoulders and looking like they'd stepped out of the cargo hold of a Boeing. If it weren't for the sight of their familiar ugly mugs, Rafe would've started praying for a fucking Hail Mary.

"Hey there, darlin'." Logan reached them first and instantly flashed Penny his signature smile. "Bet you missed the hell out of us, huh? Must've really sucked only having Ortega to talk to."

"I'm a fucking exceptional conversationalist," Rafe said dryly.

Logan scoffed. "Try that on someone who hasn't been crammed in a three-by-three foxhole with you for thirty-six hours. I had to talk to the fucking grubs to keep my sanity."

Penny laughed, giving Logan a quick hug before moving on to Trey and from there, each of the guys. Even Stone accepted her show of affection before he cut his gaze to him. "You know, when I named all the ways this op could go wrong, I didn't mean that you should go and fucking aim for every single one of them."

Rafe shrugged off the comment and diverted his gaze to the three men who didn't belong to his team. Next to him, Penny's gaze also shifted.

"No. Freaking. Way." With a laugh, she flew down the steps and toward the man with the shaved head hovering just off the shack's bottom steps. The warmth in her eyes as she wrapped her arms around the stranger turned Rafe's blood to ice.

* * *

The bonfire flames reached high into the sky, lighting the night with a warm, golden glow, and yet Rafe had never felt so damn cold. *No expectations*, Penny had said. He should be jumping for joy that he could go on with his life as he'd always meant—sans complications. But the more he thought about it, the more pissed he got—at himself, at Penny, and at the jackass across the bonfire who kept whispering things in her ear.

Vincent Fucking Franklin. The mentor. The friend. One look at the former SEAL and the image Rafe had of a middle-aged man with a potbelly and acne pits disintegrated. Franklin and his cronies, Ryker and Braggs, were easily two hundred pounds of solid muscle and bad attitude.

Penny sat tucked between Franklin and his men while Rafe's gut twisted in fucking knots with each smile she gifted the Navy SEAL. That smile could bring world peace—and he wished like hell it was being aimed at him.

He'd been dumb-shit stupid for thinking one night—or even a long string of them—would ever get Penny out of his system, or that her presence wouldn't affect him on some vital level. She was an extension of him, permanent right down to his most basic parts. But unlike with an arm or leg, there was no way to alter his way of life to make her absence easier.

It fucking hurt, and he deserved every last ounce of that fucking misery.

"You stare at the poor fuck any harder and his dick's going to turn to ice and fall the fuck off." Trey leaned back, relaxed and totally at ease. And fucking smirking. "And before you go all jealous lover and shit, you should probably know that he's the reason we were able to find your sorry ass."

Logan dropped himself onto a tree stump. "Actually, because of him and his guys, we were able to find Fuentes's little hidey-hole. But we found your sorry ass by following the trail of body bread crumbs that you left littering the jungle floor. Good job, by the way. We probably stumbled onto the compound a day and a half after you made your mark, and the place was still in an uproar."

"I had a little help," Rafe mumbled.

They'd hashed through everything over an hour ago. Back in San Pedro Sula, Alpha and Franklin's guys had nearly come to blows before realizing they were searching for the same people. And the almighty Vince and his subhuman-level contacts had pinpointed the location of Fuentes's compound in less than forty-eight fucking hours—a fact that was still making Charlie chew nails stateside.

But one thing no one knew about was Fuentes's fucking nephew. And that was because it wasn't in the intel that had been handed over by the DEA when Alpha had accepted the operation. It was a pretty big-ass piece of information to leave out accidentally. Now the question posed was where Fuentes's mole stood in the DEA food chain. And they'd be one step closer to figuring that out when they reached the Mocoron base.

Penny's laugh pulled Rafe's attention across the fire. Through the flames, he watched her shake her head and smile at something Vincent said. He couldn't tear his eyes away, could barely keep from crossing the distance and begging her to go with him someplace where they could talk. Fucking *talk*. *Him*, the man who'd rather storm a compound with guns blazing than sit down and approach a problem diplomatically.

Leaving things the way they had back in that tiny little hut not only left a sour taste in his mouth, but made him wish he could kick himself in the ass. He'd gone about it the wrong way, chose the wrong words. He fucking *lied*... because purposeful omissions were the same damn thing as spewing falsehoods.

Instead of telling her that he *wished* he could give her everything she deserved, he focused on the fact that it couldn't be done. And now it was too late. That haunted look in her eyes as she'd tried to remain cool while forcing back tears would haunt him for-fucking-ever.

"Fuck it." Rafe stood, ignoring everyone but the pair of vivid green eyes watching his departure. He allowed himself to soak in the sight of her for a minute, and then with a mental kick to his balls, he turned away.

* * *

"Christ, I need a moment of privacy and a cigar," Vince muttered as Penny watched Rafe escape toward the riverbed. "Babe, I'd be totally remiss if I didn't ask if you knew what the hell you're doing. You really up for going down that road? Going commando isn't for everyone—and I'm not talking about the fashion option."

"There *is* no road." Penny's chest ached with the truth of her words. There *was* no road, just a darkened mine with quicksand traps and projectile poison daggers. It was impassable, impossible, and not going to happen.

"Oh hell. You love him." Vincent's statement blended in with the loud drone of voices surrounding them.

"As you pointed out, falling for a man like Rafe Ortega would be an ultimate act of stupidity."

"I didn't say it in those exact words, but yeah. Basically. Yet you did it anyway."

Yeah, she did. Through the years of Trey's absence, Vince had stepped in as a pseudo–big brother and best friend—one who put the *brood* in brooding. He knew her well enough that she didn't need to tell him he was right. But not saying it aloud didn't make it any less true. To make it worse, she hadn't just fallen in love with Rafe. She'd dropped flat on her ass, rolled off a cliff, and skidded down the world's deepest ravine.

Every time she replayed their exchange in the hut, her chest felt as if it would crack open all over again. Though she hadn't *expected* words of undying devotion, she'd *hoped* for them. With her entire being.

"You're killing me with the quiet thing." Vince gently bumped into her shoulder to gain her attention. "Considering the most meaningful relationship I've ever had was with the Navy, I know I'm not exactly the right person to dole out advice."

"When has that ever stopped you?"

"It hasn't. I don't know anything about Rafe other than he'd like to loosen my jaw with a few ear-ringing uppercuts, but I know *you*. There's no way in hell you'd give your heart to someone who wasn't worth the trouble."

"I may know he's worth it, but that doesn't make a damn bit of difference if he doesn't know it, too."

"True. But maybe he's never come across the one woman who could convince him otherwise." With a playful flick to her nose, Vince urged her gaze north. "Penn, I've seen you do some amazing shit since we've known each other. Some of it was in the courtroom when you stood by your clients and helped them face down their abusers, and some of it was when we were hauling parole violators back to the jail yard. Hell, I chased your cute ass down to Honduras to find—"

"That I'd gotten lost in the jungle with a man who makes me second-guess everything I thought I ever wanted in life?"

"I was going to say, to find that there's nothing you can't do if you set half your mind to it. Smartass."

If only she could believe in herself as much as Vincent did. Penny forced her legs to lock and rose to her feet. "Wrong. I can't *make* Rafe see himself as others do. As *I* do," Penny heard herself say.

The pull to go to Rafe was more than strong; it was magnetic. But instead of taking the path of least resistance and feeling her heart break all over again, she turned back toward the huts.

* * *

Rafe had hunted terrorist cells in the middle of the Afghan desert, thwarted assassination attempts made on foreign dignitaries, and jumped from a cargo hold at thirty-five thousand feet to land in a field of pissed-off tangos. He was cool under pressure, ready to leap into action at a moment's notice, and never once would've questioned his motives.

But that was *before* . . . before Honduras. Before Penny.

She was the ultimate weapon, had the ability to get him hard with an innocent look and singe his core with just a promise of a touch. The convoluted mixture of sweet and sass was permanently etched far beneath the surface of his skin, and he didn't *want* to get it out, didn't know if he even could, but fucking up her life because he wasn't man enough to let her go wasn't an option either.

He rubbed his chest as if the pain settling beneath his sternum would go away, but it worsened. Everything about this situation sucked to high holy hell. It threw him off his game, made him second-guess every damn decision he'd made since that first fucking night.

Even without Vince making a decibel of noise, Rafe knew I-Can't-Keep-My-Fucking-Hands-to-Myself Franklin hovered at his flank. Ignoring the man's presence, Rafe dropped onto an oversized boulder and meticulously spread out his guns.

Cleaning chambers and assessing trigger mechanisms were his version of therapy. They calmed him. They were methodical and precise. He tore off a piece of his shirt and scrubbed the barrel of his Glock hard enough to take off the shine.

"What the hell do you want, Franklin?" Rafe finally asked without glancing up.

"I've heard about Alpha Security," Vincent said, his voice breaking the silence. "Even working on the civilian side, things get talked about. A lot of the world's biggest badasses are serving time in jail, or otherwise, because of you guys."

"We do our share."

"So then tell me why a world-class organization would hire a world-class asshole such as yourself?"

"You said it yourself. I'm world-class." Rafe had no intention of taking Vincent's bait—until he turned away muttering Penny's name under his breath.

Rafe jumped to his feet, hands bunched and ready for action. He'd been itching to go a good round or two ever since he saw the way Penny melded so naturally to the bastard's side. "What the hell was that, *Frankie*?"

Vincent turned back in a flash and didn't stop coming until their faces were inches apart. "I *said* that only a fucking moron would let Penny walk away. So, *are* you a moron, Ortega? You're really going to sit back and watch the best thing that could ever happen to your fucking life walk the fuck out? Be a man. Go for what you want before you end up hurting her more."

"Hurting Red is the last thing I want to do. Why the fuck do you think I'm trying to stay away?"

"And what the fuck do you think it's doing to her the longer you do?" Vince retaliated before turning on his heel and stalking back toward the village.

Hostage extractions. Unraveling drug operations. *That* was what Rafe *knew*. Forming a relationship that required openness and communication... not so much.

Why the hell did he think he needed to stay away?

The answer to Vince's question hit him like a cannonball to the gut.

Because he loved her too damn much to use her as a fucking experiment.

CHAPTER TWENTY

Even though the Forward Operating Base Mocoron meant Honduran military, American troops, and the DEA, the government facility wasn't a synonym for safety. They all knew it, which was why the joking banter of the eight men surrounding Penny slowly morphed to focused, at-the-ready stances the closer they got to the base.

Sean, in the lead, raised his hand and brought everyone to a dead stop. Safeties clicked off. Guns lifted. Her own awareness heightened, Penny slipped the 9mm from her waistband and waited.

"Easy, Red. Stay by me." Rafe drew her closer to his side.

She wasn't about to argue. Especially when with nearly no warning, chaos erupted from every angle as a dozen green camo–wearing men stepped straight out from the jungle, their high-powered rifles pointed in their direction.

"*Drop your weapons,*" the closest of the newest arrivals demanded. "*Drop your weapons now!*"

"You're going to have to do fucking better than that, my friend," Sean snapped back, no more lowering his rifle than did the rest of the team. "Why don't you lot lower *your* weapons first?"

The soldier studied Sean through narrowed eyes. Each second that ticked by brought Rafe closer to Penny's side. Eventually, he'd gotten so close that she could feel the flex of his muscles when he regripped his gun. A tense minute later, with no one eager to be the first to stand down, another man stepped out of the throng.

This one wasn't wearing a uniform. In fact, with slicked-back blond hair and a clean-cut black suit, the thirtysomething man ridiculously contrasted with everyone else's grime-covered appearances.

His gaze momentarily rested on Penny before scanning the men around her. "You must be the notorious Alpha Security," he said in English. "I'm glad that we finally found you."

"And who the hell are you?" Rafe still didn't lower his gun.

With a too-white smile on his face, the man tossed Rafe his badge and credentials. "I'm Special Agent Royce Collins. American Drug Enforcement Administration. My superiors just patched me through to a coworker of yours— a *charming* woman with the mouth of a trucker. I believe her name was Charlie She's-Not-Giving-Me-Her-Bloody-Last-Name."

"You're the AIC in Mocoron?"

"*Special* agent in charge," Collins emphasized. He turned toward the soldier who'd first demanded they lower their weapons. "Lieutenant Ramón, if you and your men will please holster your weapons...let's show our guests a bit of hospitality, shall we?"

It took a few seconds for Lieutenant Ramón to bark the order to his men, but then they started doing as directed. Collins, looking pleased with himself, nodded toward the direction in which they'd been heading. "If you all will follow me, I'll show you to our humble dwellings."

* * *

Tucked into the wildlife of the Miskito jungle with meager personnel, the Honduran outpost didn't look like the first line of defense in the Central American drug war. Only a few dozen Honduran soldiers littered the grounds, some in guard shacks while others walked the fence line with security dogs. Notably fewer in number, American uniforms and plainclothes DEA agents came in and out of unidentified, flat-front buildings. Tallied, the numbers couldn't have reached more than sixty.

It surprised Rafe that Fuentes hadn't yet assumed control of the entire fucking world if this was his opposition.

Special Agent Collins buzzed them into a modest single-level structure. The layout was comparable to the spokes of a wheel, with the main hub housing a single desk, computer, and an aging man with a scowl.

Collins nodded to the guard before leading them down one of the narrow corridors. "I have to admit I was surprised to hear your agency was called into Honduras, and more than surprised to hear it less than an hour ago from my superiors."

"I guess they felt the more eyes and ears they had on the ground, the better." Stone returned the agent's strained smile. "After all, we're all on the same team."

"Yes, but things run differently here than in the private sector. As much as I'd love to, we can't just storm the

Fuentes distribution hub and call it a day. One fuckup and the Honduran people would be on their own with him, and you could probably imagine the horrific things that would happen if we weren't here to run interference."

Rafe intercepted Stone's sideways glance with a faint nod, signaling he caught on to the oddity of the agent's statement, too. They'd been down here for months with an operational goal of finding Fuentes's operational base, and this unlucky bastard just alluded to the fact that they already knew where the hell it was.

Stone lasered his scowl in Collins's direction. "Can you explain to me again why it is that you haven't invaded his *distribution hub* the moment you located it? The longer you wait to shut the bastard down, the more chance you give him to ship Freedom to the States."

Collins turned to give Stone the full brunt of his snarl. "In case you haven't noticed, things here are rather sparse. I can't produce people out of thin air, and I can't rewrite their fucking job descriptions. And I sure as hell can't make up my own damn rules. Both my hands and my balls are fucking tied."

Rafe slid up next to his boss. "Then I guess it's a good thing Alpha owns all of their own appendages. We don't play by anyone's rules except our own. The longer that bastard stays free, the more time he has to fuck with people's lives."

Hostilities inflated on both sides. Rafe snuck a look toward Penny and immediately battled the urge to give her hand a reassuring squeeze. He knew she was thinking of Rachel. He wanted to find her, too—for Penny, for himself. In giving her back her family, he'd be making her happy, and that's all he wanted.

And more importantly, knocking heads and kicking down

doors was in his scope of practice. Everything else hovered over his head like a two-ton question mark.

* * *

Mountains of video feeds—scoured. Entrance and exit routes both for their own use and for Fuentes's—identified. Logan even shopped at the base's surprisingly well-stocked arms room like a pimply-faced teen in a video game store. The clock to Fuentes's destruction slowly started ticking down.

Once they handed Fuentes over to the proper authorities— or peppered his carcass with bullets—Rafe would be off to the next mission and Penny could move on with her life with Rachel by her side. It's what was best. Still, each time Rafe thought about it, he wanted to ram his fist through the wall.

Body still damp from his shower, he heard the first hesitant knock. Any one of the guys would've rattled the door on its hinges or burst their way through it altogether, so he knew before opening it who stood on the other side. Knowing it and being prepared for it were two entirely different things. Rafe opened the door and immediately felt like he'd been sucker-punched in the gut.

Penny had obviously made use of her own quarters. Her hair hung damp around her shoulders, and her cheeks were pink with a healthy glow. Even in unisex olive drab BDUs, she looked so damn touchable he had to cross his arms over his chest to prevent himself from reaching out.

"I-I'm sorry if I caught you at a bad time," she stammered softly. The badass commando look contrasted with the uncertainty etched on her face. Her eyes roamed over his bare chest, lingering on the towel secured around his waist.

He braced a shoulder on the jamb of the open door and

pretended he wasn't already at half-mast. "It's only a bad time if you're going to plead a case to go along on the Fuentes raid."

She glanced away with a sheepish smile. "I'm more than willing to let the professionals do their work. I'm only wearing this because it was all they had that didn't smell like jungle. Can I come in for a minute? This isn't exactly a conversation I'd like to have in the middle of the hall."

At the base of her throat, Rafe saw her heart rate flutter double time. It would probably be in both their best interests for him to shut the door... with her on the other side of it. As it was, it was going to take him until wheels up to get his head on straight. Having her standing in front of him in the flesh would make that deadline a million times harder, but not meeting it wasn't an option. This particular operation was too damn important to fuck up.

Rafe stepped aside to let her into the room but kept as wide a berth as possible. "What's on your mind, Red? If you're worried about Rachel, all I can say is that if she's there, we'll get her out."

She nervously wrung her hands together. "I know. It's not actually about the op. I know you guys will get to her."

He waited, eyebrows arched.

"I guess I just wanted to talk to you... before you left."

"Why? Think I'm not going to make it back?"

She stopped fidgeting and tightened her beautiful mouth in a humorless scowl. "That is *not* funny."

"Wasn't meant to be."

"You're not making this easy," she grumbled.

Her newly acquired boots clunked on the hard floor as she paced his small quarters. She started and stopped a few times before coming to a final halt close enough for him to smell the clean scent of soap. An errant strand of strawberry hair caught itself in her long lashes, and his hand automatically reached out to rescue it.

The entire room pulsed at the contact. *Fuckin' A*. Keeping his damn hands to himself wasn't possible. Before he knew it, he ran the backs of his knuckles up her cheek and savored the feel of her tilting her head into his touch—right until she started to pull away.

"You know what? Never mind. I made a mistake in coming here," she mumbled, turning away.

"The hell you did." He caught her arm and spun her around. She landed against his chest with a thump, and the second their bodies collided, heat spread through him from head to toe. "You came here to say something. *Say* it."

Her eyes narrowed. "Have I ever given you the impression that I like to be ordered around like a Labradoodle? Stop. Stay. *Talk*. If you ever decide to hang up your Glock for good, you could have a very lucrative career in dog training."

"*Red*," he growled in warning.

He expected another smart-mouthed comeback, and instead, she wilted in front of him. There was no other way to describe the sudden stooped shoulders or the weary-eyed look fogging her eyes. At least when she was spitting venom in his direction, he knew to either give it back or fuck it out of her. But at the quiver of her lips, he didn't know what to do...and that scared the ever-lovin' shit out of him.

On reflex, he threaded his fingers through hers and held on for as long as he could. "You'd be doing us both a favor if you got right down to the point of your visit, sweetheart."

Tears began welling in her eyes, but she held them at bay. "I just wanted to tell you that you have so much more to offer a woman than you realize or give yourself credit for. I hope that when you find that special one who completes your life, you'll follow your heart first and figure the rest out later, because if anyone deserves to be happy, you do."

Goddamn, it hurt to breathe. Each inhale stuck in Rafe's throat, collecting until his chest threatened to explode. A voice inside his head screamed that *she* was that woman, the one who rounded him out, brought things out in him he hadn't known were missing. She made him believe in things he hadn't thought about since he was a child dropped into the foster-care system—a family to protect and cherish, and the support that came with it.

The only thing keeping him from purging his thoughts and acting on his hungry greed was knowing he couldn't give her the long-term safety and security she deserved. "You're an incredible woman, Penelope Lucky Kline. And you almost make me believe it."

"Then I guess my work here is done."

Done. Final. The fucking end.

Rafe's chest fucking ached. Actually, an ache would've been welcomed. It felt like he'd been gutted and set on fire. Consumed by a rush of pain the likes of which he'd never felt before, he reached for the only thing that had the ability to take it away.

Penny.

He meant it to be a fleeting, chaste kiss. But he felt nothing innocent when it came to her. Or fleeting. When he dropped his mouth onto hers, one brush of his tongue against the seam of her lips was all it took for her to open to him— and to realize that he was goddamned tired of doing the right thing.

If she had even the slightest reservations about the direction in which they were heading, *she'd* have to be the one who took the initiative to end it, because he sure as hell couldn't, not with the feel of her in his hands.

"You have no idea how bad I wish I could be the man you think I am," Rafe murmured against her soft skin, diverting his mouth down her neck until he reached the sexy dip of her shoulder.

Penny captured his face between her palms and forced him to look her square in the eye. "I don't *think* you're him. I *know* it. And most importantly, you're the man I *need*, Rafe."

She grazed her lips along his jaw and whispered into his ear, "Let me show you how much I need you."

Rafe wasn't strong enough to say no. He slid a hand over her ass and encouraged her to wrap her legs around his waist. The second she did, his engorged cock twitched a welcome. He needed every inch of her against every inch of him. No clothing. No barriers. Just Penny's bare skin gliding over his.

He walked them blindly toward the bed, kissing her down to the mattress. Her red hair fanned out across the pillow-case, making her look like his best dream come to fruition. "You're so fucking beautiful, Red."

Rafe slid his hands beneath the stiff cotton of her shirt and up the silky skin of her torso. He dropped his mouth, kissing his way across her ribs until he reached the first bra-covered nipple. And then in a move that had her arching into his touch, he captured the bud between his lips and gave it a gentle tug.

"Mm. So responsive," Rafe hummed.

Beneath him, Penny groaned. He took his mouth off her body only long enough to pull the shirt over her head, and then his lips were back on her, flicking, nipping. He rubbed his mouth down the length of her neck. By the time he reached the delicate curve of her collarbone, he had her bra off and his hand cupping one perfect mound.

When their gazes entwined, something clicked. *Changed*. Suddenly Rafe didn't remember how to make his chest rise and fall, and judging by the widening of her eyes, Penny didn't either. This time when he took her mouth in a kiss, it was different.

This was different. *They* were different. Lust and need still threatened to drown them both, but there was something stronger hovering between them. This time when he twined his fingers into her hair, he felt *his* trembles rumble through their touching bodies.

He wanted to prove her right—that he could be all the things she deserved and so much more. But unable to find the words, he let his eyes, his mouth, and his hands do the talking. For now.

They worked together to ease the BDUs down her slender thighs, underwear and all. Layers slowly evaporated, each removal instigating a new round of caresses. He could've taken her at any point, but this wasn't about the quick thrill. It was about savoring. About showing. About living for the first time in his life.

Rafe enjoyed the sight of her naked and spread out before him. Her eyes stayed locked on his as he gently urged her legs a little wider and settled between her thighs. "I don't know what I did to make you look at me like that, sweetheart, but I'm so glad that I fucking did it."

Her hand cupped the side of his face. "You were just you, Rafe. That's all you ever need to be with me."

Her words directed him right over the edge of his control. As he stared into her desire-filled eyes, he touched his mouth to her center and relished her breathy sigh. On the second slow swipe of his tongue, she quivered.

"Rafe. Please," Penny moaned.

Sliding his hand up to play with the taut peak of her left

breast, Rafe lingered on her swelling clit before taking another pass through her wetness. Again and again. He could stay in this spot all fucking day. With the taste of Penny on his tongue, time lost meaning. Only her pleasure mattered, and he focused on every breathy moan until her body started to flutter against his mouth.

Rafe picked up the pace in small increments, taking her right to the edge—and with one gentle flick over her clit, pushed her over. Her body tightened, hips bucking up toward his mouth as he stroked her through her climax. He stayed with her for every little flutter and soft keening moan . . . right until the last quake rolled from her body.

Rafe climbed his way back up her body. "You're always gorgeous, sweetheart, but when you fly apart like that, you're unbelievable."

"You're blind," Penny panted against his mouth. "I did the best I could in that shower, but water can only do so much to wash away an entire jungle."

"There's nothing wrong with my eyesight, Red." Feather soft, he brushed his mouth over hers in a kiss that despite the gentleness of it, packed one hell of a wallop.

Penny shivered, not protesting when he tucked her knees around his hips. The change in position slid his rock-hard cock through the folds of her wetness. He slid back and did it again, this time making sure the rim of his dick brushed against her clit. Sucking in a breath, Penny canted her hips upward and encouraged him to do it again.

He teased them both for as long as he could handle, and then, making sure he had her full attention, he slid into her tightness with one slow push. They both groaned as her body reflexively wrapped around him. It was freaking heaven. A homecoming.

He dropped his forehead to hers, fighting the urge to go

too damn fast. "I don't think I can let you go, Red. God help me, but I don't think I'm strong enough to watch you go."

"You don't have to. I'm right here. I'll always be right here." She kissed his cheek. His chin. And then finally, she slid her lips over his waiting mouth. Beneath him, she rolled her hips. Her body sucked him in to the hilt. "Make love to me."

He didn't need to be told twice. They were in perfect sync, locked together as one. One thrust turned into another until the quickening of her muscles turned their movements frantic.

"Rafe." Penny's ragged sigh urged him harder... faster.

The unguarded warmth shining at him through her eyes broke his hard-fought control. Her body erupted, muscles clamping down on his cock like a vise. Rafe thrust deeper, intensifying the strong pulses with each stroke. He quickly roared his own mind-boggling release. Slick from sweat, he continued to rock their bodies together.

It took forever to come down from the high, and even when the last pulse eased away, the euphoric feeling stayed behind. The ghost of a smile on Penny's face flipped something in his chest.

His former self would've backed away from the unknown and then created a thousand-mile distance. The Rafe Penny had somehow created now molded her against the side of his body and held on tight.

The truth was a warm glow of energy that filled him from the base of his core outward. His body, heart, and soul no longer belonged to him.

They were hers.

CHAPTER TWENTY-ONE

A few short weeks ago, Penny would've never imagined being cocooned in Rafe's arms, much less the safe feeling that came with it. And it was more than knowing she was physically safe that turned her insides into a warm pile of goo. It was the knowledge that she could be herself and be *enough*—with the right person.

Hopefully with Rafe.

They'd made love for hours before exhaustion took told and Penny slept so deeply she didn't think she'd moved in twelve hours. But when they woke, Rafe had been more than willing to work out the knotted kinks in her lower back with another spectacular round of love-making.

No doubt everyone was starting to wonder where they were—or maybe not.

"You're not allowed to move even an inch." Rafe's voice rumbled the man-pillow beneath her cheek. "Actually, don't even think about moving at all, because you're not going anywhere. Ever."

Staying wrapped in his arms for an indefinite amount of time sounded good to her. As a matter of fact, it sounded like perfection. Penny propped her chin on his chest and met his sleepy-eyed gaze with an automatic smile. "I wouldn't dream of it."

"Good. Because I'll hunt you down and haul you back to where you belong. And in case you're wondering, that's right the hell here." The arm that rested possessively on her hip hugged her closer. "Get that sweet ass over here."

Penny squealed as he tugged her on top of him. Astride his still-naked body, she shimmied until the hardness of his erection brushed against her still-sensitive clit. With a groan, Rafe slid home in one tortuously slow thrust.

* * *

It was déjà vu as they silently dressed. In a methodical system, Rafe inspected the mags for each of his handguns before slipping them into his black combat vest. Already in place and tucked against each thigh were knives that would've looked lethal in any torture chamber. The thought of him needing to use any of it turned Penny's stomach inside out.

Moments before the start of an operation wasn't the time to purge feelings. Distractions were dangerous, and he and the others were about to walk into a virtual minefield. So Penny kept silent, unable to say a word even if her tongue weren't stuck to the roof of her mouth.

Weeks of worry and planning were finally ending, one way or another. But for that to happen, the man she loved and the men she'd grown to care about like brothers were putting their lives on the line.

Rafe tugged his vest into place and gave the zipper a sharp tug before turning toward her. The longer he stared, the heavier the elephant sitting on her chest became. Being in his arms made it so easy to tune out the rest of the world. Watching him transform from lover to badass commando, that world came rushing back with a vengeance.

He was in front of her in two long strides, tipping her chin up with a pinch of his fingers. "If Rachel's there, I *will* bring her back. I promise."

A buildup of emotions made it hard to breathe. "I know. Just bring yourself back, too. *Please.*"

Penny kissed him, nearly spilling her heart out at his boots with one brush of lips. It nearly killed her to back away without telling him that she loved him.

"Stay alert while we're gone. Stay close to Logan," he ordered gently. "We still don't know exactly where Fuentes has his inside man planted, and I don't trust Collins as far as he can throw a goat."

"Really? And here I was thinking it would be more along the lines of an adult-sized buffalo," Penny tried to joke.

The tight press of Rafe's mouth told her that her attempt to lighten the mood failed miserably.

When a heavy knock landed on the door, Rafe pulled it open to a waiting Trey. Dressed nearly identical to Rafe, he stood in the hall, thumbs hooked into his pockets, not looking the least surprised to see Penny walking up to his friend's side.

"Prepare yourself for a lot of whining," Trey warned her with a wink. "Logan's been bitching about being left behind."

The operator in question turned the corner. Grin in place, Logan strutted down the hall in his usual loose swagger.

"You look surprisingly okay with having to stay behind," Penny stated, suspicious of the former Marine's jovial mood.

Logan dropped an arm over her shoulder. "I'll admit I was a little put out at first, but then I saw the group that's going to be piling into the helo all sardine-like. Trust me—I'm definitely getting the better end of the deal. What do you say to you, me, and a bottle of the finest jungle wine they got on hand, darlin'? We'll make an entire night of it."

"There's such a thing as jungle wine?" Penny grinned.

"You're right. We don't need the wine to have a good time. We just need each other."

A low growl from Rafe's direction had everyone—except Rafe—chuckling. He gripped her belt loops and pulled her out of Logan's grasp and into his own, making the Marine laugh harder. "Cool down, brother. I've got *almost* nothing but the safety of your girl in mind."

Penny rolled her eyes at the level of machismo filling the small hall and wrapped her arms around Rafe's waist. When his gaze dropped to hers, she gently assured him, "We'll be fine. You need to stop worrying about what's happening here and start concentrating on what's going to happen out *there*."

"We still don't know where Fuentes has his mole planted, and I'm about to leave you in a DEA-run facility...with Collins." Rafe palmed her cheek, and instinctively she pushed her face into his touch. He waited a moment before leveling a look in his friend's direction. "I'm entrusting you with precious cargo, Callahan."

Logan nodded, suddenly a little more somber. "Like the lady said—no worries."

Penny wished that were actually true. As they collected the rest of the team and met up with Collins and the others on the tarmac, her stomach tightened into multiple fist-sized knots. Ten minutes later, she watched the helo carrying Rafe and the guys lift into the dark sky.

This was real. It was happening. After bunkering down

in flea-infested hotels and traipsing through the Honduran wilderness—which literally almost killed her with a scratch—things were finally coming to a close. It seemed to take forever to get to this point, and now it was flying by way too fast.

Though Rafe hadn't asked for it, she summoned every ounce of love and threw it into her prayers for a safe return—very much aware that they hadn't discussed what would happen between them when he did.

* * *

Penny's eyes remained glued to the black-and-white footage being transmitted from the camera on Rafe's vest. Each of the four Alpha-led teams entered the jungle warehouse—Fuentes's suspected distribution hub—from different vantage points. Screen to screen, her eyes jumped from one monitor to the other. They all looked the same. No movement. No noise except for the brief exchange of voices as the teams systematically cleared each room and moved deeper into the building.

The place looked like a tomb, the halls no less vacant than each of the rooms or the surrounding grounds.

"Where is everyone?" Penny whispered.

"Situation report, Stone Cold?" Rafe's voice called out Sean's handle but was answered with blaring silence. One beat passed, then two. "I repeat, sit-rep? Do you read me?"

"Fuck me." Sean's muttered curse echoed over the comm link as if he'd shouted it through a megaphone. "Everyone, pull back! I repeat, all teams *pull back*! Get the fuck out of the building! *Now!* Move! *Move!*"

The microphone cut out, replacing the two-way audio with a static hiss. Penny was on her feet in an instant, her stomach flipping on its side as Rafe's camera bounced with his mad-like-hell run. "What's happening? What did he see?"

Logan's fingers flew over the computer keys, cursing with each attempt to bring back the sound.

"Logan!"

"I'm working on it, darlin'. I'm working on it. Fuckin' A, Collins! These computers are pieces of shit! Know how to work a fucking upgrade!"

"Explosives...rigged...trap."

A split second after Rafe's words came online, they once again cut out. A blink later, the images on each monitor disappeared in a volcanic eruption of light and fire. That was it. One minute the entire team was there, and the next... nothing.

No sound. No visual. After the blinding flash dissipated, nothing but blackness filled the screens. Shock froze the breath in Penny's lungs, and rainbow dots peppered her vision.

Rafe was gone. Trey was gone. All of them...*gone*.

"You fucking son of a bitch!" Logan shouted. "Penny! Run!"

The shout of her name and the coinciding crash were the only things that kept Penny from hitting the floor. She turned as Logan dropped, heavy and unconscious, to the ground.

Agent Collins redirected his attention—and his gun—to her. "Alone at last. I believe we have a mutual friend, Miss Kline...and he's *very* anxious to lay eyes on you again."

* * *

Burning pain made Rafe suck in a sharp breath. *Fuck, that hurt. Everything* hurt. He flipped on his back and cursed. "Mother-sucking son of a—"

"*Rafe!*" A hard nudge followed the shout of the voice.

"Over here! *I found him!*" Another nudge. "Fuck, man. Are you dead?"

"Poke my ribs again, Hanson, and your new handle's going to be fucking Stumpy." Rafe coughed, then growled as a jab of lightning speared straight through his torso. He forced his eyes open and winced at the light Trey aimed into his face. "Turn that fucking thing off."

"If you wanted to take a nap, you could've at least waited until the work was done," Trey joked. He stepped back, offering an arm to help Rafe back to his feet.

Rafe took him up on the assist and ignored the sharp twinge in his back that came along with the abrupt move. "I think that blast could've been spotted from the fucking Hubble."

"You're not fucking lying," Stone stated as he and Chase walked up with Vince and his crew in tow. All of them looked a bit singed around the edges, Franklin a little more literally. Half his fucking pants leg was missing. "Damn glad we didn't opt for an *all-in* breach. Now the question is what set it off? Was it timing? Bad luck? Or someone off in the shadows with a remote detonator?"

"None of them," Vince interjected. "That place was rigged to blow a few minutes after entry—at least the setup I saw in the east corner of the building."

"It was the same with the west end," Chase agreed.

"So it wouldn't have mattered which entry point we chose," Stone said, stating what they all were figuring out. "The place would've blown to high hell with any of them."

Vince nodded in agreement. "Smart thing to do would be to rig every single entry point. With the amount of C-4 that was used, one trip would be all that was needed to set off a chain reaction of explosions until you have one big-ass hole in the ground."

"*You*." Chase crooked his finger at a baby-faced DEA agent. "This has been the compound you guys have been focusing on for the last few months?"

He nodded. "This entire region."

"Why?"

The kid looked at him as if he had two heads. "Because according to our footage, this is where all the activity was happening. The drug runners couldn't have advertised their presence more if they'd sent up smoke flares and wore reflective gear. There was no reason to look anyplace else."

Rafe's stomach dropped like a lead ball. He didn't give a damn that it wasn't professional or that his teammates shouted at him to calm the hell down. He fisted Doogie DEA's shirt and brought the kid to his toes. He prayed that for once in his life, his gut was wrong. "Who's the agent who *stumbled* on this intel?"

"A-Agent Collins," the kid stuttered. "He's the one who has to sign off on all missions—intel gathering, surveillance… raids."

"And what's been done with the east and northern quadrants?"

"Nothing. We've been throwing most of our focus out here."

With a disgusted curse, Rafe dropped the kid to his feet. One look at his team indicated they were all on the same page. They'd found Fuentes's inside man.

And he was back at HQ.

With *Penny*.

* * *

A steady *thwump-thwump-thwump* filled Penny's ears, ricocheting pain from her hairline to all points north, south, east, and west. She blinked, winced, and blinked again. The sharp contrast of the dim interior and brightly colored control panel seared her retinas, but it was the explosion of memories that stole her ability to breathe.

The raid.

The explosion.

Rafe.

She'd witnessed the blast, seen the screen of white fuzz, and heard the aftermath of the chilling silence. But wouldn't she have felt *something* if Rafe was gone? An ache? An all-knowing gut feeling? The irreparable shatter of her heart?

She'd always known there was a chance she'd have to let him go, but not like that. Not before she had a chance to tell him how she felt, and not because he was trying to bring back her family.

Finding the one thing people dreamed of finding and having it so viciously taken away—ripped away from her by both Collins and Fuentes—was inhumanely cruel. With Rachel, they'd taken her family, and now they'd taken her heart.

A rush of anger yanked Penny's arms toward the large shadow sitting behind the helicopter controls, but the handcuffs anchoring her to the chopper door kept her from throttling Collins in the seat next to her.

A moment after he navigated the helicopter to the ground, the agent slid her a knowing smile. "Sorry about sending you to dreamland, but it's the nature of the business."

"If you're so sorry, how about you take these off?" She jiggled the cuffs. "I mean, plastic ties and handcuffs? Isn't that a little overboard?"

"My sources tell me you have quite the lively spirit, and I couldn't take any chances. It's the same reason I had to leave your friend behind."

Logan. "I swear to God if you hurt him, you haven't even begun to see lively."

"Lucky for him, I didn't have time to inflict too much damage—just enough to make sure he's incapable of following us."

"Why?" She choked on her words. "Why are you helping a man like Fuentes? He's hurt *so* many, and if Freedom gets out to the general public, he's going to hurt so many more."

"*Money*. It can buy a man anything. A tropical island. A new life. I can buy myself a high-end whore instead of one of Fuentes's fucked-up space cadets. Maybe I'll have Fuentes make you part of my payment, huh?" Collins scraped the back of his hand down her cheek. "Just you, me, and a little bit of Freedom to make sure you don't try swimming away with the dolphins. What do you think of that?"

When his hand neared her mouth, Penny bit into the fleshy part of his hand, a brassy move that earned her a stinging slap across the face. It was worth seeing the bastard bleed as he exited the chopper and came around to the other side. Still anchored to the grip bar, she spilled onto the ground when he flung open her door.

"Get the fuck up." Collins uncuffed her, but the plastic ties still cut off the circulation to her fingers. He fisted her hair and yanked her back to her feet before giving her a hard shove forward. "Now move it."

Penny locked her jaw against the sting of tears. No way in hell was she giving him the satisfaction of knowing that anything he did to her hurt.

A warehouse structure loomed in front of them, half-hidden by the surrounding wildlife. It looked eerily like the building Rafe and the team had entered, but this one wasn't spewing flames and ash.

Collins pushed her into a stumble. Just when she

would've face-planted to the jungle floor, a set of arms caught her midfall. Relief her head had been spared another blow disintegrated the second she looked into Marco Fuentes's eyes.

"Hello again, Señorita Hanlan. I believe I told you that we'd be running into each other again." Marco's smile left Penny cold.

"Why the hell are *you* here?" Collins demanded. "And where the fuck is Fuentes?"

"I'm afraid Diego won't be able to make it to the meeting. There's been a slight shift in family dynamics."

"He didn't tell me about any changes."

"And he won't either—because he's dead."

Collins looked taken back for about five whole seconds. "This better not interfere with my payout. I performed a service that doesn't come cheap."

"And your brand of services is no longer required. Consider this your termination letter." A single gunshot reverberated off the tree line, and Collins dropped to the ground less than three inches from Penny's feet. Once again, she found herself in the sights of a gun, this time Marco's. "Now that I've dealt with that unpleasant business... with me, *mi bonita*."

"Is this the part where you tell me if I come willingly, things will go much easier?" Penny asked brazenly. *What the hell did she have to lose?* Her only chance of getting out of this alive was if she pissed him off enough that he made a mistake.

"I wish I could tell you that you'll enjoy your stay with us, but I'd hate to lie."

Marco grabbed her restraints and tugged her into the warehouse. Every few yards, he placed his finger on another electrical scanning pad. They went deeper and deeper into the building. Each hall looked the same, some leading to dead ends while others led to another set of long corridors. It was the jungle version of Fort Knox, far beyond the warehouse it looked to be from the outside.

"What makes you think you can get away with this?" Penny asked.

"Because I already have... with a shit-ton of explosives. Poof! No more Alpha Security. Beautiful, wasn't it? The explosion? So much destruction, so many bodies." He turned, catching her look of horror. "Ah. Don't worry, *mi bonita*. I assure you that your mourning for your Rafael has an expiration date. Once you've had your first few tastes of Freedom, you won't feel a thing. You'll be blessedly... empty."

Hearing Rafe's name fall from the man's lips brought the fire in her gut straight out her mouth. "Go to hell."

Bells chimed with the impact of a second slap, and with it came the metallic taste of blood. Penny didn't care. She spat into his face.

Marco didn't so much as flinch as he calmly wiped the offending spittle away. And then he was in her face, close enough for her to gag on the stench of his cologne. "*You* are going to pay both for your interference and for that of your little boyfriend. Now that my father's out of the way, I'll make *everyone* pay and pay dearly."

At her look of confusion, Marco's lips slid into a ruthless smile. "Didn't see the family resemblance until now? Being the son of one of Diego's whores didn't warrant me climbing too high in his esteem, but look at me now. Now *I'm* the one in control. *I'm* the one with all the power."

When a nearby door buzzed open, he shoved her through it. "You'll stay here until I can deal with you appropriately. I suggest you use your time wisely because I haven't figured how much of it you have left."

The door slammed shut, leaving her with nothing but a dim light from somewhere in the corner of the room. But it wasn't until she heard the loud clank of the lock slipping into place that Penny's resolve turned liquid.

Rafe's scent still clung to her clothes. His touch still warmed her skin. But he was gone. Forever. Fat tears poured down her cheeks, and the more she pictured his face, the more that dropped in a torrential downpour.

He'd believed in her. He'd taken a chance on her. He'd shown her that some risks were worth taking—no matter the cost. And she wasn't going to let him down. Fuentes—either of them—would *not* break her. Lifting her shoulders, she wiped the dampness from her cheeks and took a deep, fortifying breath.

"P-Penny?"

At the soft whimper, Penny's attention whipped to the back of the room. Shadows clung to the corners, but even in the faint light, the bodies were impossible to miss. Ranging in ages from midteens to younger adults, nearly a dozen women stared back at her. Rumpled and dirtied, their clothes hung off their frames like rags on a hanger, and they all looked to be of Miskito heritage.

Except one.

Red hair, slightly more muted than Penny's own, stood out from the mass of brunettes. Rachel's lean runner's body was gone, leaving behind paper-thin skin and protruding bones that couldn't have weighed an ounce over a hundred pounds.

"R-Rachel?" Penny stared in disbelief.

Tear streaks marred Rachel's dirt-encrusted face. She stepped forward on spindly legs, and they gave way, crumpling her slight frame to the floor. "Is that really you? Or am I imagining you?"

Rachel's tears spurred Penny from her frozen state. She flew across the room. A few of the women scattered nervously in all directions as she dropped to her knees in front of her niece. "I'm here, Rach. You're not imagining me. I'm here. For you."

Penny brushed a lock of auburn hair from Rachel's face. At the sight of her once vibrant, jubilant eyes turned dull and blank, Penny's heart shattered into a million pieces.

"You shouldn't have come," Rachel's soft voice murmured. "You should've left me here, Penn. Now we're both dead."

CHAPTER TWENTY-TWO

Militia guards stalked the periphery of Fuentes's real warehouse, badass submachine guns propped on their shoulders. They worked in pairs, monitoring the comings and goings of the worker bees loading and unloading supplies to and from a line of waiting cargo jeeps.

Furious didn't begin to describe how Rafe had felt when he and the team returned to the Mocoron base to find Collins and Penny gone and Logan just coming out of a foggy stupor. Murderous maybe, not simply furious.

The only thing that had kept Rafe from flattening the former sniper to the ground a second time was that Logan was beating himself up good enough for the both of them—and that he'd had the foresight to place a GPS tracker on Collins when the bastard hadn't been looking.

Thanks to Logan's quick thinking, the team was able to follow Collins's and Penny's footsteps, despite their three-hour head start. Three fucking hours. A lot of shit could happen in that amount of time, but Rafe couldn't let his mind drift in that direction. He was going to get Penny back—*safely*—and nothing and no one could help the fucking bastards who got in his way.

No one had ever believed in him like she did. No one had ever challenged his thoughts and beliefs, or his actions, like she did. A five-foot-two-inch temperamental sprite single-handedly made him realize that everything he thought he didn't want or wasn't worthy of was his for the asking—and that he *deserved* it.

And then he walked the fuck away.

He was a moron. *An idiot.* If he didn't get his ass kicked on this op, he'd have one of the guys punt him so damn hard their boots would bruise his fucking tonsils. And then he'd tell Penny that he loved her so much that when he pictured her not in his life, he damn near had a panic attack.

He didn't just love her. He was *in* love with her, hard and deep, and for the first time in his life that didn't scare the fuck out of him. What did scare him shitless was the thought of losing her...of being too late.

Yeah, he didn't deserve just a beating. He deserved a fifty-caliber bullet to the ass.

Every minute they waited for the go signal, the more Rafe's nerves went apeshit. "Stone, I need to get in that building right the fuck *now*."

"We'll get you there, brother. I promise," Stone said over the comm link. "SEAL-one, you ready?"

Vince's voice rumbled through the mic. "All's primed and hot. T minus five for some fireworks, kids. Hold onto your boots."

With the clock ticking down, everyone verified their positions and points of entry. Rafe's muscles tensed, ready to get his woman back where she belonged. With *him*.

As the ground shook with the first *ka-boom*, monkeys shrieked into the night. Gun aimed, Rafe took his first step toward the bunker, then his second. When two men jumped in front of him, putting themselves between him and the woman he loved, he fired off his first rounds.

* * *

Every shake of the walls pierced a new round of blood-curdling screams through Penny's eardrums. "It's okay! It's the cavalry, ladies. *Ayuda*. Help."

Penny prayed she hadn't just lied. Panic hovered at the ready, just below her seemingly cool façade, but she held it at bay. Barely. There was no way in hell she'd desecrate Rafe's name or the entire team's sacrifice by turning into a blubbering mess now.

Either Marco really pissed someone off or by some miracle, the guys survived. Thinking of Rafe, Penny's heart shuddered. Common sense told her there wasn't any way he lived through the blast, but her heart and her gut disagreed. If anyone could defy the odds, it was him. But regardless if he was behind the thunderous chaos happening outside the compound or not, Penny wasn't going to let him down.

The walls shook again, this time swaying the flickering lights above their heads. Penny was too focused on toning down the new wave of screams to notice that behind her, the locked door groaned open.

"Penn," Rachel whispered in warning.

Penny spun around, instinctively shifting in front of Rachel and the girls, and prepared to do whatever she needed to do to keep them from more harm. But it wasn't Marco. Carlotta, wide-eyed and frantic, stood in the open doorway while she stole quick glances over her shoulder. "Come. *Now.*"

Penny stayed in position in front of Rachel, mildly surprised the other woman had finally come out of her drug stupor. "Come where? How do I know you're not leading us into a trap?"

"You don't."

Penny shoved away all the emotional what-ifs and concentrated on logistics. Staying meant imprisonment, Marco, and quite possibly a life worse than death. If they ran, they at least had a shot of escape. Heck, she survived the jungle one time already. A second time would be easier, right?

Another thundering boom dusted ceiling plaster onto their heads and solidified her decision.

"Give me your hands." Carlotta produced a knife from the small of her back and gestured to the plastic ties still wrapped around Penny's wrists.

Sweat peppered Carlotta's forehead and her hands shook as she freed Penny from the restraints. Some people would've said she looked nervous, but knowing where the brunette had been, Penny recognized it for what it was— *withdrawal.*

"This way." Carlotta ushered them out of the room.

Gunfire, alternating between high-pitched pops and rolling *tap-tap-tap*s, grew louder the farther down the hall they ran.

"Hurry." Carlotta stopped in front of a scanner. Lifting her shaking hand to the screen, it denied her entry twice.

"Here. Let me," Penny offered, gently holding her hand still in front of the scanner.

"Th-thank you," Carlotta murmured softly.

"No, thank *you.*" Penny let out a sigh when the pad

beeped green and the door unlocked. "Do you have any idea who's outside?"

"Your friends."

Penny did a double take. She only had one set of friends in this jungle. Her heart nearly tripped over itself with hope that Rafe had risen from the debris and come for her. Despite the near impossibility of it, the image made her usher the women faster.

"Just keep going," she reassured the crying women. "We're almost there. I promise."

Penny ushered the last girl past when she got a brief hit of Marco's expensive cologne. A moment later, his corded arm wrapped around her neck. One by one, the girls screamed, their panicked crying turning the corridor into pure chaos.

Penny mentally prepped her head for another blow and flung it back, satisfied when the crunch of bone and string of profanities had Marco relaxing his grip.

"You dumb, fucking *puta*," Marco roared. Gripping the back of her neck in a harsh hold, he propelled her headfirst into the wall.

Blurry colors burst in front of her eyes in a starry pattern. She struck out, the heel of her hand connecting with the bridge of his already deformed nose. But with her head spinning, the impact teetered her balance sideways.

"Move and they die!" Both the threat and Rachel's sharp cry made Penny freeze.

Two of Fuentes's thugs dug their guns firmly into Rachel's and Carlotta's temples.

Marco wiped at his bloody nose and smiled. "Risking your life for these drug whores wasn't a smart move, *mi bonita*. And trust me—your life is most certainly at risk."

Another loud boom shook the foundation. "Sounds as if

I'm not the only one. No one told you that Alpha isn't that easy to get rid of, huh?"

His cold eyes flattened along with his smile. "If by some miracle your former protector is alive and well, I'll make certain that you're not. When I'm done with you, your hero won't want to touch you with a ten-foot fucking dick."

"And you think I'm just going to come with you?"

With a nod from Marco, the man holding Rachel tightened his grip on her throat. Small gasps escaped from her mouth as her fingers clawed at the man's arm.

"Don't!" Penny cried. "Stop!"

"Only you can stop it." Marco's smug smile made her sick to her stomach. "It's your choice."

The man holding Rachel hostage lightened his grip— barely.

"Don't do it, Penn," Rachel softly pleaded. Tears fell in heavy rivulets down her face, matching Penny's. "Don't. *Please*. I'm not worth it."

There was no choice to make. Penny had come to Honduras prepared to do anything to get Rachel back. This was it. Though Rachel's tears flowed even harder, Penny's slowly dried. She sent Rachel every ounce of strength she had with a single watery smile. "You're worth it and a lot more, Rach. I love you. So much. Be smart. Help *is* on the way."

"No!" Rachel screamed.

"Smart choice." Marco's fingers dug into Penny's arm and dragged her in the opposite direction.

She counted four turns and six unmarked doors until they stopped in front of the seventh. With a buzz and a snap, they were inside. Penny's heart dropped.

Sterile and cold, the large room looked like a sadistic

version of Frankenstein's lab. But it was the sight of the dentist chair from hell that rolled her stomach. Her feet skidded on the slick floor as Marco dragged her closer, but with her head still woozy, her attempts to pull away were feeble ones.

After one strong backhand across her jaw, Marco poured her into the chair and easily cinched the leather restraints around her wrists.

"There's no point in struggling," he said smugly. "Even though your friends are knocking on my back door, it's too late. It's too late for you, too late for your country. As we speak, Freedom is already on its way to your shores."

"You're harming people who don't deserve it, not to mention that you'll soon be too dead to enjoy any profits," she smart-mouthed back. As if summoned, another loud boom shook the foundation.

"*Wrong.* Those who willingly inject Freedom into their bodies or allow it to be given to them deserve the life that follows. A few drops of this"—he held up one of six filled syringes that sat on the small stand next to the chair—"and it'll be your life, too."

The hard leather bit into Penny's wrists as she tugged, but she didn't stop trying to free herself even when blood began coating her skin. Trapped and helpless, she watched Marco tap the bubbles out of the first syringe.

"We're both going to make it out of here, and you, *mi bonita*, are going to be my poster child: my living, breathing, obedient demonstration…proof for my clients of just how Freedom can fatten their already bulging wallets."

"You may as well inject me with a gallon of it, because I'll be damned if I'm going to be your obedient anything," Penny snarled.

* * *

The compound was a damn labyrinth with no obstacles. And no Penny. With Vince's and Trey's teams at his back, Rafe charged ahead, blowing locked doors with minicharges as they went from one empty hall to another.

"Am I the only one wondering why everyone's bailed on their posts?" Vince asked from over Rafe's shoulder. "Or is that the SEAL in me being too fucking curious?"

"We need to know what the hell we're up against," Rafe grumbled in agreement. "I've already been buried under rubble once today. I've hit my fucking quota."

Vince nodded. The former SEAL grabbed his team and headed toward the belly of the beast, the most effective location if someone wanted to level an entire fucking building. Again.

"*Freeze*," Logan ordered over the radio. "Ten unknowns are coming at you from the east corridor. They're slow but on the move."

Kneeling, Trey slipped a sneak-and-peek mirror around the corner. He held up two fingers to indicate that there were only two guards, armed, but with eight civilians able to get caught in the line of fire. That meant eight ways things could all go to shit if they weren't careful.

With Trey counting down the time to arrival, Rafe plastered himself against the wall. *Three. Two. One.* At zero, they moved together like they'd done on countless missions before.

Trey took out the man on the left while Rafe subdued the second with an elbow strike to the throat. They went down quick and fast, almost too easy. Around them, a gaggle of women scrambled to hide in the empty hall, all of them screaming.

"*Hey!* Relax. We're here to help you!" Trey lifted his hands in a show of innocence. "*Calm down!*"

Rafe scanned the sea of faces and immediately felt his panic level spike when he didn't see Penny among them. But there was one there that made him pause.

"Trey." Rafe caught his friend's attention and nodded toward the back of the group. The emotional tightening of his friend's jaw confirmed what Rafe had already guessed.

An auburn-haired woman that could've passed as Penny's sister cradled a sobbing girl in her arms. She cooed and shushed the young woman, but kept her wary gray-eyed gaze focused on him.

"Rachel?" Hand outstretched so as not to scare her shitless, he stepped closer. "It's okay. We've come to get you out of here. All of you. We've come to take you home."

"You're the help Penn said was coming?" Rachel asked in a murmur. The poor thing looked ready to bolt.

"We sure are, hon." Rafe took another small step closer. He gestured to where Trey's feet remained rooted to the spot, watching. "And I believe you know this big ole lug, right? We all want to get you home, Rachel."

Rachel's gaze went back and forth between Rafe and Trey. "Penny. You have to get Penny. He took her to the clinic. He said he was going to make her like…*us*." Her gaze flickered to the obviously half-drugged, abused, and malnourished group of young women.

Like fucking hell. Not wanting to stress Rachel out any more than she already was, Rafe fought to keep a lid on the burning rush of anger. "I'm not going to let that happen, honey."

"Kids," Vince's voice interrupted through the comm link, "we got a problem in the form of a fuck-ton of C-4 and barrels of chemicals that make a big-ass boom—already wired and this time with a remote-fucking-detonation system."

"Fuck me upside down," Trey cursed under his breath.

Rafe hit Rachel with the full force of his gaze. "Can you tell me where this clinic is?"

"N-no. But I can show you," Rachel stuttered. She must've read his hesitancy, because she stood a little straighter and lifted her pointed chin. "I can do it. I'll keep up. I promise."

"Trey?" Rafe let his face spell out his unspoken question.

Trey nodded. "Go. I got this. You just make sure you get our girl, Ortega."

"Plan on it."

Rafe let Rachel lead, her pace slow but steady as they navigated the deserted corridors. Each tick of the clock took an eternity until they finally stepped in front of an unmarked door. He *knew* Penny was behind it. He sensed it with a violent twist of his gut, and it took everything he had not to blow through it like some kind of crazed bulldozer.

He turned to tell Rachel to make skid marks out of the compound and was met with a level stare. With her thin arms folded across her chest, she didn't look the least bit threatening, but she did look damned determined not to move a fucking inch.

"You have no intention of leaving, do you?" he asked.

"No. Not until I know Penn's okay."

Rafe couldn't help but grin. "Moxie runs in the family, huh? Fine. But you wait here until we know exactly what's on the other side of that door. You got me?"

Finally, she nodded.

He tucked Rachel a safe distance back from the door before molding a strip of Semtex against the lock. Two seconds later, the faltered door paved his way into the sterile twenty-by-twenty room. It was a lot like the jungle bunker but with one exception—instead of a line of beds, a single reclining chair adorned with shackles was mounted into the floor.

And it wasn't empty.

Penny's gaze whipped his way. At the sight of her battered body, volatile anger burned through his veins. Bruises lay on top of bruises, the golf ball–sized knot on her forehead being the largest. Her bottom lip was split open, and a fresh welt was beginning to bloom on her right cheek. Rafe was going to make the bastard pay for touching her, and he was going to pay severely.

Tears poured down her cheeks as she stared at him in apparent shock. He needed to feel her, hold her, tell her that it was going to be okay. He took two steps in her direction before her attention shot over his shoulder.

"Rafe! Behind you," she yelled.

Marco announced his presence with a snarl. Rafe didn't hesitate. Spinning, he used the other man's forward momentum to propel him straight into the wall. With a sickening thud, his head bounced off the concrete bricks, making him stagger backward and dropping the gun that had been in his hand.

"I'm going to kill you for that," Marco growled.

"For that? Then why the fuck were you trying to kill me before?" Rafe cocked up an eyebrow, unaffected by the threat.

Marco ignored the banter, twisting his lips into a feral smirk. "I'm going to kill you. And then I'm going to start on your girlfriend. And you bet your ass I'm not going to make it quick. Maybe I'll even make you watch, *mi amigo*. Would you like that? Do you want to watch your little piece of trash beg me for a hit of Freedom? Do you want to watch her do *anything* to get it?"

Maybe the bastard wasn't so dumb after all. The thought of him laying another hand on Penny made Rafe too damn eager to shed the bastard's blood. He charged, taking a hit to the jaw that felt like little more than a fly landing. Rafe slid his Glock back into his thigh holster and embraced every ounce of anger.

He could've shot him, could've planted a bullet right between his eyes, but that was too easy. It was too quick and painless a way for the bastard to die after what he'd done and what he'd obviously planned to do to Penny. Rafe wanted the piece of shit to feel every single painful thing about to come his way.

As if sensing his determination, the smirk on Marco's face slowly slid away. *Good.*

Surprisingly, Marco didn't just stand there and take it. He fought back. Uppercuts and jabs, Rafe shook each one off. In his periphery, he saw Rachel slip into the room. She glanced his way and then hustled straight toward Penny, careful to give him and Marco a wide berth.

"Let me take a wild guess and say that you're the bastard son, huh?" Rafe purposefully kept Marco's attention on him and not the girls. It was an old-fashioned standoff, and one of them would be going down, but it sure as hell wouldn't be him. "What happened, Marco? Your mom wasn't one of Diego's favorites, and you were relegated to a life of hired help? That must've pissed you the hell off."

"It doesn't matter anymore." Marco paced the floor like a pendulum. His movements put more distance between them and where Rachel struggled to untie Penny's restraints. "Because now *I'm* calling the shots. *I* have the power and the money and the means to run the Fuentes empire the way *I* want…the way it was supposed to be run."

"Funny thing about running an empire is that you need to be alive to actually run it."

Marco bellowed and charged, but Rafe had already registered the shiny blade in his hand. He ducked, letting

Marco's arm, and the knife, fly past his face before bringing it down on his knee with a loud snap. The man's shriek echoed through the room. For shits and fucking giggles, Rafe drilled a kick straight across the bastard's knee and took out his cap.

Rafe snuck a look toward the back of the room. Penny and Rachel stood huddled together, Penny's face frozen in worry. Her concern both warmed his chest and fueled his own unease. He wanted her safe and out of the way. *Far* the fuck away.

Six long strides and he loomed over her, fighting the urge to take her in his arms. "You need to go. Both of you. *Now*."

His order was met with a brisk shake of Penny's head. "I'm not leaving you behind."

"Damn it, Red! This entire place is wired to blow any second. You need to go. I'm going to deal with Marco's sorry ass and then I'll be right behind you—I promise."

"And damn *you*, Rafe," Penny shouted back at him. She gave his chest a small shove that didn't budge him. "The last time I let you out of my sight, I thought I lost you! I nearly *did* lose you. I'm not moving from this spot unless you're coming with me."

Penny's gaze snapped behind him. "Move!"

Before Rafe could react, she rammed her shoulder into his gut, knocking him to the left while her hand grasped something on the tabletop to the right. When she stepped between him and a wild-eyed Marco, Rafe finally registered the gun in the man's trembling hand—the gun he must have picked up off the floor.

"Red! No!" he shouted.

Rafe's heart shuddered to an abrupt stop, his feet frozen in place. No one breathed. No one moved until Marco backhanded Penny so hard it sent her into a spin that knocked her into Rachel. And then it was like time surged forward in one quick burst.

"You little fucker." Rafe ripped the gun out of Marco's already relaxing hold and cold-cocked him with a brutal uppercut that dropped him to the ground. And most importantly, unconscious.

That's when Rafe saw them—a half-dozen syringes embedded into the asshole's torso. All emptied. All placed there by one quick-thinking redhead.

Rafe didn't waste a second getting to Penny. The image of her stepping in front of that gun had shaved ten years off his fucking life.

"Please tell me you're okay." His voice shook while he scanned her head to toe.

"I'm fine."

"*Red*," he said in warning.

He hated that fucking word, but it let him breathe long enough to pull her into his arms where she belonged. Nose buried in the curve of her neck, he closed his eyes and soaked himself in her warmth. "Please tell me you're okay. Again. Just say it again, baby."

Her voice quivered as she fisted his shirt and held him close. "I'm okay. But I thought you were—"

"Shh." Cupping her cheek, he soothed her trembles with a tender kiss to each visible bump and bruise. "It takes a hell of a lot more to get rid of me than a roof falling over my head."

Though it killed him to pull back, he needed to look at her. *Really* look at her, and the moment he did, that hot rage he felt earlier bubbled back, closer to the surface than before. She looked as if she'd lost a game of chicken with a semi and a few of its friends. But the bumps and cuts were superficial. What worried him was the way she braced herself for each breath.

"Do you think they're broken?" He gently slid his palm over her ribs, sensing her tense.

He watched her summon a slow smile. "I've never had broken ribs before so I don't know. But if you're asking me if it hurts worse than when I danced with Marco in that alley, then the answer is without a doubt yes. I don't think a bag of frozen peas is going to do the trick this time around."

Knowing she was in pain ripped his gut to shreds. He nodded, knowing a heart-to-heart was long overdue, but he couldn't tell her a damn thing if they were both dead heaps on the floor. He shot a concerned glance to Rachel, who, for everything she'd been through, looked alert and ready to take on the world. "You okay to make a hustle?"

"I can do it," came her soft answer.

Turning to Penny, he spread his arms wide. "Do I have your permission to be your knight in black Kevlar? No offense, sweetheart, but we have to haul ass and you don't look like you could scamper, much less fly."

She groaned out a laugh and raised her good arm. "This is going to hurt like hell either way. Your way will get us out *before* we get blown to pieces."

"That's my girl. Always the optimist." He gently scooped her off her feet, wincing at her sharp inhale. "Fuck, baby. I'm sorry."

"Don't be sorry. You're here. *We're* here. We found her, Rafe," she murmured sleepily.

He gave Rachel a quick wink to make certain she was still with them as they hustled down the hall. "Yeah, sweetheart, you did. And there wasn't a doubt in my mind that you wouldn't."

"You never doubted me. You've always believed in me."

Penny buried her nose against his neck, her voice not much more than a slurred whisper. "That's one of the reasons why I love you, Rafe. I just needed to say that out loud. I *love* you."

He nearly stumbled over his feet. Rafe didn't think it possible, but those three words, the first time he could ever recall hearing them, settled into his chest like a warm ray of sunshine. A glance down into her sleeping face and that warmth went supernova. He wanted to wake her up and tell her to say it again.

Never having anything to compare with love, he was clueless. But he *knew* this was it. He knew it every time he looked at her, thought about her. Life without her witty sarcasm and infectious smile would be cold and dark.

He needed her by his side. He wanted to watch her kick ass but also needed her safely tucked into his arms *and* in his bed. She made him invincible and weak all at the same time. And it made him realize he couldn't live happily without her.

The moment they hit open air, all hell broke loose. Trey flung Rachel over his shoulder and then he and Rafe ran like fucking hell. At the first rumble, they hit the ground. Rafe, careful to take the impact of the fall himself, coiled his body around Penny's as they tumbled. When they finally rolled to a stop, he covered her head with his arms and tucked her face into the curve of his shoulder.

"God, baby. I love you, too," he murmured into her ear, voice rough with emotion. The words flowed, sliding easily—and truthfully—from his lips. "I love you so damn much, Red. I can't even begin to put it into words."

An explosion rocked the ground. The warehouse structure they'd been in only moments before erupted into a sky-reaching inferno. Rafe shielded Penny against the wall of heat. Burning planks and ash fell down around them as shouts echoed through the din.

Rafe didn't hear a thing. Lifting onto his forearms, his heart dropped at the sight of her beautiful green eyes staring up at him. No longer cloudy or hazed with pain, she looked at him with a mixture of disbelief and awe.

"What's wrong?" *Fuck*. He couldn't breathe, holding his breath while waiting for her answer.

"I think I should be asking you the same question."

"Why?"

"Because I don't think I'm the only one who hit my head."

Rafe couldn't help but grin. With trembling fingers, he caressed the edge of her swollen lip with his thumb. "I think you heard me correctly, baby."

"My ears are still ringing a little, so you should probably tell me again. In explicit detail."

Rafe leaned down until their lips brushed with every word. "*I love you*, Penelope Lucky Kline. I nearly died a thousand deaths getting to you because I love you so much that I can't breathe when I picture you no longer in my life. And I want that life with *you*. I want a life. I want a future. I want beautiful redheaded little girls who are just like their mother—so brave and strong and abso-fucking-lutely amazing."

He caressed the already darkening bruise over Penny's cheek and prayed her tears were happy ones.

"I told myself I'd never ask you to sacrifice what you want out of life," Rafe continued, pushing through the lump of emotion clogging his throat, "but I have to. I *need* to. I need *you*, Red. I'm begging you to give us a chance, and I'll spend every damn day of my life proving to you—"

Penny silenced him with her lips. At her slight hiss of

pain, he lifted to pull away, but her hands trapped his cheeks and held him close. He let her lead, not wanting to cause her any discomfort as he slipped his hands into her hair and gently kissed her back. *This* was where she belonged. In his arms. In his heart. Everything he had, body and soul, was hers.

By the time she slowly withdrew her lips from his, his head spun. The moisture welling in her eyes matched his. It was her turn to caress his face, her fingers gently brushing over his chin and mouth.

"You don't need to prove anything to me, Rafe," Penny murmured. "Ever. And there's nothing sacrificial about loving you or wanting a life with you."

"I'm not a knight in shining armor, sweetheart. I'm bossy and overbearing, a practical Neanderthal when it comes to keeping you safe. Despite the fact you're more than capable of taking care of yourself, I want in on the action, too."

She palmed his cheek. "And I wouldn't change a single thing. I love you—Neanderthal parts and all. And if you don't kiss me right now, I'm going to be forced to take matters into my own hands."

"One more kiss and there's no getting rid of me. You'll be stuck with me. For life."

She brushed her lips against his, making his soul tremble. "That's exactly the life I want."

EPILOGUE

Lebanon County, Pennsylvania
Six Months Later

Penny nibbled her lower lip, smiling and giddy as she stood in front of the weather-beaten door. Instead of rushing through, she took a deep breath. It was done. She was finished. The next phase of her life could officially begin, and the man—at least one of them—in the building in front of her would be part of it in a very huge way.

She couldn't wait any longer. Heart trilling in her chest, she pushed through the front door of Alpha. Not yet opened for business, the former biker bar sat empty, its only occupant the fine layer of sawdust coating the floor. Plastic tarps hung in each doorway. Tables and chairs were tucked into one corner and new windows were stacked neatly along the far wall, waiting to be installed. Alpha, both the bar and the agency, was nearly done with its face-lift.

Finally.

Those that needed to find them could, but only if they

already had one foot in the door or knew someone who did. When they weren't being the official badasses behind Alpha Security, they were going to take over the lives they'd been comfortable portraying during their stint in Central America.

Bar owners. Bartenders. Bouncers. To everyone around them, they were a band of brothers, all former military, all not to be trifled with. But to Penny, they were family.

"Well? How'd it go?" Penny heard Charlie before she saw her. And then the other woman stood up from behind the bar, a crate of bottles in her hands.

"Flying colors." Penny beamed. "Nearly as colorful as your hair."

With a laugh, Charlie leaped the counter and wrapped her in a bone-crushing hug that Penny returned. "I told you that you could bloody well do it."

"You were *bloody* right." Penny chuckled.

Charlie snorted on a laugh. "You finally used *bloody* in the right bloody context. I'm so bloody proud."

Penny chuckled harder. Much to the chagrin of the guys, she and the other woman had become instant friends. Charlie didn't apologize for her colorful hair or her multiple tattoos, or for telling people the truth, regardless of its popularity. Her sharp mind and keen wit made her the perfect person to keep the men of Alpha in line, and Penny adored her to death.

No doubt sensing they were no longer alone in the front room, Charlie smirked. "We need tattoos to commemorate the occasion. I bet you that Axel down at the tattoo parlor would give us a discount if you let him put it on your arse."

"No one's putting anything on my lady's arse except me." As if summoned, Rafe leaned against the doorway.

Penny ran straight at him. He caught her easily, his palms

giving her butt a firm squeeze as she instinctively wrapped her legs around his waist.

"See? My hands. Your ass." Rafe waited a beat before lifting a single eyebrow in question. "Well? Are you going to tell me how it went or am I going to have to guess?"

With a squeal, she started peppering his face with kisses. "I did it! I *really* did it! The final is over, the credits are mine. Mine! Mine! *All* mine! You're now looking at Alpha Security's official trauma psychologist—or you will be once I complete the internship."

Rafe's coy smirk morphed into a true smile. He nuzzled into her neck and, for her ears alone, murmured, "Congratulations, Red. I knew you could do it."

Like always, a simple hug turned into a hot clash of mouths and tongue. Penny tightened her hold around his neck and let out a soft groan of appreciation...right until the mixed sound of laughter and gagging had them pulling away. Slightly.

"Maybe we should start charging tickets," Rafe teased before allowing her to slide down the front of his body. By the time her feet touched the ground, he was hard everywhere. Keeping his arms wrapped around her, he held her close enough for her to feel the erection pushing against her stomach.

Charlie shuddered. "Forget the tickets. Just do...*that*... somewhere else. Bloody hell, this is a place of business. Or at least it will be if Navy ever gets on the ball with these renovations."

Vince, now standing between Logan and Sean, shot her a glare. "*Vince* would've been done a long time ago if some snooty little English girl weren't so damn picky."

"You know what? You lot are off gallivanting for weeks at a time. If I'm going to be stuck inside these four walls more than the lot of you, then I'm damn well going to make sure it's something I want to look at," Charlie growled right back. "Get the windows done or I'm going to hire the Beau brothers to finish the job."

"Like hell. You just want to hire them so you can watch their asses while they work."

She shrugged. "Your point is what?"

Trey stepped between Vince and Charlie moments before suspected bloodshed. "All right, kids. Don't make me put the two of you in separate corners." With a small smirk, he dropped a kiss on Penny's cheek. "Congratulations. I think this calls for a party by the lake. What do you think? Swimming, beer, and barbeque?"

"That sounds great." Penny looked up at Rafe, her smile mirroring his. "I want to call Dr. Phillips and see if Rachel would be okay coming out with us. Is that okay with you?"

Rafe gently guided her mouth back to his. "It would be more than okay, baby."

Penny squeezed him tighter. God, she loved him with every inch of her being. He'd been by her side, her mountainous support as they found both medical and emotional help for all the women that had been trapped in the warehouse bunker. He and Charlie had helped her find Carlotta's family... who lived in New York... and who *hadn't* named her Carlotta, but Nora.

And thanks to Alpha's connections, Rachel was in a government-sponsored rehab facility less than an hour away. It would be a long recuperation process, her battle with Freedom sometimes needing to be fought minute to minute... but if anyone could fight it—and win—it was her. Knowing that both Fuentes men died in Honduras and couldn't hurt another soul helped the darker times seem just the smallest bit lighter.

It would be a long road to normal—Penny's *new* kind of

normal, one that involved a new family and a new job. As a trauma psychologist, she'd help the people Alpha saved *after* the bullets stopped flying. It was an exciting new chapter in her life, and she couldn't wait to get started.

Penny lifted to her toes and kissed Rafe until her head went dizzy. "Can you and I have our own private celebration when everyone goes home?"

"Red, we can have our own private celebration every damn day of the week. As a matter of fact, I encourage it... *demand* it even." Rafe feathered his mouth against hers.

"Jesus. Get a hotel room," Trey grunted to the chorus of everyone else's chuckles. "That's basically my little sister you're groping in front of me, Ortega."

"Learn to look away, brother, because there's no way in hell I'm ever going to stop touching her or let her venture out of my sight. And speaking of... we'll meet you guys out at the lake."

Before Penny could ask what he meant, she found herself thrown over Rafe's shoulder like an economy-sized bag of potatoes. This time, there were no gag, no handcuffs, and no blindfold. This time, she could see exactly where she was going... or would have if Rafe's smackable ass weren't in the way.

And that was straight into the future with the man she loved.

Nurse Elle Monroe never expected
to see her one-night stand on the
steps of her clinic. But Alpha
Security operative Trey Hanson isn't
back for a repeat performance. He's
come to save her from heavily
armed guerillas—and maybe to steal
her heart...

A preview of *Holding Fire* follows.

Elle stared, transfixed, on the clock behind the airport's claims counter. Each twitch of the second hand took about five years off her life. Being a month shy of her birthday, she estimated she had roughly ten and a half seconds until the coroner needed to be called. Twelve max, with a little bit of luck, but luck seemed to be in short supply.

Her normal patience was at an all-time low, sucked into a black hole right along with her personal hygiene and her luggage. Twenty hours in flight time from Thailand to New York was to blame for the first. The latter was entirely the fault of the airline.

"Next." Behind the counter, the gray-haired hospitality worker never bothered looking up at the next traveler.

One more person. One more step. The closer Elle got to the cracked yellow Formica counter of the claims department, the more that surface looked like a goose-feather pillow. *To leave or not to leave.*

Jeans. Shorts. Granny panties. All cotton, no sexiness. Everything in her suitcase could be easily replaced by her modest paycheck and the nearest discount store. She could call it a loss and find the nearest hotel, be damned the health department reports.

With a deep sigh, Elle looked around the open room. People littered the airport, bulky suitcases bouncing behind them as they scrambled to their destinations while others coveted blankets and pillows and looked to be settling in for the duration. On the left, two children tackled the legs of a tall, slender woman dressed in desert camouflage.

A smile ghosted over her lips...and froze. That *tingle*, the one she'd felt the moment she and Shay unloaded from the gate—the one that came with the ardent focus of someone's attention—took root in the pit of her stomach. When she sensed it earlier, she blamed the paranoia on her long hours of travel and lack of sleep. But the prickle of awareness came back tenfold, turning her head and stopping at the man leaning against the far wall.

Elle did a double take. It wasn't Trey. It couldn't be. She'd left him back in Thailand without so much as her last name, much less her travel itinerary, yet every second her gaze stayed narrowed on the stranger across the room, her heart pattered a little faster.

Jeans encased his thighs perfectly. Not tight. Not baggy. No doubt if he turned around, the rear would look as impressive as the front. Both his face and his hair were disappointedly half hidden by a baseball cap and sunglasses, but they had the same strongly chiseled jaw and sexy blond scruff that made her want to throw every razor known to man straight into the garbage.

Even though he never looked away from his paper, his

lips twitched almost as if sensing her visual appraisal. That smirk. Those lips. The tight stretch of a long-sleeved T over a chest wide enough to land an airplane. Elle nearly collapsed into an X-rated memory of how lips nearly identical to the stranger's had pleasurably ripped away all her sensibilities only a scant few days ago.

Standing in the middle of a busy airport definitely wasn't the time to give in to a never-ending mental replay of her time with Trey. When her turn came up at the counter, she gave them all the information they needed in the hopes of reconnecting with her suitcase, and then with a "Have a nice day" and her single carry-on, Elle bounced off the chest of another traveler.

On reflex, she reached out to steady her victim. "I'm *so* sorry."

"*Shut* it," a low voice snarled.

Oh, hell no. Exhaustion mixed with an insane need to shower off the last twenty-four hours made her head swivel to Mr. Attitude. Normally she would've taken a step back and gone on her merry way, a side effect of her upbringing. But she was eight hours past polite, and people who wore sunglasses indoors annoyed her to no end—unless they were sexily coy and leaning against a wall.

She narrowed her eyes, wishing him to squirm at least the smallest bit, but there wasn't so much as a flicker of remorse. "It was an accident. I said I was sorry. There's no need to be a jerk about it."

"Actually, there is." Mr. Attitude clamped a hand around her upper arm.

"Ow. Hey, watch it!" She tugged and he tightened his hold.

He leaned his large body way past her personal boundaries until his mouth brushed against her ear. Elle cringed.

"I told you to shut. The hell. Up." He emphasized each word and punctuated it with a nudge to her ribs. It took a moment to register the cool steel as a gun. "If you so much as twitch, sputter, or look at anyone cross-eyed, I won't hesitate to make this very bad for you."

Elle forced bile back down her throat. Yeah, she had luck—*bad* luck that smelled worse than a skunk den. "I should probably warn you that I don't have any money. Well, I have about ten dollars' worth of Thai baht, but that's about it. And maybe a fuzzy breath mint."

"I don't want your money, Miss Monroe."

His grip tightened as he steered them away from anyone who would remotely care what was happening. And let's face it: this was one of the busiest airports in the country. No one was going to notice one travel-ravaged blonde and a tank of a man, probably not even if she stripped down to her cotton undies and streaked through the terminal.

Her armed captor kept the barrel of the gun snug against her side as he directed them to the airport exit.

Elle's heart went from a steady thunder to an apocalyptic roar when it finally sank in. *Her name.* He knew her name, knew she'd be returning to the states *today.* At *this* airport. Elle Monroe, certified trauma nurse, wasn't exactly a hot commodity for kidnapping, which left only one other reason...and a desperate need to get away.

Elle whipped her head from side to side in hopes of catching someone's eye, but everyone was too involved with their own travels. Even the station cop clear across the room seemed to be dealing with a minor scuffle between two passengers.

"So I'm your meal ticket, huh?" Elle kept talking, hoping someone would eventually catch on to her dilemma. "You obviously need me alive or you wouldn't be going to all this trouble to get me out of here. I could scream bloody murder at the top of my lungs."

"I wouldn't recommend it. Not only could you get hurt in the process, but you could get a lot of innocent people hurt, too. You wouldn't want that on your conscience, would you? And what about your friend? You don't want anything to happen to Miss Chandler while she's in the bathroom. And just so you know I'm not bluffing, it would be the bathroom directly across from the newspaper stand—the one with one working stall and a dripping faucet."

Oh God. She wouldn't jeopardize Shay's safety or that of any other innocent bystanders, but she also couldn't continue to let this man lead her straight into whatever hellish nightmare he had planned.

She needed to think. She needed her own plan. She needed—

Elle's gaze snapped to the far wall where she'd last seen Mr. Tall, Ripped, and I-Can-Flick-a-Man-with-My-Fingers-and-Send-Him-Across-the-Room.

Her baseball cap–wearing stranger stood in the same spot, but instead of leaning against the wall, he stood erect, newspaper tossed to the side, and was looking straight at her, twitching smirk nowhere to be seen.

"Keep up." Elle's captor tugged her closer to the exit.

She dragged the tips of her toes in hopes of slowing him down even the slightest bit. When she looked back to her looming stranger, he was gone.

Panic seized her throat, making it nearly impossible to breathe. Even though her life plan was currently one big question mark, she knew it didn't involve ending up in an unmarked burial plot somewhere near LaGuardia Airport.

The second she felt the cool January air slide through the glass exit doors, she locked her legs and forced both herself and her captor into a stumble. A small bit of space was all she needed to plow-drive a fist straight into his man goods.

He released her arm to deflect the blow. Thank God for those hospital-sponsored defense classes. Anticipating her new freedom, she snapped her tennis shoe straight across his kneecap. The man howled, his legs buckling for a split second when a whir of black zipped by her shoulder.

Sounds of flesh on flesh sent her gaze backward just as her wall lounger's fist connected with her captor's jaw. Much to the horrified fascination of nearby travelers, the two men exchanged punch after punch. People stopped and stared. Across the lobby, the uniformed cop finally looked their way. But with one final blow, her stranger put Mr. Attitude down on the ground—and then Elle found herself in a completely different set of hands.

"Walk faster." Her stranger hustled her through the sliding doors and into New York's as-fresh-as-can-be air, one hand resting on the small of her back. The tingling touch was far better than the other's bruising grip.

She opened her mouth to object, but he cut her off. "Save the questions for when we're not about to become target practice."

Elle's head spun around and she realized her savior had a point. Her would-be abductor stood in the airport lobby, sunglasses off and gun twitching at his side. She'd seen those eyes before... *and* the scar that slid down his cheek.

Cold dread licked up her spine. She couldn't pull her gaze away, watching as the man from the Thai alley lifted a cell phone to his ear.

Her stranger turned her focus back to him and the looming SUV half-parked on the drop-off zone's sidewalk. "Get in the car."

Elle's feet screeched to a stop. "Yeah, I may be blonde, but I'm not stupid. What makes you think I'd get into a car with you any more than I would with him? Thanks for helping me back there, because I've obviously landed in the Twilight Zone instead of LaGuardia, but if you want me to get in there"—she gestured to the door he held open—"then you're going to have to physically toss me in there and sit on me."

Elle met her rescuer glare for glare, except hers was directed into his mirrored sunglasses. He was larger than he looked even from across the room, the top of her head barely reaching his shoulders.

"If you think that would be a deterrent for me, sweetness, you're mistaken. And as for manhandling you into position, I'd be more than happy to cover your body with mine, but I sure as hell wouldn't be sitting on you. Now get. In. The. Car. *Now*."

That voice. His smell. Familiarity tugged at her memory while her body shifted into a pheromone-driven DEFCON 1. Elle's eyes widened in recognition, but she didn't know how it was possible. Or why. First the man from the alley and now…*him*.

She teetered sideways, would've face-planted on the sidewalk if it hadn't been for the hands pulling her against a strong, wide chest that didn't belong to a stranger. She didn't need to imagine what he looked like beneath his clothes. She knew. She knew how his body felt against hers, knew that each touch felt like she'd touched an exposed electrical wire. Those hands especially had given her a lifetime's worth of happy-place memories.

With trembling hands, Elle slid the sunglasses off her wall lounger's nose and stared into the same green eyes in which she'd allowed herself to get lost in a dingy Thai bar.

And in the room above.

And in the bed in that room.

Elle Monroe, humanitarian nurse and ever-responsible daughter of a United States senator, stood in front of her one and only—and forty-eight-hour recent—one-night stand.

ABOUT THE AUTHOR

April Hunt blames her incurable chocolate addiction on growing up in rural Pennsylvania, way too close to America's chocolate capital, Hershey. She now lives in Virginia with her college sweetheart husband, two young children, and a cat who thinks she's a human-dog hybrid. On those rare occasions she's not donning the cape of her children's personal chauffer, April's either planning, plotting, or writing about her next alpha hero and the woman he never knew he needed, but now can't live without.

You can learn more at:
AprilHuntBooks.com
Twitter @AprilHuntBooks
Facebook.com

Fall in Love with Forever Romance

MISTLETOE COTTAGE
By Debbie Mason

The first book in a brand-new contemporary series from *USA Today* bestselling author Debbie Mason! 'Tis the season for love in Harmony Harbor, but it's the last place Sophie DiRossi wants to be. After fleeing many years ago, Sophie is forced to return to the town that harbors a million secrets. Firefighter Liam Gallagher still has some serious feelings for Sophie—and seeing her again sparks a desire so fierce it takes his breath away. Hoping for a little holiday magic, Liam sets out to show Sophie that they deserve a second chance at love.

Fall in Love with Forever Romance

ONLY YOU
By Denise Grover Swank

The first book in a spin-off from Denise Grover Swank's *New York Times* bestselling Wedding Pact series! Ex-marine Kevin Vandemeer craves normalcy. Instead, he has a broken-down old house in need of a match and some gasoline, a meddling family, and the uncanny ability to attract the world's craziest women. At least that last one he can fix: He and his buddies have made a pact to swear off women, and that includes his sweetly sexy new neighbor...

THE BILLIONAIRE NEXT DOOR
By Jessica Lemmon

Rachel Foster is surviving on odd jobs when billionaire Tag Crane hires her and whisks her away to Hawaii to help save his business. As things start to get steamy, Rachel falls for Tag. Will he feel the same, or will she just get played? Fans of Jill Shalvis and Erin Nicholas will love the next book in the Billionaire Bad Boys series!

Fall in Love with Forever Romance

HEATED PURSUIT
By April Hunt

The first book in a sexy new romantic suspense series from debut author April Hunt, perfect for fans of Julie Ann Walker, Maya Banks, and Lora Leigh. After Penny Kline walks into his covert ops mission, Alpha Security operative Rafe Ortega realizes that the best way to bring down a Honduran drug lord and rescue her kidnapped niece is for them to work together. But the only thing more dangerous than going undercover in the madman's lair is the passion that explodes between them...

SOMEBODY LIKE YOU
By Lynette Austin

Giving her bodyguards and the paparazzi the slip, heiress Annelise Montjoy comes to Maverick Junction on a mission to help her ailing grandfather. But keeping her identity hidden in the small Texas town is harder than she expected—especially around a tempting cowboy like Cash Hardeman...

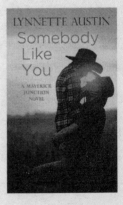